DELIVER ME FROM MY ENEMIES

SHARON OLIVER

URBAN CHRISTIAN

www.urbanchristianonline.net

Urban Books
1199 Straight Path
West Babylon, NY 11704

Deliver Me From My Enemies copyright © 2009 Sharon Oliver

ISBN- 13: 978-1-60162-983-8
ISBN- 10: 1-60162-983-4

First Printing March 2009
Printed in the United States of America

10   9   8   7   6   5   4   3   2   1

Distributed by Kensington Corp.
Submit Wholesale Orders to:
Kensington Publishing Corp.
C/O Penguin Group (USA) Inc.
Attention: Order Processing
405 Murray Hill Parkway
East Rutherford, NJ 07073-2316
Phone: 1-800-526-0275
Fax: 1-800-227-9604

DEDICATION

In memory of Ernest Price.
Be at peace, my friend.

ACKNOWLEDGMENTS

To my Heavenly Father, *I love you, O Lord, my strength.* *(Psalm 18:1)*

To my childhood friend, the very, very funny Mrs. Mary "Debra" Bowman. To Sharniece Moore, thanks for all the zingers, quips, quotes, advice, ear to hear and shoulder to cry on. You both make me laugh out loud! And last, but not least, Angela Taylor, thank you, thank you, thank you!

To my Urban Christian family, it really is like a family affair. May the Lord continue to bless each and every one of you and make those crooked paths straight. May you know your Jonathan from your Judas.

To everyone else, may the Lord keep you and bless you.

And if you ever find yourself on the floor (crushed by life's circumstances) don't get up the same way you went down. Be yourself because everyone else is taken.

DELIVER ME FROM MY ENEMIES

PROLOGUE

August 30, 2004

After an emotionally charged homegoing service for her cousin Tina, Charlotte Morley found herself staying at Turtle Island, South Carolina one week longer than planned.

Tina's parents, Charles and Francine Morley, were understandably devastated by her death, and to make matters worse, Tina's twin sister, Terry, left behind a note, revealing she had been masquerading as Tina and was involved in a money scheme with Reverend John Cedric Holiday. In fact, it was Terry who had eloped with Greener Pastures A.M.E. Church's pastor, the late Reverend Holiday, and together, they had run off with all the money from the church's bank account.

Rather than face time for fraud and identity theft, Terry chose to desert the family again, skipping her sister's memorial service. No one from Greener Pastures attended the memorial service for Reverend Holiday, which was held in his hometown of rural Georgia. Even the few loyalists vowed not to attend.

As if all of this weren't enough, Charlotte was still reeling from the news about her Uncle Charles's double life as a married man living on the down-low.

She looked out the kitchen window to check on her paternal grandparents, Edmund and Mattie Mae Morley. They were sitting on a picnic bench talking with her parents, Esau and Betty Morley. Charlotte's parents decided to stay a few extra days after coming down for the funeral to provide family support. Still grief stricken after burying their daughter in a family plot at Greener Pastures Church's cemetery, Charles and Francine went back home to the D.C. metro area immediately after the service.

In spite of other recent tragedies, which caused a morose atmosphere, Charlotte was proud of her accomplishments while on the island. In particular, the praise and worship team she pulled together from a handful of local singers had morphed into a group to be reckoned with. Thanks to another cousin, Jeff, who was able to preach the first Sunday after Reverend Holiday's dismissal from the church, many folks not only heard a true word, but were saved as well. Her best friend, Timmi, also came for a little rest and relaxation after the breakup of a relationship, and she, too, found herself being used by God and getting some answers to a few questions of her own.

All in all, Charlotte could not dismiss the fact that she saw where God was at work through it all. The telephone mounted on the wall rang. As soon as Charlotte picked up the receiver and placed it to her ear, the caller hung up.

"That's the third time this week," she said out loud in disgust. She had a strange feeling it was Terry.

The telephone rang again. "Hello," Charlotte answered. This time it was her Aunt Francine.

"Charlotte, this is your Aunt Francine," the shaky voice said. "We've heard from Terry."

Charlotte gasped as her eyes shifted to a stack of mail on the kitchen counter. On top of the pile was an envelope addressed to her. The sender's name and address made her gasp again. Charlotte had a strange feeling that days ahead seven days would be just as eventful as the last.

1

*To everything there is a season and a time to every purpose
under the heaven*

Ecclesiastes 3:1

Thirty-one-year-old Charlotte Morley could tell it was
going to be one of those lazy kinds of late summer mornings, evident by the cloudy overcast and her snail's pace.
The motto *carpe diem* was the furthest thing from her mind.
In fact, she pictured spending the rest of the day lying in a
hammock with a piece of straw hanging from her lip and
enjoying a fine September day.

She spied through the smoke-tinted glass at Walker's
Auto Garage to see if the mechanic had finished working
on her grandfather's truck. Instead, she found a young Bob
Marley knockoff with the same long, fat dreads and yummy
cashew pigmentation working non-stop beneath the hood
of a green Ford Explorer.

Although Charlotte was anxious to read the letter tucked
away in her leather satchel, she opted to do a quick study of
her surroundings first. Leon Walker, Sr. was not only the
best auto mechanic in town, but his establishment was the
only black-owned auto body shop on Turtle Island, and it

was no secret that such an enterprising feat had richly and quickly fattened his bank account.

She let her eyes tour the waiting area that consisted of four white wicker club chairs along with one very out of place metal folding chair. Charlotte guessed that this small seating arrangement was of no major concern since most customers tended to linger around the garage to chat with the mechanics and other customers. The walls were painted a bright sky blue with a collection of white fluffy chiffon-like clouds stenciled about, reminding Charlotte of her computer's screensaver. A handsomely made cobweb suspended from the ceiling and laid claim to the southeast corner of the room.

A heavy pair of faded navy-and-cream striped drapes with silver blue sheers in the middle hung from the window. The lone potted plant that kept the magazines company on the chrome and glass table could cry for water no more. It was beyond dry. Charlotte had a sudden craving for a grilled cheese and tomato sandwich, but had to settle for a cup of caffeine instead. As Charlotte helped herself to the strong, freshly brewed coffee, she heard a very familiar voice behind her.

"Hey, there!" Nora 'Sista' Jones cheerfully greeted as she entered the premises. Strutting two paces behind her in a pair of wrinkled grayish-blue overalls was the shop's proprietor, Leon Walker, Sr., more commonly known as Walker. Immediately, Charlotte noticed the strong resemblance between Walker and his son, Junior, the mechanic working on the truck.

"How y'all doin' today?" Walker asked, whisking past Charlotte after nearly knocking Sista down to the floor. The wooden floor boards made a loud squeaking noise as Walker marched across the room accompanied by his clanking keys, which were grouped together by a plastic coil key chain wrapped twice around his wrist.

"Shucks, this ole clock done went out on me again," he said, looking up at a wall clock. "I told that boy of mine to get a new clock three weeks ago. Sometimes I think Junior is one hot dog away from a picnic. Either one of y'all got the time?" Walker asked as he placed his collection of keys on the countertop.

Annoyance was written all over Sista's face. She was as irritated as a teething baby. She rolled her eyes up toward the ceiling, thinking Walker wasn't sharp as cheddar himself at times. "Half past my elbow accordin' to my fist," she answered sarcastically. Touché!

That was classic Sista, a comical and sprightly character.

"And why was you so close up on me comin' through the door? You was up on me like you my girdle or somethin'. You almost knocked me down," she added.

Walker winked at Charlotte as he removed the clock from the wall. "Come on now, Sista. You know I was not trying to knock you down on purpose." He was obviously proud of his ability to rattle Sista's cage. "I'm sorry. I was in a hurry. I promised this fella I'd have his car ready by noon. Anyway, how come you don't like me? What have I done to you?"

"Oh, you ain't done nothin' to me. I like ya just fine. 'Specially since Mattie Mae married Edmund instead of you!" Sista snapped gruffly, her sagging breasts heaving beneath her blouse. She strummed her fingers along the windowsill, frowning at the day's worth of dust choking the windowsill and the blinds.

Walker was one of Charlotte's grandma's gentlemen callers back in the day. She could not imagine her grandparents, Edmund and Mattie Mae, being married to anyone else aside from each other.

Charlotte ran her fingers through her hair. She desperately needed to take a comb to her head since her hair saw fit to stick out like curly fries all of a sudden. Her pink sundress was so faded that it was hard to tell if the dress was supposed to be floral or polka dot. And to top it all off, her ashy knees resembled snowcapped mountains. Charlotte could not forgive herself for leaving the house looking that way. She had hoped to zip in and out of the garage before her grandfather needed the truck, and without being seen by half the town.

Given Walker's profession, Charlotte could understand his appearance. Black smudges covered his hands, and his khaki uniform was covered in oil, grease and God only knew what else.

Sista, however, was another story all together. Sista knew how to dress and *could* dress well since her children kept her closets stocked with nice, expensive outfits. She was decked out in a pair of burgundy, green and beige argyle polyester knit britches that were too short to be pants and too long to be capris. Sista, at times, simply just did not care.

Now, feeling a little self-conscious about herself, Charlotte pulled a small bottle of oatmeal and honey lotion from her bag. She squeezed out a liberal amount and rubbed over her chalky white knees to control the ashiness that had started to spread at an alarming rate. She squeezed out a second helping and slathered her elbows for good measure.

Every few seconds, Walker would look back and give Sista a good up and down inspection. "Why you holdin' on to the past, Sista?" Walker asked through his thick mustache. After placing fresh batteries inside the clock's compartment and hanging the clock back on the wall, he then slipped the opened pack of batteries inside a drawer, nearly jamming his thumb in the process.

"I ain't holdin' on to the past," Charlotte heard Sista insist. "You the one still livin' in the past. You called yo'self a playboy back then, and you still call yo'self a playboy. If you ask me, Shirley Mae shoulda left yo' behind a long time ago." Sista took a few steps forward, made a sharp left turn and plopped down in the chair next to Charlotte.

"Why you so worried about my business? You must want me for yo'self." Walker grinned slyly, winking again at Charlotte. Charlotte grew curious as to why he winked so much, considering that he did indeed behave like a true flirt.

"Who want yo' po' behind, Walker?" Sista raised her voice, clearly outraged by the insinuation, yet able to have the grace to blush the color of a red russet potato.

"You must want my po' behind." Walker released a hearty laugh that came straight from his belly as he proceeded through the door which led to the garage. He seemed totally unaffected by Sista's ability to use words for arsenal.

Sista sucked her teeth and turned to face Charlotte. "How are you, Charlotte?"

"I'm doing well, how about you?" Charlotte replied.

"Other than my feet sproutin' corns, bunions and onions, I'm doin' just fine. Listen. I saw Edmund's truck out there and I thought he was in here. John Edward is out there gettin' something done to his car. I told him I wanted to run in here and talk to Edmund, but I can talk to you." Sista cocked her head sideways to roll her eyes at Walker, who was busy chit-chatting away on the telephone.

"I'm curious. Why do you dislike Mr. Walker, Miss Sista?" Charlotte asked, hoping the question would lead to information regarding his former relationship with her grandmother.

Mattie Mae often beamed like a beacon of light whenever

Edmund came in the room, and said on more than one occasion that she felt her name was safe in his mouth. Their marital relationship was ideal to many.

"Oh, I don't hate Walker or nothin' like that. He knows that. We just cuttin' the fool. Although, back when we was young and he called himself likin' Mattie Mae, I could not *stand* him! I knew Edmund was fool 'bout Mattie Mae and I knew Walker was nothin' but a plain ole fool. All the girls was crazy 'bout Walker too. He was tall, dark and handsome; and he had that good hair. Plus, he always worked on a job, so you figured he'd be a good provider. Walker probably got enough money saved up to use for toilet paper."

Charlotte sensed a 'but' coming. Sista popped a piece of hard candied mint in her mouth and moaned, "The problem wit' Walker is the women loved him and he loved the women. He wouldn't know how to stop cheatin' if there was only one woman on earth. He'd find a way to cheat on *her*."

"God, I hope not," Charlotte said flatly. "Surely, he has changed by now."

"Changed?" Sista nearly shouted at the top of her lungs. "Baby, that's an old root and the only thing you can do with an old hard root is kill it. Walker can't help it, I suppose. He's a womanizer just like his daddy, Henry, was. Henry met his end in a watery grave, and there was talk about how he got there too. Now that's something to think about."

"I imagine so," Charlotte moaned before covering her mouth to yawn.

"But I just like to mess wit' Walker. You know, he can near 'bout fix anythin' 'cept that loose screw in his head. Anyhow, his wife, Shirley Mae, don't seem to mind his cheatin' ways, so I guess I shouldn't mind either. They got plenty of money and she don't want for nothin', so maybe that's why she can turn her head the other way. I heard that he lets her handle the purse strings."

"Oh, I'd bet she would rather have a faithful husband. As old as Mr. Walker is, I would have thought he'd have all of that out of his system by now. But I have to say he really is attractive for his age. I can only imagine how he looked back in the day." Charlotte rubbed her chin. "Let me guess. I bet he and his wife were probably one of the cutest couples on the island."

"They were a cute couple. I admit that," Sista said. "I even admit that Walker still looks good, but Shirley Mae used to be such a pretty girl. Now she looks like sin."

"Miss Sista, that's not nice," Charlotte scolded.

"I mean all that worryin' she used to do when Walker ran the streets took a toll on her."

"You sure don't have a problem with saying what's on your mind."

"I sho' don't! I do not believe in bitin' my tongue or swallowin' my words, and if you ever see me quiet, that means I'm either sick or somebody got a gun in my side. Just thank God Walker didn't turn out to be yo' granddaddy. Listen, I ain't get a chance to talk to Mattie Mae yet. How is she?"

Although Charlotte was only half listening, she did hear Sista's question and it sent shivers down her spine. *How is she?* Surely that had been the burning question on everyone's mind lately. Usually, Edmund and Mattie Mae Morley's home was filled with joy and laughter. Recently, it had turned into a house of sorrow, forcing the family to inhale more than its fair share of trouble and grief.

Charlotte then vaguely heard Sista say, "When it rains, it sho' does pour." And considering all that was going on in their family, she couldn't think of a more appropriate cliché.

2

My son, if sinners entice you, do not consent.

Proverbs 1:10

A strange scent from the garage wandered in the reception area. It was a dizzying cross between cod liver oil and hickory chips burning on a grill. Charlotte felt nauseated.

She looked around and found Sista standing at the door, keeping it slightly ajar with her foot, and listening to her son, John Edward, complain.

Once the clean-shaven John Edward finished whining of his reoccurring blackheads, whiteheads and oily skin, Sista suggested he try an inexpensive application of pure lemon juice on his blemished face. "I know yo' skin is oily enough to fry chicken in, but God did put things on this earth to help us. You can even drink some yarrow tea for oily skin, John Edward."

After listening to John Edward mull over the idea of purchasing a costly astringent from the local drugstore, Sista suggested again that he go home and simply apply some lemon juice or alcohol on the troubled areas. She then curled up the corners of her mouth and shook her head as if to say John Edward was not the sharpest pencil in the box.

Sista fidgeted about, expressing her need to go prepare a decent meal for her neighbor, Ms. Mamie. She went on to inform John Edward of her having found the senile Mamie feasting on a plate of dry sardines, scorched rice steeped in butter and a tall glass of buttermilk during a recent visit.

"And you know she's hard of hearing," Charlotte heard Sista say. "Mamie is about as deaf as a piece of wood."

Sista looked tired. Poor thing. Due to lack of proper sleep, she had developed raccoon eyes. The gloomy dark circles almost gave the appearance that Sista wore sunglasses. But she had been a godsend in the Morley family's time of need.

Charlotte checked the time on the clock Walker had just hung on the wall, and figured she may have enough time to read. First, she took the opportunity to clean out her purse, tossing out an old movie ticket stub, dried out tattered tissue, old grocery receipts, an old tube of apricot lipstick and Post-its with telephone numbers belonging to persons that escaped her memory. She tossed out a crumpled offering envelope from her church, Greater Faith Center, located in her hometown of Washington, D.C. Seeing the envelope only stirred up her desire to get back home and return to her duties as the senior minister in the Women's Counseling ministry.

Charlotte carefully unfolded the slightly crumbled letter written to her by her aunt, Ramiyah. She slowly smoothed out the creases and started reading:

Dear Charlotte,

I hope this letter finds you in good health and good spirits. I can't believe I'm writing you. I guess it takes something like this to happen to make people communicate with one another. I don't know if Jean or Betty has kept you up to date about my incarceration. I am so grateful that Jean has agreed to take care of my babies for me, but she is getting up in age and I will soon have to reconsider my options for their guardianship.

You probably don't know all the details about that night or about the events that led up to it. I guess it doesn't really matter now. I may have been christened Ramiyah Patterson, but in here I'm just #0195823234, thanks to the penal system.

I did not sleep well last night, not with all the screaming, crying, pleading and obscenities bellowing over my head and beneath my feet. Talk about acoustics. They have excellent surround sound in prison. Sometimes I think I can feel the inmates' emotions sink into my bones, right down to the marrow, and eventually seeping into my very spirit.

Every night when those steel doors clank behind the guards, and I lay down in my tiny cot, my filthy environment is just another added distraction to keep me from peaceful slumber. Confession: I know I'm not supposed to hate anyone, but I really did hate that curmudgeon of a judge who so harshly sentenced me. I hated my poor excuse of an attorney who must have ordered his law degree from a JC Penney catalog. Most of all, I hated my dead husband, who swore that he loved every fiber of my being with every fiber of his. That was a lie straight from the pits of hell. I hated Ma and JT, and last, but not least, I hated myself.

Truth of the matter is, I'm disappointed in myself for allowing the devil to convince me to marry Cole, only for me to end up killing him. Now look at me. I'm serving time. So, where is the devil now? Undoubtedly, off somewhere recruiting more dumb souls like mine. I hated myself for not listening to you in the first place. But I am, by the grace of God, slowly getting past all this hatred.

Hindsight is definitely twenty-twenty. I mean, sin is truly ugly when you think about it with all its masked drawing attraction, only to result in pain and destruction.

Pray for me, Charlotte. Pray for my strength. Pray for my protection. I've already heard horrid stories about the butches (including some of the guards) in here, and I've got to tell you, I'll kill again to keep from being raped.

Cole had raped me emotionally for years and I promise you I WILL NEVER go through that torture again, nor will I worship another human being again. After all, it's not like Cole was a miracle worker who taught me how to breathe or eat solid foods.

It's time you know the truth since I have no pride left to hide behind. Besides that, you deserve to know the truth. All I have now is time. Time to wait, time to talk and time to rot. Well, time to talk through letters, at least.

You warned me not to marry Cole. Do you remember that? I thought he was the "one." He had job stability and money. He was well known, well liked and he wanted me. Me! And at the age of thirty-three (at that time) I felt privileged to be wanted by such a man.

What I didn't know was that Cole had such a short attention span and wouldn't want ME for very long. After about two years into our marriage, I reluctantly agreed to join him in participating in swap meets (and I'm not talking about California flea markets either) and YES . . . some black people are into this sort of thing.

Our little clandestine "meetings" were usually held at the palatial second home of a well-known award-winning R&B singer and his B-list actress wife. Out of respect for this couple's privacy, I'll keep their names confidential, but will continue to pray that they repent before the Lord sees fit to expose them publicly. Although it wouldn't be too hard to guess their identity if the ownership of this home was common knowledge. At other times, we'd rendezvous at a dark, dingy underground club that was secretly owned by one of our local politicians. So much for scruples.

You have to understand, I was desperate to keep my man. I simply was a desperate, insecure and pathetic fool. No woman should subject herself to such humiliation. I should have been his and his alone and not treated like a basket of bread that was passed around as an appetizer.

I thought we did well in keeping up appearances though. Didn't you think so? Didn't our family portraits look good enough to come with wallets? Our smiles could not have been more perfect if someone had pasted them on. Well, as you know by now, we were not those Brady Bunch-Huxtable type folks in those pictures.

And another thing, now that I think about it, this is not my first time in prison either. I had been in prison for the past five years. Only I did not share it with a bunch of, well, a garden variety of women. No. My prison was a six-bedroom house in an exclusive, almost totally lily-white neighborhood, run by a sadistic husband.

Did you think I lived in an ivory tower? I did, I suppose. After all, it is a privilege, especially for black folks, to live on Eau Claire Street. I lived in a palace with gold handcuffs secured snugly around my wrists. Pretty-up the ugly, problematic life.

Truth be told, I'd been in prison long before I married Cole. I'm sure you don't know, but you, Charlotte, had been a lifeline with all your wisdom and godly attributes growing up.

But in all fairness to Cole, everything is not entirely his fault. I allowed myself to be a Stepford wife. For the record, Cole didn't start beating me until the last six months of our marriage. By that time, I had handed over my life to him.

There is a big difference between not being able to see and choosing not to see. Either way, when it came to Cole, I was blind in one eye and could not see out of the other. Funny. Not once did I ever attempt to drag out my suitcase and flee.

Did I ever even think about it? No. My mind was too numb to be wrapped up in rational thought.

He only fought me twice before that fateful night. The first fight was because I contracted a sexually transmitted disease. Charlotte, I can only compare my life to that of a forsaken mute living in a house where all windows and doors are sealed tight, no ventilation or incoming air.

After our second knockout-drag down fight, I was determined that there would not be a third time. Three strikes, he was out! Because I caught a STD, he wanted to beat the crap out of me. What was he thinking? With our lifestyle, how could I have not caught a disease? Again, stupid! I am blessed to be alive. Even though I had become an overly submissive wife, I had had enough abuse that night. Oh, I know. There is nothing wrong with being submissive, right? You mentioned once that the Bible says that we are to be submissive to one another. Problem was, I was submissive to the wrong man.

For over three years, I've endured more pain than anyone should have to. It was never enough for Cole. Women would call the house consistently and he would stay gone for days on numerous occasions. And do you think he had an explanation when he got home? No; of course not. I, the wife, was not worthy of an explanation. Then again, in my heart, I knew his excuse.

During the last six months of our marriage, I was an absolute wreck. That's why I did not come to D.C. to visit you last year. I knew you would be able to see through the façade. It amazes me how you were always able to do that. You saw through Cole from day one. I chose to wear blinders while he lorded over me.

Anyway, I was so distraught last year until we had to hire a full-time housekeeper to look after three-year-old twins, Coby and Chance. I just couldn't do it anymore. I spent most of my time in bed, and when I did get up, I would drink straight vodka on the rocks to self-medicate.

In the beginning, whenever Cole had plans for us to attend one of those Sodom and Gomorrah–type sessions, I would get semi-drunk by night. But five months before Cole's death, I would get fully loaded in order to cope. Survival.

As I write this letter, hot stinging tears are starting to blur my vision. Charlotte, I can only imagine the shock you must feel while reading this, and I haven't even told you the shocking part yet. Milk for now. Believe me. You couldn't handle the meat right now. I apologize if it seems like I'm teasing, but I'm trying to sort through this mess myself. You do not know how many times I wanted to come to you for help.

There were times when I would pick up the phone to call you, only to place the receiver back on the cradle. Maybe if I had the courage to have done so, I would be home raising my children. At least I would be enjoying freedom. Perhaps I should end here and let you digest what I've written so far.

It's chow time anyway; not that that's anything to look forward to. I could really sink my teeth into a nice piece of grilled salmon with some mozzarella cheese right about now. Most of the meals here look like oatmeal and taste like cardboard. Write me back soon and let me know how everyone is doing. I'm sure I will be the main topic at next year's family reunion. Are you going?

Write back soon.

Love Always,

Ramiyah aka #0195823234

3

*A wise man will hear and will increase learning; and a
man of understanding shall attain unto wise counsel.*

Proverbs 1:5

After Charlotte had finished reading the letter, a feeling
washed over her that could best be described as wistful. She
felt compelled to go back and linger over every sentence
written with its flurry of words. She had no idea that Ramiyah had been involved in a swinger's lifestyle. Ramiyah was
her mother's youngest sister. Jean, the oldest sister, raised
Ramiyah and their brother, Wendell, after their mother died.

Ramiyah's letter, which poignantly reflected on her tragic
life, was yet another reminder of the turmoil in Charlotte's
family. The Morleys and their church family had recently
been rocked by scandal. The pastor had been banned from
the church because of stealing, and then he secretly eloped
with Charlotte's cousin, Terry. The pastor had been killed
in a fiery plane crash that also claimed the life of Tina,
Terry's twin sister. Now Terry was on the run again. At least
this time she had informed her mother that she was okay,
but would not disclose her location. The grieving Morley
family wanted answers. However, Charlotte held on to a
sermon she remembered her pastor preaching some time

ago. *"Sometimes we just don't get answers on this side of heaven."* Although the conceited twins used to walk around as if they founded the free-world, no one felt that Tina or the pastor deserved such a horrible death.

Charlotte sensed that she was slowly being prepared for Ramiyah's complete story and wondered why this information had not come out during the trial. A jolting chill ran down Charlotte's spine.

Charlotte was grateful that her parents had chosen to remain on Turtle Island for another week before returning to their home in the nation's capital. Poor Edmund and Mattie Mae had gone through so much over the past few weeks with the deaths of friends and their granddaughter, Tina, that they really needed the support of family and friends.

"Mr. Edmund's truck is ready," Junior announced dryly as he crunched on a granola bar. He walked past Charlotte in an urgent manner.

Even though Charlotte could see that Junior strongly resembled his father, he did have one tiny flaw. His eyebrows were so close together that they appeared to be in danger of becoming one. The big unibrow look threatened to take Junior off the attractive men's list by at least one notch. However, his broad torso, which was practically bursting through his shirt, made up for the unibrow.

Charlotte grabbed her belongings and followed Junior to the cash register. The total cost rang up to a mere five dollars. The look of surprise gave Charlotte away.

"Mr. Edmund is a long time customer. That lock was no trouble to fix," Junior explained as he broke open a roll of coins. Junior's breath smelled loudly of peppermint and his mammoth-size afro threatened to make his head topple.

"Thank you," Charlotte said, handing him a five dollar bill. "You have a nice day."

"You too," Junior, who was unashamedly admiring Charlotte's walk, replied from behind the cash register.

Charlotte pretended not to notice, but she did, and felt that Junior's glances were somewhat assaulting and intrusive. Once outside, she instantly spotted the truck parked near an air pump and vacuum center.

"When I get back in this car, don't you tear outta here like you crazy, John Edward," Charlotte heard Sista order. "I ain't tryin' to learn how to walk and talk all over again. In other words, I ain't tryin' to test God to see if He is able. So, you drive like you got some sense."

Sista turned around and saw Charlotte leaving. "Tell Mattie Mae I'll be by later today," she yelled from inside the garage while shaking a few corn chips from a bag into her hands. John Edward looked up from the hood of his car and waved.

"I will." Charlotte waved back. She had completely forgotten about Sista's question concerning the family's welfare and could not remember if she had answered or not. No matter. Everyone knows that when tragedy comes knocking at the door, you just do the best you can, with God's help.

Charlotte drove away slowly from the lot of Walker's Auto Garage. Thinking about the family's drama, she wanted more than anything to help her relatives. "Lord, please give us a breakthrough," Charlotte pleaded earnestly. "We need one. But in the meantime, Lord, thank you for the grace to go through it."

As she neared her grandparents' rugged, gravel laced lane, Charlotte slowed down to let a pack of stray dogs cross the road. It was late August, too early for leaves to fall, yet she noticed that the ground was almost covered in goldenrod, burnt orange and russet foliage.

Parking along the side of the house, Charlotte noticed her mother pulling a handful of stubborn weeds from the ground. Mattie Mae and Betty moved about laggardly in the garden. Noting that her father's vehicle was not in the yard, Charlotte assumed that he and Edmund were probably out somewhere together.

Betty straightened up, pulled off her yellow, pink and orange striped garden gloves and stretched for a moment while Mattie Mae continued to mill about and toil in the dirt. Mattie Mae loved her son Esau's wife as if she were her own daughter. The mother-in-law and daughter-in-law team had formed a strong alliance and worked well together over the years.

With all that had happened recently, Charlotte realized that Betty had not briefed her on what had been happening with Ramiyah. Charlotte went in the house and proceeded upstairs to the guest bedroom in search of her journal. There was much to write. Moments later, she was sitting down with pen and journal in hand.

"Charlotte," Betty's voice called out from the top of the stairs. "You've got some more mail from Ramiyah." Betty had a worried look on her face as she entered the bedroom. The twinkle that had once been was now gone and replaced with sadness. There was not much life in her mother's eyes.

"I forgot to tell you about that sofa store near our house."

"Sitting Pretty?" Charlotte asked.

"Right," Betty replied. "They will be having a going out of business sale soon, if you're interested," Betty said, nervously handing Charlotte two envelopes addressed from a Women's Correctional Center.

"Really?" Charlotte stared blankly at the envelopes. "I wonder if they have any suede sectionals. Then again, I don't need to be making two major purchases right now. I can barely afford to take a trip across the street. I need a new car, remember? I may look into it when I go back home."

Betty nodded and Charlotte continued.

"I was thinking about trading in my car for an SUV, but that means I would literally be leaking gas."

"You sure would. Gas prices are outrageous," Betty said, one corner of her mouth curved upward.

"By the way, Ma, we haven't had a chance to really talk since you've been here. It's been so crazy around here, and now, all of a sudden, I'm hearing from Ramiyah. She had not spoken to me much since she got married. Actually, I'm the one who weaned off because I never approved of that marriage. I had no idea her life had been such a living hell. So, it's a little shocking to be receiving mail from her."

"Ramiyah is in prison, honey. She's just reaching out for support. She knows you love her." Betty inched closer to the door.

"Of course. I know this." Charlotte shrugged her shoulders, deciding to drop the matter and adopt Betty's sentiment. Big loose curls spilled about Charlotte's face.

Betty started toward the stairway. "We'll talk later," she promised. "Right now, I need to go help Mattie Mae in the kitchen."

Charlotte sighed wearily and said nothing. Words lodged in her throat. This once close-knit family of hers was becoming unrecognizable.

After dismissing the notion to finish writing in her journal for now, Charlotte chose to read at least one of the letters Betty had hand delivered to her. After deciding to read in date order, she stretched out across the bed and tore open the tightly sealed envelope that had the earliest postmark date.

Charlotte raised her arms to stretch a bit. She looked at an old scar on her elbow as if she was seeing it for the first time. It was an ugly reminder of the consequences of not paying attention when going down a flight of concrete stairs. Moreover, it reminded her to simply pay attention, stay alert and be discerning.

Feeling too uncomfortable to read in a prostrate position, Charlotte sat up, leaning her head against the headboard. "Lord, give me strength," she whispered weakly. Charlotte pondered on how tough life must have been for Ramiyah and how depressing it must be sitting in a jail cell. After unfolding the three-page letter, Charlotte began to read.

4

I applied mine heart to know and to search and to seek out wisdom and the reason (of things) and to know the wickedness of folly even of foolishness and madness.

Ecclesiastes 7:25

Dear Charlotte,

As you can tell by now, Jean sent me your grandparents' address. I was so sorry to hear about the Morley family's devastating loss. Also, I pray that Terry is convicted in her heart for what she has done.

There is nothing like making a bad situation worse. There were times when I wanted Cole dead. Wished for it. Hoped for it. Almost prayed for it. Never imagined I would cause it. I've adopted, and since dropped, the lowly victim stance.

Anyway, I had a dream last night. It was about my father, JT. Well, actually, it was about his brother, Uncle Chester, and what Uncle Chester had to say about JT. Before I tell you about the dream, yesterday afternoon I was sitting out in the "yard" and I guess God brought a memory back to me. I had forgotten all about Uncle Chester until yesterday.

Anyway, I'm sleeping peacefully and all of a sudden there was Uncle Chester with those dark spooky eyes of his. Those eyes used to scare the you-know-what out of me. He had eyes *much like yours, deep and piercing. However, your eyes are not spooky. They're intoxicating (smile). You were blessed with a pair of friendly eyes.*

As I was saying, I suddenly remembered how Uncle Chester smelled like liniment and rotten gas all the time. Not the Exxon or Shell kind, but the beans and cabbage kind of gas. Next thing I know, my eyes are opened and I'm left wondering why I'm having flash backs of Uncle Chester.

Before I forget, I have a friend here named Monica who's been helping me deal with my issues. Monica is Caucasian and her story is the stuff that country music is made of. Sorry, I sound so scattered, but her story is truly an amazing story. I promise.

In case you're wondering why I'm writing you, it's because you're the closest thing to God in our family I've got, and I want and need your advice. The night I killed Cole was not because of any physical blow he gave me. It was because of an emotional blow.

In due time, I will tell you the full story. Okay, back to last night's dream. I dreamed I was in Salt Lick, Tennessee at Great-Grandma Nancy's house. I was a little girl, sitting on that raggedy back porch with Uncle Chester. The one thing that puzzled me about the dream was why Uncle Chester was there. Great-Grandma Nancy was related to us on our maternal side and Uncle Chester was related to us on our paternal side. He was JT's brother. I don't even think Uncle Chester knew that side of the family. Anyway, in the dream, Uncle Chester bluntly told me that Ma hung herself and that God had called JT to preach ever since he was a little boy. Now, since I know the family rarely mentions JT, and just in case you've forgotten, JT was your grandfather. That monster sired me, Jean, Betty and Wendell.

In the dream, I was laughing hysterically at the state-

ment about JT being called to preach, but Uncle Chester continued with his story as if he had my undivided attention. He said that because of JT's wickedness, the devil would have a terrible stronghold over our family that would cause great devastation and heartache. That's when I stopped laughing in the dream. Uncle Chester had scared the pants off of me.

Nevertheless, according to Uncle Chester, God will have His way and in due season, two righteous seeds will spring forth from JT's loins and carry out the work of the Lord. At first, when I woke up this morning, I was thinking somebody should have taken an iron skillet to JT's head a long time ago.

But if this is true, who are those two righteous seeds? Well, for one, I think you are, being that you're a minister. Perhaps the scoundrel left a legacy after all. Well, that's all for this letter for now. However, I want to leave you with this question. Who do you think is the other righteous seed? SMILE.

Love,

Ramiyah

"My God!" Charlotte said to herself. Now she remembered why and when her mother had gone through that bad depressing patch. She remembered hearing of Betty's meltdown during the anniversary of her mother's, Gladys Patterson's, suicide. Charlotte was barely out of diapers when it happened. She even vaguely remembered Uncle Chester and was old enough to know the difference between passing gas from time to time and a continual wind.

Charlotte did not know her maternal grandmother, Gladys Patterson, nor had she ever met her grandfather, JT Patterson. He abandoned the family before Ramiyah had been born and no one talked about him fondly whenever his name did come up. Now Charlotte was curious as to why Ramiyah felt the need to spoon-feed her family history.

"Charlotte! Charlotte! Yoo-hoo, colored girl! I know you're up there, 'cause Miss Betty just told me so," the male falsetto voice called out. "Are you decent up there? I don't care if you are or not. You don't have anything that money can't buy no way."

Charlotte slid the letters, along with a few sheets of stationery paper, pad and ink pen, inside the deep pockets of her dress. She tilted her head sideways to see who the orator of that statement was. Moments later, standing before her was this smartly dressed, cocoa brown linebacker of a man with frosted, permed hair, manicured nails and smelling like Coco Chanel.

Charlotte jumped up and screamed with excitement. "Hiawatha? Is that you?" She ran up to Sista's son and hugged his neck tightly while he gave her a peck on the cheek. Charlotte might not have approved of Hiawatha's gay lifestyle, but ever since her childhood visits to Turtle Island, she always enjoyed his company.

"It is me in the flesh and I bring you greetings in the matchless name of Hiawatha Samson Jones. Girl, you know Mama ran out of names when she got to me, didn't she?" Hiawatha wrapped his arms around Charlotte's tiny waist and then gently pushed her away to get a good look at her. "Look at you! Still petite. I bet you weigh about a hundred pounds soaking wet and stand five feet tall in three-inch heels."

Charlotte felt silly for blushing, but blush she did. She could not help it.

"Looking all Annie Mae-ish in your little country house-coat-slash-frock."

"Sundress," Charlotte corrected. "It's called a sundress." Charlotte twirled around.

"Oh, sundress, moo-moo, whatever. You know they did not teach you to dress like that in D.C." He sniffed. "And you smell like a little doll baby."

"A doll baby? A doll baby does not have a smell."

"Yeah, they do. When my niece was little, she used to sprinkle baby powder on her doll's bottom. Don't worry. Plastic and talcum is a clean pleasant scent to me."

"Well, I'm glad." Charlotte chuckled. "I was afraid I needed to go back and shower again."

"Naw. You're fresh and so clean-clean. Girl, I haven't seen you since hatchet was hammer. So, what's been going on with you? I heard you're a minister now." Hiawatha sat down in the Queen Anne chair. Charlotte leaned against the dresser.

"You heard correctly. I am an ordained minister." Charlotte did a curtsy. "One might say that I got a revelation about my genesis and made an exodus from my past. Being a minister does not make one perfect, so don't go putting me under a microscope."

"What do you mean?" Hiawatha smiled.

"Oh, I know you. Just letting you know ahead of time that I am not perfect and the blue bird of happiness does not land on my shoulders every morning."

Hiawatha grinned and leaned forward. "Okay. Tell me about your ministry."

"Well, being a divorcee, my ministry mainly deals with counseling divorced women, abused women, women with is-sues in general."

Hiawatha raised his eyebrows. His eyes were bright with admiration.

"Did you bring your dog?" Charlotte asked, referring to Hiawatha's beloved brown and white Jack Russell terrier.

"On the bus?"

"Oh, that's right. Miss Sista did say you were coming

down on the bus. And since when did you, Mr. Hotshot
Record Exec from New York City, choose the bus for your
mode of transportation?"

"Only because I decided I wanted to see the countryside.
I know that's unusual for me, given that I have first class
tendencies."

Charlotte giggled.

"But I don't own a car. No need for one in New York, and
I didn't rent one because I was not up for that long drive
alone. Although little dude down in advertising did offer to
help me drive if I would drop him off in Clarendon County
to visit his grandmother."

"Why didn't you take him up on his offer?"

"Because I *let* him drive me to a release party once and
the brother drove so slow I wanted to take the steering
wheel from him and drive us into a median just so the
medics could come and airlift us to our destination."

Charlotte cracked up. "Well, regardless of how you choose
to travel or how much you spend on traveling, I must admit
that money looks good on you."

"Thank you. Thank you." Hiawatha stood and took a bow
before primping and posing in front of Charlotte. Then he
sat back down. "It's been a long time since I rode the bus
and it will be a long time before I ride it again. Do you hear
me?" Hiawatha shook his head in disgust and started fanning his chest with his hand. "But that's another story. Anyway, I left pooch with a friend. Guess what that crazy dog
did?"

"What?"

"The other day when I came home, I caught Ms. Thang
walking down the hall with a knife in her paw, barking
about she was going to end it all."

Charlotte looked puzzled and then realized that Hiawatha was pulling her leg. Laugh lines formed on her face.

"Gotcha! Seriously, I think my pampered pup is gay. He's always switching around the apartment like a little queen." Hiawatha grinned, proud of his teasing.

"Okay, Lord. Is this an opening to witness to Hiawatha?" Charlotte asked beneath her breath. *If so, give me the words to say.* Nothing. She sensed the time had not yet come, but the time would come while she and Hiawatha were in South Carolina. "So, how long are you here and what's been going on with you?" she found herself asking.

Seizing the opportunity to shine, Hiawatha crossed his legs and folded his hands over his knees. Encircled around his pinkie finger was a dazzling platinum and black onyx ring. He caught Charlotte marveling at the ring as if it were a rare blue diamond, stolen from an Egyptian tomb. "Charlotte, remind me to give you this little bauble I've got stashed in my bag. You know how I loves my jewelry," he said. "Anyway, business is booming. I'm here to conduct a little personal business. Oh, before I forget, you remember Ms. Mamie's granddaughter, Tawny?"

Charlotte nodded, signaling that she remembered the girl.

"Well, Tawny goes to the same hair salon I go to, The Shampoo Bowl. I ran into her the other day at the Bowl and tried to hook Tawny up with my hairstylist, but noooo! She wanted the new girl to do her hair, and get this; the new girl's name is Lista Reen. I kid you not. Now, what was *her* momma thinking?" Hiawatha's body jerked as he laughed uncontrollably.

"I don't know what kind of style Tawny was going for, but when she left the salon she had blond tresses that were sweeping the floor. Most ridiculous. She looked a hot mess. Why she wants to look like Rapunzel is beyond me. Other than that, she looks fabulous. Remember, she was ill-favored without any war paint on her face. She's lost all that weight and I know you remember how well nourished she was. I used to think that Abdul the Tentmaker made all of her clothes."

Charlotte grabbed Hiawatha by the hand in an attempt to get him up from the chair. "You are a mess, Hia. Let's go downstairs before you have me repenting before the Lord. You got me laughing at folk."

Always the show-off, Hiawatha raised his arms and play-fully flexed his muscles, pumping them like Texas oil drills. "Repenting for what? It ain't nothing but the truth. Tawny lost so much weight, I swear she must wear a size nine months. She looks good though. Not Halle Berry good or drop dead gorgeous, but she's no plain Jane either."

Without thought or effort, words involuntarily gushed from Charlotte's mouth. "Hia, how is your mother with your homosexuality?"

Hiawatha patted Charlotte gently on her hand. "Chile, Mama will be all right. I've been this way for over twenty years. She gives me the same treatment she gives everybody else; a piece of her mind and a whole lot of her mouth! Mama discriminates equally and that's a good thing in a way, but it still won't change a thing with me. My thing is, you do *you* and I'll do me. I am what I am."

And you're not what you think you are, Charlotte said to herself.

5

Behold, how good and how pleasant it is for brethren to dwell together in unity

Psalm 133:1

Mattie Mae and Betty were in the living room, slumped down in their seats, listening to Sista tell them some saga about her seemingly endless supply of medication. Despite Sista's annual checkups consistently rendering bills of good health, she stood in the living room holding several brown prescription bottles that brandished her name.

"Look at her," Hiawatha whispered to Charlotte. "My mother, the drama queen. They should prescribe medication for her advanced stage of nosiness." Hiawatha stood with his hands on his hips. "My mother has more drugs in her medicine cabinet than a pharmaceutical company, and it's costing us a fortune too. Between me and my siblings, we shell out enough money on Mama's medicine to purchase a small island in the Caribbean. That's one of the reasons why I'm down here. I plan to have a little talk with her doctor, 'cause you can't tell me some of that ain't nothing but some sugar pills, honey." Creases formed crookedly on his forehead.

Betty, who was the first to see Hiawatha and Charlotte, pointed to Sista and said, "Come and join us, you two. Your mother is a character, Hiawatha. I just love her."

"She's a mess all right," Hiawatha agreed, knowing that his mother always had a knack for spinning a good yarn and calling it as she sees it.

Ignoring her son, the highly animated Sista continued on with her show and tell. "Now, my sister over in Columbia takes more pills than me. I'll never forget the time the doctor had her on something that made her skin like fish scales. Her face was all blotchy."

"That would be Aunt Annie, the pill popping serial spouse," Hiawatha whispered in Charlotte's ear. He then pretended to pop a pill in his mouth and swill back water to wash it down. "The woman went down the aisle at least five times, and all of her marriages ended before the ink dried on the license. Some of Aunt Annie's medication was probably for stamina to keep up with all those young husbands."

Charlotte struggled to keep a straight face. Sista feigned a dizzy spell as she described the side effects caused by another prescription she took for hay fever. After each exaggeration, she would place a medicine bottle on the table.

"Now, these pills are antibiotics the doctor gave me a while back when I had a cold and sore throat. I couldn't tell if they stopped my throat from hurting or not, 'cause they made my mouth numb. It felt like I had cotton in it." Sista frowned at the last bottle in her hand.

"My goodness. All of this medicine must cost you a small fortune, Sista," Betty said, reading some of the labels on the bottles. "But I'm sure Medicare or Medicaid helps some."

"They won't allow me to have Medicaid; talking 'bout I got too much money in the bank and income from rentin' out some land. How can they decide what's too much money for me to have? They don't know what I have to do wit' my money." Sista rested her last medicine bottle on the edge of the coffee table.

"It's a shame all right," Betty said sympathetically.

"I'm blessed to have chi'ren who help me out, but some folk don't have help and they can't afford to pay for their medicine. My mama used to say a rich man can get his ice in the summer, but a poor man has to wait until wintertime."

"Ain't that the sorrowful truth," Mattie Mae said, taking time from enjoying a cup of dandelion tea. The matronly Mattie Mae placed her tea cup and saucer on the end table to secure the bun at the nape of her neck with a hair pin. "Even back then I'd bet a woman would wear her petticoat in public if she could help afford to take care of her family."

Sista folded her arms and gave a smug look in agreement.

Mattie Mae took a sip of tea. "Sista, you sho' you don't want some of this tea?"

"Nooo! I don't mess wit' tea too much. The last time I drank any tea was that Sleepytime tea. Darn thing almost put me in a coma. But I tell ya, spendin' all this money on medicine just don't make no darn sense." Sista sounded outraged. "The other day, I had a toothache and I just rubbed some whiskey on my gums."

"You still ended up goin' to the doctor," Mattie Mae pointed out.

Sista giggled. "Yeah, I did. But you know it just reminded me how things have changed."

Mattie Mae nodded her head in agreement.

"When we was comin' up," Sista continued, "we didn't have much, but we didn't worry about not havin' enough, 'cause families used to share wit' one another."

"That sho' is the truth," Mattie Mae said, rocking back and forth. "What we had, you had. We really didn't lack for nothin', but nowadays you bet' not ask folks for anything, 'cause they'll look at you like you're crazy."

"Miss Betty and Ms. Mattie Mae, as much as I enjoy your company, not to mention that of my mother's, I would like to have a little private discussion with Charlotte, if you don't mind," Hiawatha stated. "If I stay in here much longer with Mama, it would be too much fire in the hole." Hiawatha grinned mischievously at Betty as he stopped short of leading Charlotte outside.

"Well, go on then," Sista said, blushing. "This is grown folks conversation anyhow and that does include Charlotte. She's welcome to stay." Sista grinned at Charlotte, making it obvious to see where Hiawatha inherited his mischief.

Hiawatha placed his index finger on his lips as a gesture to his mother to tone it down some. Mattie Mae and Betty giggled as Sista rolled her eyes at her effervescent son.

Sista and Hiawatha both enjoyed being the center of attention to the point where it often seemed like they were competing against one another. To get Hiawatha out of her hair and out of the spotlight, Sista started to recall Hiawatha's beginning, a story he was tired of hearing.

"I stayed sick when I was pregnant wit' Hiawatha. That boy's got a head made of concrete." Then Sista's voice started to crack as the subject changed. "I saw signs early on and tried to ignore it when I caught him wearin' my clothes."

It was the first time Charlotte had ever seen a crestfallen Sista.

Hiawatha could not get out the door fast enough.

Charlotte feared the porch swing was not sturdy enough to hold Hiawatha's large Mr. Universe frame, but it did, though barely. She offered to go back inside and bring him something to eat and drink, but he politely refused, pointing to his protruding belly and noting that he was on the verge of passing for a six-months-pregnant woman.

"Have you talked to Ramiyah lately?" he asked out of the blue.

"You remember Ramiyah?" Charlotte was astounded since Ramiyah had only been to Turtle Island a couple of times when they were kids.

"Girl, I can remember things as far back as when I was five. But yeah, I remember that skinny little girl with the long pigtails, braces and freckled face. She's not that much older than us."

"It's funny you should ask about Ramiyah. I was just reading a letter from her when you came upstairs. She and I didn't keep in touch that much after she got married. I didn't go to her trial. All I know is that she and Cole got caught up in some kinky stuff and now he's dead and she's in prison. Cole had threatened to leave her for one of her so-called girlfriends, Anjenette. To my understanding, there was some sort of argument and Ramiyah shot him."

Hiawatha's face lacked emotion. "Yeah, well, I got a little more information on that from Cha-Cha." Hiawatha noticed Charlotte's furrowed eyebrows. "Don't tell me you don't remember Preston Chambers from down the road. He used to live only a howdy and a half, as Mama would say, from Ramiyah."

"Who?" Charlotte asked in a nonchalant tone.

"He used to play hopscotch with you. Well, he calls himself Cha-Cha now. Come on, now! Don't look so shocked. As much as that boy loved to play hopscotch and jump rope you didn't think sugar was all up in that tank?"

"Oh, yes. I remember him now. How is he?" Charlotte wanted to laugh, but couldn't. As funny as Hiawatha was, he only confirmed the fact that the chances for women being found by men who wanted to be with *only* women was getting slimmer by the milisecond.

Hiawatha cleared his throat. "Baby girl, Cha-Cha is doing Stevie Wonderful. That boy is merrier than Christmas. He's big time with his event planning business and travels all over the place. Although I don't know how he does it since he rarely gets up before noon. But somehow, he is making that paper."

"Paper?"

"Yen. Shilling. Peso. Deutsche mark. Ruble. Money. However you want to say it."

Charlotte chortled. "Gotcha. Anyway, I don't know how people can sleep past noon. Unless I'm sick, once that sun shines in my room, I'm up."

"I know, right. But he's fabulous and knows absolutely everybody and their momma. Well, he used to live in Tucson. Now he's in New York. It's a shame his brother chose a life of crime."

"What do you mean?"

"He steals clothes for a living and then sells them. Girl, that stuff is hotter than the noonday sun in August in the Bahamas."

"You know you're crazy, right?" Charlotte chuckled.

"Yeah. Anyway, I wish I had known what was going on with Ramiyah sooner. My brother, Luke, is a paramedic. He would have driven to Arizona in that ambulance and put Cole in the back of that thing. Nobody would have ever known what happened to Cole."

"Aside from his thriving business, how is Preston doing these days?"

"He's okay. But do you want to hear something for kicks and giggles?"

Charlotte hunched her shoulders nonchalantly.

"Girl, the last time I saw Cha-Cha, he looked like the entire Village People. And he needs to stop getting those injections in his lips. The boy's lips were puffier than cumulus clouds, plus he piles on all this thick mascara and dark *guy-liner* around his eyes. It makes him look ghoulish. Anyway, I met him for drinks a few weeks ago and he was drooling like an invalid. How hard is it to drink liquids while keeping your mouth closed? I was tempted to buy him a bib. But then again, with those lips of his, I guess it is hard to swallow."

Hiawatha hissed as his brother, John Edward, drove by, blowing the horn. "You know my brother's girlfriend has a four-year-old son by some other dude, right?" Hiawatha said, getting off track. "The kid was with John Edward when he picked me up from the bus station. So, the kid asked me how old I was. I asked the little crumb-snatching yip-yapper how old did he thought I was."

"What did he say?" Charlotte asked. Knowing that Hiawatha had a flair for crudeness, she braced herself for his outrageous answer.

"Fifty! Fifty years old! I know I don't look twenty-one anymore, but fifty!" Hiawatha huffed. "The devil *is* a liar!"

"And what was your response to the little boy?" Charlotte started laughing, already convinced that Hiawatha gave the child a smart-alecky answer.

"I told that rascal I was the same age as my tongue but older than my teeth! Let him figure it out. You know me. I seek validation, not ridicule."

"Okay, he's only a kid," Charlotte pointed out.

"Aren't we all?" But Hiawatha knew he had more on his mind to discuss with Charlotte besides his age.

6

A merry heart doeth good like a medicine, but a broken spirit drieth the bones

Proverbs 17:22

John Edward had circled back around and was now driving onto the Morleys' property. Grinning wider than the state of Texas, he parked and got out of his car and gingerly walked along a stony path toward the front porch, stopping briefly to tie his shoelaces.

"Boo!" Hiawatha bucked his eyes and shouted gleefully.

"Man, what's wrong with you?" John Edward asked.

"No. The question is, what's wrong with you? Walking like you're afraid somebody's going to bite you."

John Edward was not as buffed as his older brother, and was slightly shorter. His bowlegs presented a perfect arch. He waved Hiawatha off before burying his hands in his pants pocket. "Hey, Charlotte," he greeted just before playfully punching Hiawatha in his shoulder.

"Hey to you too, John Edward. You came to visit us or to pick up your mother?" Charlotte asked, raising her hand to shield her eyes from the sun.

"I came to chill wit' y'all for a minute." John Edward took a seat in the corner. "Nellie Moss said she saw you earlier today." John Edward slapped Hiawatha on his knee. "She said she offered you a penny for your thoughts and you ignored her."

"Doggone right I ignored Nellie with her nosey self." Hiawatha squinted his eyes and pouted. "My thoughts are worth more than a penny. My thoughts are worth millions! And where are you coming from anyway?"

"From one of my boys' house. We were over there just trippin' about his cousin's ghetto wedding."

"Oh, yeah?" Hiawatha's interest peaked. Much like his mother and brother, Hiawatha also had a natural bent for prying and gossip.

"Yeah. The mother of the groom had on this see-through cream-colored blouse and you could see her blood red-size double-D bra underneath it. People started shoutin' out to the folks in the wedding party when they marched in the church."

"You are lying!" Charlotte was tickled, yet disappointed in such a blatant display of ignorance and lack of social graces. "Now that's tacky."

"No, straight up," John Edward said. "The so-called wedding photographer is a cousin of the groom and he was taking pictures with disposable cameras. Not a digital camera. Not a Canon, Minolta or Nikon. Dude used disposable cameras."

Charlotte closed her eyes and shook her head.

"The bride's uncle looked to be almost eighty years old. He had his silk shirt unbuttoned all the way down to his gray-haired navel, and then he had the nerve to have six gold chains around his neck. One of the chains was a Mercedes medallion. But worse than that—"

"What could be worse than that?" Hiawatha asked.

John Edward started laughing. "Man, the uncle was talking all loud during the wedding, telling the groom not to do it; to lift up the veil and take a good look at the bride. He told him to think about how the children will look."

Charlotte and Hiawatha roared. Charlotte laughed so hard she feared wetting herself.

"Give us the what-what. How did the bridesmaids look?" Hiawatha asked, cracking up and doubling over.

"Some of them looked okay. I mean, they had on nice dresses, but they were strapless and some of them girls were thick! I don't mean Coca-Cola thick, but NFL hard body thick."

"Yeah, buddy! When you have shoulders like a line-backer, you can't pull that look off," Hiawatha said as he propped his feet up on the ledge.

"The groomsmen wore . . . what do you call those things they wear around their waists?" John Edward asked, tugging on his shirt sleeve before scratching his forearm.

"Cummerbunds," Charlotte answered.

"Yeah, well they were fake Gucci designer cummerbunds."

By now, Hiawatha and Charlotte were laughing until tears streamed down their faces. It was at this moment when she realized that John Edward was just as hilarious as Hiawatha. Then again, they had Sista, the ultimate comedian, for their mother.

"Well, what about the bride?" Hiawatha asked.

"Uh-uh." John Edward held up his hand. "You don't *even* want to know. I'll say this and drop it right there. The bride came down the aisle wearing these yellowish cat eyes contact lenses that you buy from the beauty supply store."

"Get out!" Hiawatha screamed. "I bet she looked like she had yellow jaundice."

"Did you take your girlfriend?" Charlotte asked, still trying to picture it all.

"No, and I'm glad I didn't. Mary would not have been ready for that. Oh, and after the reception, how about the bride and groom drove off in the groom's tricked out '68 Chevy. Man, it was crazy!"

"Oh, my God!" Hiawatha cried out. "What about the reception?"

"The food was good. I ain't gonna lie. We put a hurtin' on that food, but there was no wedding cake. They had all these different kinds of pound cakes they bought from the grocery store."

Not being able to contain himself any longer, Hiawatha screamed, sprang to his feet and sat down again.

"I heard that the groom had come into some money, but then he lost it all gambling," John Edward remarked.

"Well, you know what they say." Hiawatha had a twinkle of mischief in his eye.

"What? What do they say?" John Edward asked, sounding suspicious.

"Heir today, gone tomorrow."

"Boy, you stupid." John Edward chuckled.

Then as though a light bulb had been turned on in his head, Hiawatha turned toward Charlotte and asked, "Tell me something before I forget. What is this madness involving little Miss Terry? Scandalous! I ain't trying to downplay Tina's death or nothing like that, but has Terry lost her freaking mind?"

Charlotte heard Hiawatha, but was slightly distracted by the aroma of coconut pies baking in the oven. She realized that Mattie Mae, Betty and Sista were no longer within earshot and must have moved their conversation to the kitchen.

"Earth to Charlotte," Hiawatha commanded, waiting for a reply. John Edward appeared anxious for an answer as well. He fidgeted in his seat and toyed with a twig until he gave it one fatal snap.

"I'm sorry. I don't know what to say about Terry."

Suddenly, Charlotte's cell phone rang, and much to her delight, the bright neon display pad showed that the caller was her best friend since childhood, Timmi.

"Timmi! What's really going on, girl?" Charlotte answered the phone. She could hear a baby crying in the background. "Where are you? I can hear a baby going for it."

Hiawatha and John Edward went inside to give Charlotte some privacy and to grab a bite to eat.

"Yeah, I know. I'm in a hotel lobby. I'm pretty sure the baby needs his diaper changed, because he smells really ripe right about now. The mother has another kid in a stroller. The kid looks to be about six years old. Now to me, if you are so big that your legs are dragging the floor, then you don't need to be riding in a stroller. Let me stop. I can't talk long, so how are you doing?"

"Good. How about you?"

"I'm doing great. Any word on Terry yet?"

Charlotte sighed. "Well, you know she ran away again. She didn't even stick around for her own sister's funeral or for her husband's funeral."

"After stealing her own sister's identity and then with Tina dying, I guess she didn't have the guts to hang around. I would have dragged her little behind straight to jail, or at least court," Timmi said staunchly.

Charlotte sighed again. "Yeah, girl, I felt like taking her out myself. You can run, but you can't hide from God. Uncle Charles and Aunt Francine said there will be no more pacifying Terry."

"That has to be hard on them, but Terry needs to learn," the attorney in Timmi said.

"I know. Changing the subject, tell me something good." Charlotte was all too ready to change her somber mood.

"Okay. Guess what city I'm in."

"I give up. Where are you? What city?"

"New York City, baby!" Timmi blurted. "Your cousin, Jeff, invited me up to be his date tonight at the African American Legendary Ball! It's going to be held at the Waldorf."

"His date? Did I miss something?" Charlotte was confused and excited at the same time. Even though Jeff and Timmi had only recently met and they were friendly at best, Charlotte saw no indication that the two were interested in each other, although she secretly hoped they would be. Nevertheless, Jeff was a good man. A real good man. The kind that was hard to find, because lately, really good men were dropping off like flies. "When did you two start dating?" Charlotte asked as she envisioned Timmi in a long flowing gown that swept the stairs as she was descending and giving the illusion of her floating her way down. "When did you two start dating?" she asked again after not getting a response.

"We're not."

The call dropped.

7

Trust in the LORD with all thine heart and lean not unto thine own understanding

Proverbs 3:5

"Daddy, where have you guys been?" Charlotte asked as he and Edmund got out of the truck. Esau looked like a farmer in his denim overalls and boots. He and Edmund were covered in dust from the field.

"How is everybody?" Edmund asked as he proceeded toward the house. Both Hiawatha and John Edward professed to be doing well.

"We were helping Busta Watkins put up a fence, little Mattie Mae," Esau answered Charlotte.

"How is he?" she asked.

"You know what? I'm not really sure. Every time we talked about his daughters, Busta would quote scripture from Second Timothy or somewhere," Esau replied. Edmund, who had a bad case of hiccups, went inside the house as Esau continued. "I don't know what that was all about. It was really strange."

"I don't know either, but I do know this: it's all right to quote scripture, but unless it is inspired by God, it may not apply to a particular situation," Charlotte stated.

"What do you mean?" Hiawatha asked.

"You have to know that you *know* what the Lord is speaking to you specifically when you're reading, quoting or applying the scriptures," Charlotte replied, sounding fairly certain of her answer. "For instance, if you're out there lost in the woods without any water, I doubt God is going to tell you to take a stick and strike the nearest rock. Those instructions were for Moses. Now, God may actually tell you where a stream is located."

"God may actually speak? Audibly?" Skepticism rose in Hiawatha's voice.

Undaunted and knowing that Sista raised all of her children in the church, Charlotte refused to believe Hiawatha's act of being brand new to the things of God. "Yes, if He wants to. God speaks in many ways. Often times when you attribute something as your gut feeling or instinct, it is really the Holy Spirit giving you unction."

Esau nodded in agreement as he, too, went indoors.

"If it weren't for those two having the same physique, you couldn't tell that Mr. Charles and Mr. Esau were brothers," Hiawatha noted. "Speaking of which, you know I can't stand your Uncle Charles, right?"

"Why not?" Charlotte asked, all the while thinking how much nerve Hiawatha had to admit to her face that he did not like someone in her family. But it was Hiawatha and she was not offended. Aside from Timmi, no one else would get away with that statement.

"Because. If he had been on the real about himself, maybe some of this crap would not have happened." Hiawatha rolled his eyes and sucked his teeth. "Please! Nobody had to drag me out the closet. In fact, I flew out. Sequins, bows and all."

Charlotte noticed the smirk on John Edward's face as he

leaned back in his chair. It had been at least ten years since she had seen Hiawatha, and yet it was painfully obvious that he knew much more about what was going on in her family than she did. "You knew about my uncle?" she questioned.

"Girl, please!" Hiawatha rolled his eyes. "I recognize my *sisters*, okay. Don't tell me you didn't know! Is your gaydar antenna broken or something?" Hiawatha was about to make another comment when Mattie Mae came to the screen door and invited them inside for lunch. Hiawatha and John Edward could not resist the offer and pleaded with Charlotte to join them, but she declined in order to finish reading her mail.

Out on the highway, a group of rich, white elderly townspeople rolled by on their golf carts, gabbing, laughing and enjoying themselves. In recent years, masses of New England snowbirds had flocked to Turtle Island, making it their home.

The transplants took great delight in living on the beachfront in their bungalows since they were used to breathing ocean air. Charlotte waved at them and prayed for their safety since most of them were prone to run through red lights and stop signs.

Amidst the sounds of laughter and chatter coming from the dining room, Charlotte closed her eyes and drew a deep breath before opening the letter she retrieved from her dress pocket. After slowly exhaling, she opened her eyes and began to read.

Dear Charlotte,

Please keep me in your prayers. Do not ever stop. Anyway, Neil (as she calls herself, but her real name is Nell) and her spineless flunky, Lisa, are our resident bullies. Recently, they cornered Monica in the laundry room and roughed her

*up a bit. Monica is all right. She's got a black eye right now
. . . walking around here looking like that dog from the Little Rascals.*

*On second thought, please pray for Nell and Lisa also.
They need Jesus in a big way and to stop all this terrorizing.
Now, let me tell you a little about Monica's story before I tell
you about our ministry. THAT'S RIGHT! Our ministry,
or should I say, the Lord's ministry.*

*Monica is serving time for killing her three kids. Me and
my ignorant self had asked her how come white women tend
to eat their young. You know what she said? No race is ex-
empt from doing evil and asked if I hadn't paid attention to
the fact that African Americans are in the news for committing the same crimes as everyone else. And she's right.*

*Monica's story is not your typical "my husband done left
me" blues. She's been on lockdown for five years now. She
had lost her home, her job, her dignity and has no family to
speak of, except for an elderly aunt who lives in a nursing
home in Michigan. After several months of living in her car,
which was about to be repossessed, and tired of struggling to
provide food and shelter for her kids, she saw no other way
out for them.*

*The cold winter months were coming, and one day, she
just decided to leave her children in the car, in an abandoned
garage, with the engine running. Carbon monoxide. She
lied to them by telling that she was going to get them something to eat, knowing there was no more money and she was
exhausted from begging and being rejected. Monica never
went back. She couldn't face seeing their dead bodies. Now,
why she didn't kill herself also if she felt so hopeless, I do not
know. That always amazes me.*

*A former neighbor recognized the kids on the news and it
didn't take long for the police to find Monica. In fact, I think*

she turned herself in. Monica was wrong. The system failed her. It's all crazy. Anyway, she's turned her life around.

Now, from what I can tell, Neil and Lisa have a serious problem with us reaching out to women to accept Christ, but we refused to be stopped! We still meet every Wednesday night and attendance is increasing even though we just started this a month ago. Last week, three women accepted Jesus Christ as their Lord and Savior. Isn't that good news?

Guess who visited me recently? Hiawatha. He used to come to Tucson to visit Cha-Cha, who used to live down the street from me. Small world, isn't it? We've been keeping in touch ever since. Hiawatha has been sharing some things with me and I've been trying to talk to him, but he's not convicted in his heart yet. At least, I don't think so. But I do sense something is going on with him.

You know what, Charlotte? Although I'd give anything to get out of this sewage and be with my boys again, I love rolling up my sleeves and working in this ministry. Who would have thought, huh? Do you suppose I am the other righteous seed? Well, I've got laundry duty. Tomorrow, I suspect I will be a writing machine cranking out many letters. Do not be surprised, and please don't be annoyed when you get an avalanche from me. So, take care.

Ramiyah.

Now, Charlotte was really mystified. Hiawatha, whom she had not seen in years, not only kept in touch with her imprisoned aunt, but apparently, chose Ramiyah as a confidant as well. She wondered. Could this be why she wasn't given a word to speak into Hiawatha? Had Ramiyah been given charge to minister to him? One thing for sure, Charlotte was definitely happy about Ramiyah's prison ministry and was determined to help her in every way possible.

"Lord," Charlotte called out while looking up, "we, as women, are receivers and bearers by nature. We tend to hold on to grudges, memories and strongholds; things that can lead to violence, such as the case with my aunt. It's like these negative things are stuck in our teeth. Father God, free us. Release and restore. On behalf of my aunt and all women, I lay this at your feet, for they are nothing but distractions that hinder us from walking the righteous paths you have set before us. Father God, take control over all that concerns us. It is yours, in the mighty and matchless name of Jesus, I pray. Amen."

Charlotte folded the sheet of paper in half and tucked it inside her pocket, hoping to remember later to place it in her billfold behind the checkbook.

8

*My son, hear the instruction of the father and forsake not
the law of thy mother; for they shall be an ornament of
grace unto thy head and chains about thy neck*

Proverbs 1: 8 & 9

Out of the corner of her eye, Charlotte spotted two humming birds taking flight and chasing each other in the air, flapping their wings wildly. Over to her left, a small speckled rabbit ran across a field of tall cornstalks burnt to a crisp by the penetrating sun. Charlotte had loved Turtle Island and its inhabitants for as long she could remember.

She used to try to imagine her ancestors arriving at this strange land on human cargo ships, fearful as they docked along the Carolina coast; fearful as they witnessed white traders and wealthy merchants grin joyously while signing documents prerequisite to their trading. She wondered which of the sturdy oak trees her forefathers, whose lives did not rival the value of dogs, hung from, lynched whenever the spirit of another man moved him to call for such action.

She wondered how easy or how hard it was for her ancestors to adapt to eating new vegetation and killing wild and unfamiliar beasts. Charlotte also wondered if her great-great-great grandmothers and their sisterhood of friends found moments of peace when they congregated together

to pick cotton, shuck corn, snap peas, can peaches and deliver each other's babies.

She wondered how her great-great-great grandmothers
and their circles of friends handled their pain whenever a
husband, child, or any other family member was snatched
and consigned to another master. No doubt, the hardship of
plantation life had hardened and conditioned many hearts
to this new way of life.

She thought of how her people could so easily detach
themselves emotionally, and how some men could walk out
on their families or responsibilities as if a master were still
around leading them off to be sold. Regardless of the history of the nomenclature of Darkie, Niggra, Negro, Colored, Black and currently, African American, Charlotte was
proud of her people, despite the trials.

Charlotte took a moment to relish the peace and tran-
quility at hand. Hearing a noise, she turned her head. Sista
closed the door behind her.

Except for the sound of a plastic bag filled with yarn
dropping on the porch floor, Sista quietly joined Charlotte
and pulled out a pair of knitting needles. Peering over her
gold-rimmed glasses, Sista said, as she straightened the cush-
ion in the Morris chair, "They tell me you've been getting
mail from yo' Aunt Ramiyah."

Charlotte carefully mulled over the best possible response to give. Should she be brief with Sista or nip the
topic of conversation in the bud? "I have." Charlotte opted
for brief.

Sista looped a cord of lime green yarn over the needle.
Her knitting had a consistent rhythm of movement. She
peered over her glasses once more. "It's a shame she messed
up her life like that."

"I'm sorry that things had come to this, but believe it or
not, Ramiyah seems to be getting a new lease on life in

prison." Charlotte knew that Sista's sole purpose for bringing up Ramiyah was to find out what was in those letters.
"You know, Miss Sista, Moses was a murderer, and look at
how God used him. Ramiyah and another inmate are over-
seeing a women's prison ministry and are doing quite well
in ministering to others."

"Well, I hope she's found the Lawd. It seems to me that
every time somebody goes to jail, they suddenly find religion, or they become a lawyer. I guess some folks make you
put a knot upside their heads and some folks just need
killin'," Sista protested with a pout.

"The thing about this is that people are usually hard-
headed and stubborn. We don't recognize our need for God
until we hit rock bottom. As long as life is fine, we don't give
God a second thought, so He knows what it takes to get our
attention."

"Ain't that the truth," Sista agreed.

"By the way, how is Miss Mamie doing?" Charlotte chose
to make her point and quickly change the subject. "Grandma
told me she had been sick."

"She's in bad shape. When I was over there the other day
to wash out a few things for her, she was havin' trouble
movin' her bowels, and when she finally did go to the bathroom, that scent walked down that hall like a human being."

"Oh, my God!" Charlotte laughed. Hard. So hard, her
stomach started to cramp.

"It was awful." Sista grinned mischievously as she continued. "Neighbors can only do so much. Her family needs to
come down here and see about her. Mamie offered me some
candy, couldn't remember where she put it and come to find
out she was laying on top of it!"

"What?" Charlotte tried not to laugh. Even she knew
that Mamie's once sharp mind was now weakened by old
age.

"Yeah. When I went to help her turn to her side, there was the Wal-Mart bag peeking from underneath her tail. Do you think I ate that candy?"

"I'm sure you didn't." Charlotte chuckled. "Miss Sista, when we were at Walker's Garage the other day, I overheard you talking to John Edward about some home remedies."

"That's right."

"Grandma is good about that too, and using or even knowing about home remedies is becoming a lost art."

"You got that right," Sista agreed. "For some women, cooking and cleaning is a lost art. They got time for everything else."

"Since I've got you here, I want your advice."

Sista's face lit up. "Ask whatever you want."

"Several women in my women's ministry group suffer from various stomach ailments and I'm sure it's largely due to stress."

"Yeah, and stress can kill you too."

"I know. What do you recommend?"

"Well, let me think." Sista shifted her eyes to and fro. "Raspberry leaf tea is good for loose bowels, and snacking on sunflower seeds helps with constipation. Of course, prune juice, fruits and vegetables help keep you regular. Oh, and drinking a glass of water with a dash of cayenne pepper in it is supposed to be good for ulcers."

"Really?" Charlotte had now developed a habit of keeping pen and paper on her person. She pulled out a piece of paper and pen from her dress pocket and quickly jotted down the information. "What is good for bruises?"

"Bruises!"

Charlotte did not respond.

"I don't understand how these women are letting some man knock 'em around like some spinnin' top! They need to learn how to gut 'em like a fish!"

"Uh-uh, Miss Sista. That's not the way to go."

"It's the way to go if it will keep yo' butt alive. Especially if you got chi'ren to raise. At least scare 'em up a bit so they'd think twice befo' raisin' their hands at you again. Anyway, the only thing I can think of for bruises is an ice pack and rubbing some witch hazel on the bruise."

"Okay. You'd be surprised at how many people don't know about those home remedies."

"I doubt if I'd be surprised. As you know, some of my chi'ren is real light skin like their daddy. They look like butter. When they was little and hurt themselves playin', I would rub some moist sugar on the spot to keep it from turnin' so black and blue."

"Really? Sugar? Did that help?"

"Who knows? We did the best we could wit' what we had. Somehow, things turned out all right. My chi'ren hemmed and hawed about my home remedies, but I wasn't studying them."

"Mama, why are you out here interrogating Charlotte? I know that's what you're doing," Hiawatha scolded as he came out the door. He looked back at John Edward, who was walking close behind him, and shook his head.

"Whose mama is that?" John Edward joked as he proceeded down the steps. "I'm fixin' to go."

Sista looked at John Edward disapprovingly. "You just eat and run. That's all you do. I tell you the truth. Trying to keep you still is like nailin' Jello to a wall," Sista said in a sharp tone after snapping a yellow plastic barrette on the end of her braid. While cross-stitching the yarn between the knitting needles, and without skipping a stitch or pricking a finger, Sista caught Hiawatha laughing at her. "You know I ain't studyin' you, Hiawatha."

Upon noticing a child's barrette clamped in his mother's hair, Hiawatha flashed a mischievous grin. "A child's hair barrette? What's next? Just don't you go putting a pair of cotton panties on your head tonight. Women all across America go to bed with scarves tied around their heads, and my mama still wears bloomers on hers." Hiawatha waved as his brother charged down the lane.

Both Charlotte and Sista laughed.

"I'm sho' Charlotte done seen panties on Mattie Mae's head befo'. How you know she don't wear 'em on her head?" Sista asked.

Hiawatha threw up his hands.

"You better thank the Lawd yo' mama still got hair! I don't have to put my hair on a wig stand or put my teeth in a glass," Sista stated as she pointed her finger at Hiawatha. "Look here. I just remembered something. Do you still have that neighbor wit' the baby livin' upstairs over you? I don't want to come up for a visit if that bad little rascal is still there."

"Oh, Lord, yes!" Hiawatha threw up his hands in disgust. "And I have complained to the superintendent I don't know how many times." Hiawatha turned to face Charlotte. "This girl who lives upstairs from me has a two-year-old son."

Sista started snickering.

"I don't know if the child wears lead shoes or what," Hiawatha continued to explain. "But every morning he gets up and runs through that apartment like he's training for a marathon. Just running back and forth. Back and forth, from one end of the apartment to the other. I would take a broom handle and bang on the ceiling and the mother would have the nerve to bang right back! I've gone upstairs and talked to her politely about this."

Charlotte doubted that he was polite. Hiawatha flailed his hands in the air again and said, "And of course, she said she'd take care of it and didn't. Lying vixen. I wanted to trick slap her!"

"Hia, that's not nice," Charlotte interrupted. "Be sweet. Although it does sound like you're living with a nightmare on *your* street."

"I am, and she *is* a vixen!" Hiawatha snorted. "Well, she's a video vixen at least, and that's church, baby! I don't know when she or that baby goes to sleep. Being in the music industry myself, I know dancing in videos means she has a crazy work schedule. She's in everybody's video, shaking her groove thang! Obviously, she has no home training or consideration for people living underneath her. Just downright inconsiderate! I'm seriously thinking about buying a brownstone over in Brooklyn anyway."

"She certainly sounds inconsiderate," Charlotte agreed. "But remember, people cannot discipline their children in areas they're not disciplined in. How can they? Children only know what they see or what they are allowed to do. Either she's not cognizant of it, or she just does not care."

"The heifer just does not care," Hiawatha stated. "And then to top it all off, she had the nerve to complain about my dog, claiming *she* can't get any sleep because of my dog's incessant barking. That's a lie and she knows it."

Betty appeared to be cheerful as she joined the clan. Despite looking haggard of late, Betty Morley was quite attractive for her age and still had her youthful figure. Even Esau prided himself for having a wife who could transform herself into a most stunning creature when attending social events.

"You guys talking about these girls in these videos?" Betty asked after overhearing the conversation.

"Yeah, Ma," Charlotte answered. "And it just gave me an idea for the next basic life skills class I'm teaching in the fall.

I've got to stress to these young girls the importance of dress, especially when going for a job interview or even attending church."

"These young girls today don't leave nothin' to the imagination," Sista chimed in as she continued knitting.

"I agree with you, Sista," Betty seconded. "Unless you're a baby needing your diaper changed, I don't care to see any more butt cheeks."

Charlotte noticed the faraway look on Hiawatha's face. "A penny for your thoughts," she said jokingly.

"Girl, don't play." Hiawatha chuckled. Suddenly, his cell phone rang to the tune of "It's Raining Men." Charlotte was not totally surprised by his ring tone selection.

"This is Hiawatha Jones speaking," he answered. After listening to the voice on the other end, he said, "Sir, we've not ironed out all the preliminaries yet for that label. But what you or your friend can do is send us your bio and a demo so that we'll have it on file. If we like your stuff, we'll contact you. In the meantime, just keep checking our website to see what's going on, okay? Later, man, and good luck to you guys." Hiawatha pressed the end key on his phone, rolled his eyes and sighed.

"Do I have to ask?" Sista grinned.

"No, little Miss Nosey," Hiawatha said. "Charlotte, you might be interested in this, being in the church and all. Our record company is about to launch a brand new gospel label. Of course, first, we're going to sign established artists who are looking to switch labels. But eventually, we'll sign new talent. So, keep your ears open."

"Oh!" Charlotte sounded excited. "You know what? I heard that our choir is looking for another contract deal. I'll try to find out."

"Do that for me. Anyway, this dude on the phone says he's from Iowa and he and his partner are into gospel rap."

After checking the time on his watch, Hiawatha looked at his mother and asked, "Well, Miss Sista, are you ready to go?" Sista nodded her head as Hiawatha got up to help her from the chair.

"Tell Mattie Mae that we're leaving," Sista said as she left, arm-in-arm with her son.

"I will," Charlotte obliged. Charlotte noticed that Betty looked sad. "Ma, what is wrong?"

"Nothing really," Betty replied slowly. "I mean, look at all that's happened. It's been a grievous time."

"That's true. It has been difficult," Charlotte reasoned. But she couldn't shake the sense that Betty was holding something back. Charlotte flinched as she heard the Holy Spirit say, "Unveiling."

9

*For God speaketh once, yea twice yet man perceiveth it not.
In a dream, in a vision of the night, when deep sleep falleth
upon men, in slumberings upon the bed*

Job 33:14 & 15

Later that day, Edmund and Esau sat in the living room, barely talking above a whisper. Despite the family's recent loss, Edmund did seem to be in better spirits as he reached for reading glasses from the coffee table. Edmund seldom wore his glasses, since they had a tendency to slide down his nose and were almost thick enough to see into the future. Esau smiled dotingly at his daughter as she walked past. Charlotte fondly remembered moments between her parents where Betty was fiercely determined not to have a spoiled brat and Esau fought to mollycoddle his only child.

Charlotte decided to go in the kitchen to get a drink. Mattie Mae stood in front of the back door fully engaged in a telephone conversation. "Sista, I don't know what I'm gonna do wit' you," Mattie said in a frosty tone into the receiver.

Charlotte walked softly over to the cupboard where she retrieved a glass and a packet of Crystal Light. After pouring herself a full glass of cold water, Charlotte tore open, poured in the contents of the packet, and proceeded to stir. Just as Charlotte was about to leave her grandmother to her telephone conversation, Mattie Mae beckoned for her.

"Charlotte, Hiawatha wants to say something to you."

Charlotte reached for the receiver. "How may I serve you?" she asked, tilting her head to the side to hold the receiver in place on her shoulder blade.

"Ma can't even wait until we get home to call Ms. Mattie Mae. Abusing my cell like that. Charlotte, I forgot to ask you if you wanted to hang out tomorrow. Well, actually, I need a ride into town, and then maybe we can have lunch. Wait a minute. Hold on for a sec, Charlotte. I've got another call."

After a few moments, Hiawatha came back on the line. "Girl, people really think you're stupid!"

"What's wrong?" Charlotte was curious.

Hiawatha laughed. "This guy just called me *claiming* his name is Sean Pennington and he's a representative from Score Records, wanting to know if we'd be interested in signing two men. He was acting all hyped about this hot gospel rap duo from, get this, Iowa. This Sean person claims the duo, who call themselves David and Jonathan, is creating a hot buzz in the industry already."

Charlotte laughed. "Well, if he is a record mogul or whatever, and the duo is so hot and *that* talented, then why doesn't he sign them?" Charlotte glided her tongue across her teeth. "Hold up. Did you say Iowa? What are the chances that David and Jonathan are taking turns calling you?"

"Exactly! And how come I've never heard of this David and Jonathan?"

"Well, you can't say your job is dull, can you?"

"Nope. I sure can't. Dealing with ego maniacs, divas and diva wannabes is never dull, but my assistant tops them all.

She called earlier whining about this, that and the other. All that girl does is whine, whine, whine. One of these days, I am going to give her a chilled glass to go with it. All I ask for is some decent support from her and not all that complaining. That's all."

"Hia, maybe she's under a lot of stress." Charlotte made sure her tone sounded encouraging.

"I'll admit, her job can be stressful, but sometimes she whines as a cover up for something she didn't do. She's just special."

"What do you mean?"

"Well, she does that to garner sympathy. Today, for instance, I found out that she forgot to send a CD to *Fresh* magazine. Now, this CD is Honey's latest project and her music reviews are to coincide with the reviews for her upcoming movie. It's all strategy, baby. All strategy."

"I'm sure."

"Granted, Honey is a publicity whore, but the industry is buzzing about her being an Oscar shoo-in. Her reviews need to be out there; and *Fresh*, like everybody else, has a deadline to meet."

"Okay, you need to stop it. I started to buy Honey's CD when I was in Wal-Mart the other day. I heard a couple of the tracks and it sounded really nice. Aside from gospel music, of course, I love smooth, jazzy CDs."

"Why didn't you get it? You would have probably paid less for it at Wal-Mart."

"Yeah, but I would have paid a price by standing in that long line. I hate long lines. Speaking of young singers, not long ago I read this article about girl groups from the sixties. And I tell you, behind some of those smiles and gowns were some very depressing stories. The one topic that stuck with me was this feature about Tammi Terrell. She used to sing duets with Marvin Gaye."

"Yeah, 'You're All I Need To Get By' and 'Ain't Nothing Like The Real Thing.'" Hiawatha cleared his throat.

"Right. Personally, I think her story would make for a very interesting movie."

"I bet it would. Even I can recall some of the rumors I heard straight from the wagging tongues of some industry veterans. Anyway, let me let you go. I'll talk to you later. How about we go into town tomorrow? You may have to drive."

"That's fine with me. I'll talk to you later," Charlotte replied. She wasn't one to faithfully follow secular news, but even she knew that Honey positioned herself in front of camera lenses more than bugs flew into headlights.

As soon as she hung up, Charlotte thought she heard the Holy Spirit say, "Read II Samuel 4:10."

"Okay, Holy Ghost. As soon as I finish this letter I will read it," Charlotte replied as she went upstairs to her bedroom.

After remembering a previous paper cut to the finger, Charlotte carefully picked up a sheet of paper from the table. With ink pen in hand, she started drafting a letter to Ramiyah.

Dear Ramiyah,

All things considered, how are you and Monica? How is the ministry coming along? I have some materials I think you can use, and as soon as I get back home, I will send them to you. May I suggest that you study the Book of Esther? Queen Esther was not imprisoned, but she had been chosen to help save a people . . . just like you. While your surroundings are not ideal and certainly not plush, God obviously chose to use you in this setting, nonetheless.

Also, I have two books that I think will be a blessing to you and others. One is an autobiography of a woman who had been battered for years by her husband. I don't want to give the story away, but the book really ministered to the women I counsel. They were truly inspired by the writer's awesome triumph.

The second book is entitled, Destined for the Wilderness. *I think this book will benefit you the most by guiding you in your calling.*

Wait. There is more. There is nothing like some praise and worship music. I will send you some Richard Smallwood, Hezekiah Walker, Israel Houghton, Chris Tomlin, Yolanda Adams, Vanessa Bell Armstrong and Fred Hammond CDs, and a few of my pastor's sermon tapes. Namely, "This Too Shall Pass," "Trouble, Transition and Triumph," "Living in a Dying World," "Why Jesus Came" and "Why Me?" If I think of anything else, I will send that also. I hope you will look forward to receiving these.

As for the prison bullies, all I can say is God has His timing and His methods. Just hold on. I would not be surprised if the Lord will have those two assisting you in the ministry one day. Better yet, He may have them taking over after your release. Hallelujah!

I love you, Ramiyah, and believe your stint in prison is only temporary. Know that God is able.

Charlotte could feel her brain activity slowing to a crawl and she wanted some rest. As the night wore on, her eyes grew heavy and her fingers went limp. She soon began to dream. In the dream, she was a child, wandering around in her parents' bedroom. A lone candle on a tea caddy burned and flickered in a dark corner. She checked herself out in the dresser mirror, disappointed at the sight of braces clamped around her teeth. She could even see her face in the shine of the recently polished silver-plated brush and comb set.

The dresser was lined with fancy bottles filled with

strong perfumes, which made her sneeze. Startled by the flapping noise made by a window shade, Charlotte spun around and found herself drawn to a covered object in the windowsill. She went over and lifted the fringed material, discovered a family photo album hidden beneath the cloth, and dusted it off with the palm of her hand.

Charlotte opened the book and was frightened by what she saw. Nevertheless, being precocious and hoping that the next page was more promising, she mustered up the nerve to continue. But she gasped as she flipped through page after page. Polaroid snapshots of family members with bloodshot eyes filtered throughout.

She recognized a picture of Betty's mother, Gladys. She was dressed in a navy blue double breasted jacket with big brass buttons, matching navy blue skirt, a white derby-styled hat with a navy blue brim, white gloves, sensible shoes and a purse large enough to pass for a sea bag. She was poised against a fake street background complete with a sidewalk, street lamp and a convertible Studebaker. Gladys could have easily been mistaken for a naval officer on shore leave. Gladys had a grumpy look on her face.

However, there was one picture in particular that frightened Charlotte the most. It was that of a shadowy figure standing as erect as a statue. Printed on the top were the words *generations of stains*.

Charlotte jolted in her slumber, breaking free from the nightmarish view. Soon, she drifted back to sleep, wondering just exactly what the dream had meant. If it had any meaning at all, she was sure God would reveal it.

10

*A friend loveth at all times and a brother is
born for adversity*

Proverbs 17:17

It was early Saturday morning, and Charlotte arrived at the
mailbox in the nick of time. Just when she was about to
place her letter to Ramiyah inside the mailbox and lift up
the attached flag, she noticed a wave of steam rising from
the hot tarmac. Behind it was the U.S. Postal truck, traveling slowly up the road.

Charlotte waited until the mailman reached the Morley
mailbox. Like clockwork, Mr. McNeal, curmudgeon extra-
ordinaire, drove his route faithfully each day, looking as if
he were nursing a long-term grudge. Charlotte bid him a
cheerful good morning only to receive a grunt and a handful of parcels in return. Perhaps the moody Mr. McNeal
perceived the residents on his route to be as dull as the
route itself.

Taking no offense to Mr. McNeal's less than charming
ways, Charlotte sifted through the sales papers and advertising flyers before discovering that she had not one, not two,
but three letters from Ramiyah. She wondered if Ramiyah
even had time to write to anyone else. For a split second,

Charlotte thought she heard Mr. McNeal say goodbye as he drove off to make his next delivery.

Anxious to read one of Ramiyah's letters, she positioned the rest of the mail under her armpit and ripped opened the envelope marked #1. Thankful to have the house all to herself, Charlotte went to her room to read. She turned on the ceiling fan to cool the already humid bedroom before settling down in the big comfy chair and propping her feet up on the bed.

The first envelope was rather thick, with the first sheet of paper having a short note written by Ramiyah, saying:

Charlotte, I've purposely numbered the envelopes, so I hope you read the letters in order. Actually, the note is not mine, but a letter written to me from Hiawatha. I talked to him a few months ago and he said it was okay to share it with you. By the time you receive this, he should be in South Carolina.

Charlotte felt a little uneasy. She unfolded the pages and noticed that Hiawatha's letter was dated three months ago, right after Ramiyah had been sentenced to prison. Charlotte began to read:

Greetings 'Miyah,

I was in D.C. recently and I put some flowers on your mother's grave like you asked. The plot was looking quite dog-eared. Since Miss Betty is the only sibling living in D.C. now, I wonder why she's not doing the perpetual care thing. I guess taking care of Miss Gladys's resting place is the last thing on her mind these days, huh?

Well, let me get out of family business. Yes, I spoke to Cha-Cha, with his little ashy self. But that's another story. Let me address the advice you so poignantly and freely gave me in your last letter. What do I have to be ashamed of? God is a God of love, isn't He? I wouldn't think that God would want me to live a lie.

I tried the heterosexual thing. Briefly. That wasn't for me. I'm glad that you've found some solace, even though it took prison to get it. But trust me. I'm at peace with myself and have finally found someone that I love, and he cherishes and adores me. The only thing that ticks me off about the relationship is that he's married.

Since when did being married become the new gay trend? All of these brothers claiming to have MBAs should tell a sister that what it really means is that they're "married but available." They've got MBAs all right. Right along with their PhDs (piled up high and deeper). Alas, I guess dishonesty is here to stay.

And the thing that gets me is that I wasn't even attracted to him physically. Stupid me. I thought he had intelligent eyes with compassion to match. He had neither.

Are they treating you right in the big house? Never turn your back on Big Bertha to pick up the soap. Stay away from the birls (girls who want to be boys) as much as possible.

By the way, as for me personally, I ain't mad at ya for putting Cole out of his misery. You just did God and His army of angels a big favor by singlehandedly taking the devil out. I hope Cole saw the bullet coming right before it landed between his beady little eyes.

Justice was served when you pulled the trigger. Cole was just lowdown. He wasn't on the down-low, was he? 'Cause if he had never traveled down my road before, I bet he had thought about it. I always suspected Cole was a little freaky.

What exactly happened that night anyway? I read in the paper where it said that he was leaving you for another woman, Anjenette. Didn't she live across the street from Cha-Cha? Was that the final straw for you?

I am at peace with myself. If I die and go to hell, so be it. It has been hell here on earth at times anyway. However, I do not believe I'm going to hell when I die. I attend services at God's house. I have a healthy respect for God, try to treat everybody right and believe that God loves me. Basically, I am a good person. If He was so angry about my "sin," then He would have done something about it. Don't you think? He has not.

But I ain't mad at ya. You have your opinion and I have mine. It does not negate the fact that I'm glad we've formulated a friendship these past couple of years. Stay in touch until the next time. Love, Peace & Collard Greens, Hia.

Charlotte briefly pondered over Hiawatha's defensive letter.

"Charlotte?" Hiawatha called out as he stomped up the stairs. "Did you forget our conversation on the phone last night? We're going into town to watch the town folk?"

Charlotte quickly put the letters away. She tidied up the dresser and grabbed her makeup pouch. "No. I did not forget." Charlotte's answer was so absolute as she steadied her hands to apply the eyeliner. "And you know good and well we're not going into town to laugh at people." Charlotte found her compact of pressed powder on the dresser and touched up her foundation.

"Maybe you're not going to gawk or laugh . . . ouch!"

Charlotte turned around to see what caused the outburst. Apparently, while walking up the stairs, Hiawatha had broken one of his delicate fingernails as he strummed his fingers along the bars of the banister. She suggested that he get something from the first aid kit located in the bathroom to doctor his bleeding finger, which he hurriedly proceeded to do.

Charlotte could hear the water running in the sink. Soon,

Hiawatha emerged with the nail that had been peeled back like a lid on a tin can now removed and replaced with a Band-Aid. She briefly debated whether or not to ask Hiawatha about his friendship with her aunt. Eager for answers, she made her decision. "Hia—"

"Girl, where are your kinfolk?" Hiawatha interrupted.

"Ma and Grandma went to the mall and Daddy and Granddaddy are back over at Busta Watkins's house to help him with some carpentry work." Charlotte belched. "Oh, excuse me. Hia, when did you and Ramiyah become such good friends?"

"Well, me and little Miss 'Miyah got chummy about two years ago when Cha-Cha was still living in Tucson. It was a hoot how we met up. Cha-Cha and I drove down the street on our way to pick up his friend. And there she was, standing in the yard watching her boys play."

"You were shocked to see her, huh?" Charlotte slid her hand down the rail as she went down the steps.

"I was," Hiawatha said as he followed, carefully protecting his hands by keeping them in his pockets. "But you know what shocked me even more?"

"What?" Charlotte reached for the keys on the coffee table once they had made it down the stairs.

"When we got to Cha-Cha's friend's house and that man opened his mouth . . . oh, my God! The dude had so many missing teeth I could see his tonsils! Soot. That was his nickname."

"Soot?"

"Yeah, you know, like chimney soot, black ash."

"Hia, that's not nice."

"Naw, you got it wrong. That is his nickname. I didn't give it to him. The boy *is* one gorgeous blackberry. Don't you know black is beautiful? He just needs to keep his mouth closed. Soot was telling us about the time a neighbor took his six-year-old nephew to church with her. Apparently, it's a well-known fact that the boy is bad and does not come from a God-fearing family. Needless to say, he had never been to church before.

"Sometime during church service, the child belted out a curse word and the pastor asked the neighbor to take him out. The boy looked up at the neighbor and said, 'Y'all knew I was a devil. What did you bring me to church for?'"

"He's used to being called that." Charlotte shook her head in disbelief as she nudged Hiawatha out the front door.

"I guess they called it like they saw it, Charlotte. I mean, he is bad. This is the same little boy who stuffed his nose with a couple of raisins just before they went to church."

Even though Hiawatha was not the "ideal" suitor, driving along the countryside with a male companion did remind Charlotte of happier times, like the year *before* her marriage. She missed sharing candlelit dinners with someone she was not in a platonic relationship with. And the last time she shared watching the sun rise or set over the crest of some hill was when she went on a camping trip with the kids from children's church. It was far from being a romantic moment.

Charlotte observed Hiawatha as he checked himself out in the mirror. An immaculate dresser, he was undoubtedly ultra metro-sexual, if there was such a thing. Charlotte wondered why Hiawatha chose a pricey Jhane Barnes suit to wear into town. "Hia, is there any place in particular you wanted to go? I feel so under-dressed in my denim dress and sandals and you're dressed to impress."

Hiawatha placed a ten dollar bill in the car's ashtray. "Honey, the only place to go on this desolate piece of land is

Waller Street. Don't worry. You look marvelous! It's just that I don't bum it even when I'm slumming."

"True that. Even when we were kids you didn't," Charlotte agreed. "But still, why are you *so* dressed up?"

"Because I like to give a good dog and pony show." Hiawatha snapped his fingers.

"Okay. You got a meeting with the movers and shakers at City Hall or something?" Charlotte asked as she sped around a slow moving tractor. "By the way, what is this money for?" Charlotte pointed to the folded bill in the ashtray.

"Gas. Unless this car is moving by the power of my essence, I don't expect to ride for free."

"You're blessed to be a blessing, Hia. Where is our first stop anyway?" Charlotte made a left turn onto Main Street.

"Busta's Beauty and Barber Shop. One of my old high school friends works there." A buzzing sound came from Hiawatha's pants pocket. "Whew, chile! I'm vibrating," Hiawatha said, fanning himself before answering his cell phone.

Charlotte tossed questions around in her mind as to how to approach Hiawatha. Since he gave Ramiyah permission to share his letter, she could only assume that he would not mind talking to her about matters most intimate.

"Have a good day, man!" Hiawatha nearly shouted as the phone's signal started to fade. "Girl, you're not going to believe this." Hiawatha seemed aggravated.

Having been oblivious to his conversation, Charlotte looked at Hiawatha curiously. "Believe what?"

"This man claims he's a deacon at Bishop Spicer's church in Texas and he wanted to know about our gospel label; when, how, who, and all that. Anyway, you know it was that same little dude from Iowa, right? Then again, it could have been his partner. Still, it was the same exact questions. He'd better stop harassing me, like his calling is going to make us draw up a contract. Plus, who says we would even sign him on anyway?" Hiawatha protested. "I'm telling you. Folks are in it for the money, 'cause you can make a crazy salary. Talk about bling. Even my dollars don't make sense."

"How did he get your number?" Charlotte parked across the street from the barbershop.

"Oh, like an idiot, I forwarded all my calls from my office phone to my cell and now, Beavis and Butthead keep calling me."

"Not too bright, are they?" Charlotte turned the engine of the car off and got out.

Just as Hiawatha, who was only a few paces ahead of Charlotte, was about to step up onto the curb directly in front the barbershop, he felt Charlotte tug on his coattail.

"I read a letter that you wrote to Ramiyah," Charlotte stated, but Hiawatha did not hear her. A young lady crossing the street had recognized him and called out his name.

Charlotte found her mind drifting back to Timmi's phone call the other day. She wanted to call Timmi, but decided to give her and Jeff some uninterrupted time together before asking for the latest scoop.

She turned her head slightly. Hiawatha was heavily engaged in his conversation with the woman. Suddenly, Charlotte felt someone bump into her. She quickly spun around and saw that it was her grandfather, Edmund.

"Grandpa! You are a sight for sore eyes," she said, noticing his face was lightly streaked with sawdust.

"So are you. We just keep seein' each other in passin'."

"Where is Daddy?"

"Oh, he's still at Busta's house. I came into town to get some bolts and screws from the hardware store." Edmund had always been proud of the fact the he and his sons possessed crackerjack carpentry skills.

A patrol car from the town's fleet of three pulled up alongside Charlotte and Edmund, nearly plowing into the parked car in front of it. It was Turtle Island's Chief of Police, Alford Pettigrew. Edmund watched and waited as the man struggled to free himself from the seatbelt.

A friendly man, Chief Pettigrew was viewed by many as being a chronic talker, a motor mouth of sorts, who looked for trouble where none existed. Thanks to a large upper frame complete with an overlapping belly and eyes as icy blue as Alaskan glaciers, Charlotte found Chief Pettigrew to be a far cry from nondescript.

"How are you, Edmund?" Chief Pettigrew asked before popping an antacid into his mouth.

"Oh, just fine, and yo'self?" Edmund replied.

"Can't complain." Chief Pettigrew towered over Charlotte and appeared to be sizing her up. His face was as red as a cherry tomato. Not sunburn red or alcoholism red. Just flushed—red as a cherry tomato.

"Chief, this is my granddaughter, Charlotte," Edmund introduced proudly.

Chief Pettigrew tipped his hat and rushed out a hello before switching from concerned lawman to a doting grandfather himself. "That reminds me," Chief Pettigrew said as he pulled out a small photo from his wallet, "you remember my boy, Rusty, don't you?"

Edmund nodded as he took the photo. The Chief tried to pull his pants up around his waist for a snug fit, but it was useless. "This is Rusty's little girl," Chief Pettigrew said with an equal amount of pride.

Charlotte leaned forward for a closer look. She instantly noted that the child appeared to be about five years old and was cuter than a thousand button mums. The little blond-haired pixie was graced with a mop of curls that perfectly framed her face. She also had those same captivating eyes as her grandfather. However, the child's milky white skin could use some sun.

Then the chief shoved a photograph of a rather scary-looking child in Charlotte's face, introducing the boy as his grandson. "Isn't he adorable?" Chief Pettigrew asked, examining Charlotte's facial expression.

Dear Lord, forgive me. I know you made us in your image. All things are made good in your sight. Please don't let my face say this is horrid. Charlotte felt as if she might as well have been subjected to sitting in front of a searing lamp bulb while strapped to a lie-detector. No matter what she said, no matter how kind, she feared Chief Pettigrew would see right through her response as she continued to study the photograph of the brooding boy with a dark black pageboy haircut, gothic clothing and commanding scowl. There were no redeeming qualities. She refrained from asking if it was a mock up of a book cover for another *Omen* sequel or something by Stephen King.

"Grandchildren are precious," she managed to say, even though she was sensing the child might be exposed to some ungodly practices.

"Yes, they are. Each one is different," Chief Pettigrew agreed.

Charlotte now felt as though he may have been reaching out for an opinion, having some suspicions of his own.

"Well, I just stopped over here to pick up some lunch from the diner," the Chief explained, his stomach roaring like a lion. "Hey, Edmund, did you hear about my deputy making an arrest last night at Piggly Wiggly? They hired another janitorial company to do their cleaning and one of the gals got caught stealing."

"Is that right?" Edmund said with disgust.

Chief Pettigrew scratched his head and swirled his tongue around in his mouth. "Of course, the supervisor of this company was embarrassed and apologized for this, but ain't that the darnest thing? It's hard to find people you can trust these days."

"Well, that's just one of those things, I guess," Edmund said, shrugging his shoulders. "A crook steals. That's what they do and then you lock 'em up. That's what you do."

"Yeah, I guess you're right, Edmund. Well, listen, you take care of yourself, and it was nice meeting you, young lady."

Charlotte nodded as she observed Chief Pettigrew hurriedly enter the diner to beat the lunchtime crowd, wiping his sweaty brow with the cuff of his shirt sleeve. It was indeed hot. The temperature had been flirting with heat stroke–inducing Fahrenheit all morning.

Charlotte blew her grandfather an affectionate kiss as he went on his way, then she went about hers. Edmund whistled as he fumbled around his pockets for his keys. Whistling was usually a habit of his whenever he had something on his mind or was at peace. As soon as Edmund turned to look back at his grandchild, displaying that grand smile of his, Charlotte felt assured that this time he was simply at peace.

11

*He becometh poor that dealeth with a slack hand; but the
hand of the diligent maketh rich*

Proverbs 10:4

Prior to entering the barbershop, Charlotte and Hiawatha
were met by two elderly gentlemen sitting on top of wooden
crates. The men were enjoying a friendly game of checkers,
anticipating and studying each other's moves. Intently focused
on the game, the men spoke without shooting a glance in
Charlotte and Hiawatha's direction.

"What's going on, man?" Junior asked as he leaped up
from the barber chair to shake his high school classmate's
hand. Hiawatha pulled back the partially opened screen
door. "Long time no see. I didn't get a chance to see you the
last time I was home."

"Yeah, man. I heard you came through. That's been about
two years ago now."

An old gospel song was blasting on the radio. The bass
was so loud that Charlotte thought she could actually see it
thumping and battering its way through the case. Thank-
fully, one of the stylists kindly lowered the volume.

The stylist looked at Charlotte and said something, but
she talked so fast that Charlotte did not understand a word

she'd said. "That song has become the national anthem for many black women," the stylist said with neck-breaking speed before she returned to her customer to resume working on the frizzy ends of the woman's unevenly shorn hair.

She stood beneath a hanging basket, careful not to knock over the shipment of boxes containing hair products. Overall, Charlotte thought the depressingly drab shop's white-washed walls could use a punch of color. An extreme makeover, a nip and tuck here and there was definitely in order.

She observed two men exchange pleasantries before catching up on each other's lives. Charlotte also noted that Junior seemed genuinely interested in what Hiawatha was saying. Hiawatha had a style that deliberately demanded attention be drawn to him, and his cheerfulness was contagious.

Charlotte admired one of the female customer's newly coifed hairstyle as her stylist tightened her grip on the curling iron. The woman obviously took care of her crowning glory on a regular basis. However, the customer's full head of healthy hair was not the only thing Charlotte noticed. The woman's eyebrows were arched so high that it was hard to tell if she looked surprised or spooked. The black eye and quarter-size knot on her forehead were also hard to miss.

After Junior left, Hiawatha escorted Charlotte to a seat in the waiting area. "I'm checking out my investment," he whispered in her ear.

"Investment?" Charlotte inquired.

"Yep, gotta chase that paper. I plan to buy this shop from Busta." Hiawatha snapped his fingers and flailed his arm in a zigzag motion. "Greetings and salutations, everyone."

It was clear to Charlotte that there were a few people present who were turned off by Hiawatha's outlandish behavior, while others were highly amused. Only one person seemed totally oblivious to Hiawatha's presence. Hiawatha proceeded to a booth belonging to one of his former classmates. Although the barber politely shook Hiawatha's hand, he did not seem all that glad to see Hiawatha.

It made no difference. Hiawatha strutted about unabashed as if he already owned the place. There was one thing definite and constant about Hiawatha: He was prideful and wore it like a badge.

One roly-poly of a barber could not take his eyes off of Hiawatha. He draped a white towel across his shoulder and shot Hiawatha a dirty look while scoping him from head to toe. The remaining two barbers chatted quietly amongst themselves. Meanwhile, Charlotte could not take her eyes off the barber with the weird mustache and eyeglass lenses that were thicker than the London fog.

Charlotte had to admit that Hiawatha was some kind of sharp in his Jhane Barnes suit. "My God, does she ever blink?" Charlotte mumbled to herself after glancing at a female client who had a fixation on Charlotte's hair.

Moments later, Charlotte discovered why. The stylist lifted the wig from her client's head, revealing a small tuft of hair on the top of the woman's head. The client was not ashamed to have this part of her appearance disclosed publicly. Charlotte briefly watched the stylist skillfully massage the woman's scalp with the tips of her deft fingers.

A very pretty stylist donning a red wig accidentally bumped into Charlotte in a mad dash to retrieve some dry hand towels. She quickly apologized before returning to her dripping wet client. The stylist was an absolute whiz with a blow dryer, even though one arm was in a cast.

Suddenly, a short and stocky loud-mouth man came into the barbershop. "How is everyone doing today?" the man asked, resting his hands in his pockets.

Unenthusiastic tones of "hello" and "hey" echoed back to the man. "How are you, Randy?" Hiawatha asked the man as he ventured toward the front.

"I am doing exceptionally well. Everything is going along congruously. Don't tell me this is . . . is that you, Hiawatha?" Randy asked as he sat in one of the barber chairs squinting his eyes.

"The one. The only. Nice to see you, man," Hiawatha answered as he gently grabbed Charlotte's elbow and practically pushed her toward the door. Hiawatha did not seem to be thrilled about Randy's presence.

"Likewise. You look like you're doing well yourself. You have a prosperous glow about you. All homo sapiens must take care of themselves. Am I right?" Randy said.

"What did you say?" Hiawatha furrowed his eyebrows and grinded his teeth.

Discerning that Hiawatha was offended by the comment and Randy was confused by Hiawatha's reaction, Charlotte quickly took control of the situation by gently nudging Hiawatha out the door and saying goodbye.

"Hia, what did you think he said?" Charlotte asked as Hiawatha led her toward the town's most popular eatery, Joe Green's Place. The diner's outdoor structure was made of a strange, but charming mixture of clay, brick and crawling English Ivy vines, as well as the attorney's office next to it. The two-story brick building dated back to the turn of the century.

"He made some wisecrack about homosexuals taking care of themselves." Hiawatha made no effort to hide the anger in his voice.

Hiawatha and Charlotte entered the virtually empty diner.

"No, he didn't. First of all, aren't you a homosexual?" she

asked. Hiawatha nodded his head, but before he could mouth off, Charlotte continued. "Then why were you offended? Actually, he did not call you a homosexual. He said homo sapiens. He was talking about mankind."

"Okay, that's what I get for not paying attention. The thing everyone knows about Randy is that he has one year of community college and thinks he can pass himself off as some sort of intellect just because his vocabulary surpasses that of a four-legged mammal. By the way, lunch is on me."

"Your treat? Oh, I forgot you were bringing down that kind of cash," Charlotte joked as she pushed Hiawatha through the door.

"Right. Hey, did you see the lady at the shop with the pink skirt and pink shoes on? That was so five minutes ago."

"I did see her," Charlotte acknowledged.

"And I thought big hair died around the same time as black and white TVs. And as for her hairstylist, I didn't know if she was trying to grow dreads or the head of Medusa. These people need me. Anyway, I'm glad we're inside. It's so hot out there I thought I was going to faint," Hiawatha said.

"When we go back out and you think you're going to faint, let me know," Charlotte said.

"Oh, you will know because I'm dragging you down with me."

Charlotte gasped after a customer passed by, leaving with his food order and a strong, musty body odor to boot. Her eyes started stinging and she was all too grateful that Hiawatha had not commented on the man's personal hygiene.

As they took a seat at a table by the window, she noticed another customer half-sitting on a stool, watching with fascination as the cook firmly pressed his burger on the grill with a spatula.

Mary, the longtime girlfriend of John Edward, brought them each a complimentary glass of iced water and a small container of lemon wedges. Mary's fading cranberry color lipstick took nothing away from her ingratiating smile.

"Are y'all ready to order yet?" she asked, pulling a pencil from behind her ear. Mary's dyed and frosted hair reminded Charlotte of a Carolina sunset.

Mary had worked at the diner since the tender age of fifteen. Over the years, she had developed, prematurely, varicose veins around her thick calves and her arches had already fallen. She looked much older than her twenty-eight years.

"Hmmm, give me second, Mary, but don't go away. I think I've narrowed it down," Charlotte said, pondering over the menu's tempting dishes. "Okay, I'll have an old-fashioned hamburger with everything except pickles and onions; a small order of seasoned French fries and a glass of iced-tea. Thank you."

Mary waited patiently until Hiawatha finally ceased from vacillating between choices. "I'll just have the same thing," he said. "By the way, I hope my brother is treating you right, Mary." Mary nodded as she walked away with their orders.

Hiawatha dropped a lemon wedge in the glass and stirred it around with a straw. He took a sip of water and frowned. "This place seems so eerie. I can't believe Mr. Joe and Ms. Lily are gone." He lifted his glass as if he were about to make a toast to the late owners, who died shortly before Tina. Their deaths were the first devastating blow dealt to Edmund and Mattie Mae. It hit Edmund especially hard, since he and Joe had been friends for several years.

"I know." Charlotte took a sip of water from her glass. "I really had no idea Busta wanted to sell his business."

"He's not yapping about it much, I don't think, but yeah,

he wants to sell. Every year I say I'm going to start my own business, and every year, before you know it, I'm buying a new calendar and had not taken that risk." Hiawatha turned his head to see who had slammed the door so hard until it practically bounced back off the wall. It was Otis and Nellie Moss, two Turtle Island natives that could fuel Sista's ire like no other.

"Leave them alone, Hia," Charlotte cautioned. "I can see the wheels turning in your head."

12

Whoso loveth instruction loveth knowledge; but he that hateth reproof is brutish

Proverbs 12:1

"Chile, I have no intentions of bothering those two. Them is Mama's special friends." Hiawatha chuckled, knowing full well that Sista and the Mosses did not get along. Otis, who was as drunk as ever, winked at Charlotte as he passed by. Nellie turned up her nose at Hiawatha, complaining to Otis about her chafing thighs.

"Oh, no she didn't!" Hiawatha huffed. "I *was* going to leave them alone until Miss Thang turned on her royal rudeness. She ain't the only queen in this joint. And, I *know* she don't want me to say anything about that girth of hers."

Charlotte grabbed Hiawatha firmly by the wrist and struggled not to lose her patience with him. "Hia, listen."

"What?" he snarled. By this time, Mary arrived with their burgers and fries, and an unopened bottle of Heinz ketchup.

"Oh, do not snap at me," Charlotte cautioned Hiawatha, hoping that he would not cause a scene.

She thanked Mary for her service before Mary walked away from their table. Mary thanked Charlotte and Hiawatha for their patronage. A small bottle of mustard slipped from her hand. She chased the bottle only to watch it roll across the floor and finish up at the baseboard.

"We are here to have lunch, not have some WWW match," Charlotte continued to insist as the delicious aroma of fried chicken insisted on making its way up to her nose. "You and the Mosses will not be hurling insults at each other in here."

Hiawatha pretended to not be paying attention.

"Now, before we went in the barbershop I mentioned to you that I read a letter you wrote to Ramiyah."

"Right?" Hiawatha squirted dollops of ketchup and relish over his burger.

"What are you and Ramiyah discussing so much that she felt it necessary to forward your letter to me?"

Perhaps for the first time in his adult life, Hiawatha struggled for words. "I guess . . . I guess I should start at the beginning, 'cause you're gonna ask anyway."

"Probably," Charlotte stated as she munched on her thick, juicy homemade burger. She caught the juices dripping down her mouth with a napkin. Joe and Lilly Green, the late owners of the diner, may be gone, but the legacy of the diner's good food and prompt and friendly service remained.

Hiawatha's face literally lit up as he delved into his burger. He chewed his food slowly, deliberately and almost systematically. "Ms. Lilly must have taught Mary how to cook, 'cause her mother sure can't. I remember one time her mom sent over a plate of food to my mom when she was sick. I sampled some of it because it looked so good." Hiawatha paused to wash down his food with his drink. "All I know is, looks can be deceiving. Unless you've got an appetite for prison food." He paused again after noticing Charlotte's facial expression, which stated that she was in no mood for his stalling.

Hiawatha sighed. His glass of water glistened in the sunlight. "Okay. Ramiyah and I became really good friends over the past couple of years. In the beginning, I didn't know that Cole was strong-arming her into this risqué lifestyle, but I always suspected something was not quite right." Hiawatha's Rolex glistened from underneath the cuff of his shirt as he placed his elbows on the table and rubbed his hands together.

"I'll cut to the chase," he continued. "A couple of years ago, I got sick. My mother doesn't even know this, so please do not say anything to anyone about this."

Since he did not ask her to make a promise or swear on a stack of Bibles, Charlotte did not offer a commitment to keep a secret. She had always tried to be careful about making promises, because sometimes promises had to be broken. The fact that Hiawatha mentioned sickness made her hesitant to commit to a promise. She stared at him with a vacant look.

Suddenly, Nellie Moss cried out. "Why didn't you say you didn't have any money befo' we came up in here? You done drunk it up, didn't you?" Otis looked stupefied as Nellie lashed out at him. Mary and the other cook merely went about their mundane chores as Nellie angrily coasted Otis toward the door, this time, carefully easing it shut.

"Those two will never change," Mary mumbled as she wiped down the table next to Charlotte and Hiawatha. "Nellie thinks she's so slick. She knew Otis didn't have any money when they came in here. They always tryin' to get somethin' for nothin'. It's a doggone shame."

Charlotte waited for Hiawatha to continue his story. Once Mary left to go to the cash register, Hiawatha resumed. "I was diagnosed with the alphabets three years ago." Seeing the puzzled look on Charlotte's face, he clarified. "I tested HIV positive."

Charlotte was hoping that she had shown no emotion, no shock or disdain. She remembered the time she had to counsel some mothers of a group of students at a high school when it was discovered during a blood drive that many of the students were HIV positive. The screams and the cries in the school hallway still rang in her ears.

"I'm fine now. The doctors can't find a trace," Hiawatha reassured her. "Go figure."

"Go figure? No. Praise the Lord for that miracle. That was nobody but God. You do know that the Lord is *the* healer, don't you?" Charlotte's voice cracked.

"I know, but here's the deal. During that time, I was strapped for cash because of a legal bind I was in. Plus, I was in between jobs and was behind on some bills, but that's another story. Long story short, I needed money for medicine and Ramiyah loaned it to me.

Charlotte nodded, for she certainly was familiar with seasons of more than enough and seasons of not enough.

"Back then, I wasn't bringing home enough cash. You know what I'm saying? My dollars didn't make sense nor did it look like it would change. I've since paid her back, of course. Well, over the course of time, Ramiyah started confiding in me about this couple-swapping mess she and Cole were into. I didn't say anything, 'cause who I am to judge, right?"

Charlotte merely listened intently as she tried, without success, to chew her ice quietly. Hiawatha looked her squarely in the eyes and said, "But then when she killed Cole, all I could hear was my mother's mouth talking about reaping what you sow and paying for sexual perversion. Of course, I'm paraphrasing, 'cause she don't know the term *sexual perversion*, but you get my drift."

Hiawatha appeared to be uncomfortable and started

squirming in his chair. At first, Charlotte thought it was because she was a woman of God and he was feeling guilty, but on second thought, Hiawatha was too cocky to show guilt about anything unless God truly was doing a work in him at this hour.

"Since Ramiyah's incarceration, she has challenged me spiritually," Hiawatha said, clearing his throat.

Charlotte began to speak candidly. "And does this spiritual challenge have anything to do with your lifestyle and dating a married man? I still find the timing of getting these letters coinciding with your arrival here interesting. Ramiyah knew I was here in South Carolina and she knew you would be coming here. Interesting."

"Now, even you know timing is everything."

"Oh, no question," Charlotte agreed.

"When I was diagnosed, my attitude was that I was going out with a bang. I was not reckless sexually or anything like that. I just partied all the time. I was still in love with a married man who left me high and dry when I was sick and thought I was dying. I'm over him now. He was vermin, a common bottom feeder, and he treated me as if I was some type of fleeting amusement."

"He was married, Hia. The man was never really there for you in the first place. Not only that, as a Christian, you know I go by the Word of God, right?"

"Now, don't you go getting all sanctimonious on me too. I had resented Ramiyah because I thought she had commissioned herself as God's Holy Messenger. My God is a God of love and He loves me."

"Let's get something straight. Ramiyah is now a messenger of God and so am I. Hia, it's true that God does love us, but He does not like some of the things we do. Just like any parent who loves his or her child and teaches them right from wrong. I am not gay, but I'm not perfect either. There are some things about me that God is not pleased about as well."

An indignant Hiawatha took a deep breath and made a loud sigh. "Well, all I know is that some of these so-called Christians are out here living the same life I am."

"And you're right; but again, God does not approve of some of the things we do. I don't care who it is. We all will have to stand before God one day and give an account, and I don't think He will be interested in us pointing fingers at Ray-Ray, Pookie or Reverend Dr. Bishop John Q. Public. When you get a chance, I want you to read Romans 1:26-32."

"Here we go with the scriptures. How come every time something goes down that Christians don't like, y'all go quoting scriptures? Y'all use God for a convenience."

"Y'all. What y'all?" Charlotte tried to remain cool. "Everybody uses God for their convenience, as you put it. You told me that *you* go to church. Why? You told me that God loves *you* too. If you believe that God exists, then study and believe what He says in His Word—the Bible. Look, I do not make or enforce the rules and I'm not perfect." Charlotte held her ground. Exasperated, she asked, "Did you not hear anything I just said?"

"I did," Hiawatha answered in a lowly voice.

"Think about this for me. We both know that many people say they believe in God or even call themselves Christians, yet over half of them are offended by scriptures. Why do you suppose that is? Does that make sense?"

Hiawatha could not answer.

"We can't pick and choose what we want to believe about God. By doing that we make ourselves the deity."

Charlotte wasn't sure if she had gotten through to Hiawatha, but unbeknownst to her, she had. Hiawatha was taking every word spoken to him into consideration.

13

Take heed to yourselves, if thy brother trespass against thee,
rebuke him; and if he repents, forgive him

Luke 17:3

During the remainder of the drive back to the Morley residence, Hiawatha remained quiet for the most part, thinking. Or sulking. Gone was the person known for his ostentation and snappy deliveries. Gone were the smirks, wisecracks and mischief in his eyes. Sitting beside her now was a man so out of character, until Charlotte almost regretted what she had said. Almost.

Lord, was the timing or the words not right? she asked without moving her lips. In her spirit she heard the word "Wait."

While driving along Route 321, Charlotte spotted the old Dixon farmhouse that once belonged to the family of Turtle Island's beloved mayor. The plum and pear trees were loaded with fruit and the farmhouse was in shambles. A broken window shutter drooped down like a hangnail. Its former glory had vanished along with the once grand circular driveway now covered with wild grass and weeds. Also missing was the little black Sambo statue that used to stand guard in the front yard, offending and infuriating passersby on the highway.

Most townsfolk cheered when Delbert Dixon lost his home to foreclosure many years ago. Not even his bootlegging liquor profits could save his hide. Delbert, a mean cuss who served as a magistrate judge during the 1950s, resigned under a spotlight of scandal that nearly ruined the Dixon name.

Oddly, it would be his eldest grandson who would bring honor back to the name and revitalize the town several years later. When asked why not restore the old Dixon homestead, his reply would always be, "It's best to leave ghosts where they are."

Not far from the farmhouse was an old dilapidated outhouse, halfway concealed by a grove of shade trees, bramble bushes and poison ivy that grew to new heights with each passing year.

Just a short distance beyond the willowy pine trees, Charlotte could see Turtle Island Beach. The resort area had been founded by the late Amos Wright, the son of slaves. The property was deeded to him after the ailing owner moved to Ohio to live with his son. The rest of Turtle Island's white society chose to lounge around trendy beaches as far away as Europe and as close as south Florida. When he grew to be a young man, Amos Wright took his forty acres and a mule and the help of a few carpenter friends and turned the beach into an oasis for Black America.

He spruced up the rundown homes and rented them during the summers and catered events for the flock of vacationers. Amos then turned his small fortune from this business venture into an even larger one by starting an African American hair product enterprise. By the time Amos Wright turned thirty, he had netted over two million dollars in cash, stocks and property.

Eventually, Amos's sons took helm of the business and moved it, along with their father, to Los Angeles. Amos

Wright died in Los Angeles at the ripe old age of ninety-six, with his children and grandchildren having no interest in the South or what it stood for.

Recently, Amos Wright's great-great grandchildren, who had not squandered their monetary inheritance, decided to commit to reclaiming and revitalizing their legacy. Except for one small section where white sand had been covered with beach erosion, debris and garbage tossed by drunken adults and partying teenagers, the beach was turning into a major tourist attraction rivaling the likes of Martha's Vineyard and Cape Cod.

The Wright Empire could have attained a minor increase in wealth years ago by accepting checks waved in their faces by developers in exchange for their land. But Gladys Wright-Frazier, Amos Wright's great granddaughter, peddled a few ingenious ideas of her own and persuaded her kin to "keep it in the family." As it stands, Turtle Island Beach demanded the admiration and respect of onlookers. Undoubtedly, this new venture would increase their fortune vastly, even with the risk of their coastal property being the gateway for hurricanes.

Charlotte smiled. She remembered the stories her grandmother told of local African Americans hitching up their mules to the wagons on Saturdays to go to the beach for a game of baseball on the nearby grass and have a community picnic. The women would dress in their finest cotton dresses. Men, musclebound from years of plowing in the fields, came eager to play nine fun-filled innings. The elderly would sit in the now dismantled gazebos for shade and comfort while others gathered around the open pits or covered picnic area.

After the game, everyone would settle down to the previous winning team's choice of fare, which usually consisted of fried fish, shrimp, crab cakes, salmon cakes, diced cucumbers soaked in vinegar, salt and pepper, fried green tomatoes, stuffed bell peppers, fried potatoes with onions, deviled eggs, corn pudding, carrot and raisin salad and Ms. Lutie Bell Johnson's famous baked chitlins with green onions served over a bed of rice. Dessert would be heavily frosted cupcakes, bread pudding, blackberry cobbler and sweet potato pie. Charlotte thought it would be nice to see those days relived again on the island.

Once neglected beach front property, Turtle Island Beach was getting an attractive facelift thanks to a Victorian style bed and breakfast that was in mid-construction and would house an upscale reception hall and chapel for weddings. To the right of it was a pampering spa salon complete with masseuses, facialists, manicurists, pedicurists and featuring Wright Brothers hair products, homemade soaps, shampoos and body butter derived from the essence of herbs, flowers and other natural ingredients. Over the past three years, this new line of products had boosted sales and sky-rocketed the Wright family into such an astronomical net worth that Amos Wright and his ancestors would have never dreamed possible for Africans brought to a foreign land, whipped and manipulated into submission. There was even talk of a golf course joining the ranks of this resort landscape, symbols of the Wrights' success.

The view of the beach now became obscured and was swallowed by the pine trees. A road crew worked diligently, paving a road which bled onto the beach. Traveling in front of Charlotte and Hiawatha at a snail's pace was an elderly gentleman whose head barely reached the top of his headrest.

"Bless his heart." Charlotte laughed. "It's hard to tell if somebody is even in that car."

"Lord, have mercy," Hiawatha said. "My nephew can move faster than that on his Big Wheel."

"We've got to have patience. As soon as this car passes by, I'll go around the man."

Finally, the ice had been broken. They had, albeit trivial, dialogue between them.

The old man seemed to drive even slower, forcing Charlotte to toss her patience in the wind. She whirled the steering wheel around in a circular motion, floored the gas pedal and swerved past the man, narrowly missing a Dodge Dakota pickup truck that was stuck halfway in a ditch where a collection of litter had accumulated. Hiawatha tilted his head back and tightened his grip to feign riding at warp speed as they narrowly avoided hitting a Caterpillar tractor hoe that was on its way to rape some land.

As soon as Charlotte turned into the driveway, Hiawatha perked up. "Lord, look at Mama. Sometimes I think she really lives here with Miss Mattie Mae and Mr. Edmund."

Sista was sitting on the porch, talking to Mattie Mae and Betty.

"Charlotte, I want to talk to you some more about some things," Hiawatha said in a low tone.

"We can. Whenever you're ready," Charlotte obliged.

"Not right now. Mama, with her meddlesome self, won't give us any peace." Hiawatha unfastened his seatbelt once the car was in park.

"We can go up to my room. I want to read another letter also. Miss Sista, my mother and Grandma will be out here talking anyway." Charlotte got out and locked arms with Hiawatha, glad that he was no longer angry or hurt.

"Ooh, your mama let you have boys in your room?" Hiawatha joked. Charlotte pinched him on the arm. "Ouch," he yelled. "Girl, you sure do like to pinch folks, don't you? Okay, we can talk after you've read your mail."

"Where yunna been?" Sista asked almost before they got within earshot.

"Why, Miss Nosey Rosey?" Hiawatha said as he opened the door for Charlotte. "And how is everyone else doing?" Hiawatha leaned over to give Sista a kiss on her cheek.

Sista rolled her eyes at Hiawatha before setting her sights on Charlotte. "Y'all been at Busta's?" she asked, expecting Charlotte to answer truthfully and without any sass.

"Yes, ma' am." Charlotte knew that Hiawatha did not disrespect his mother. The two of them were just so much alike and knew it. Sista never needed coaxing to voice her opinion, just an open door.

"I was just tellin' Mattie Mae and Betty that Hiawatha bought the place. I sho' hope he don't bring all that ol' mess here."

"And what mess might that be, Mama?" Hiawatha grimaced.

"All that ol' imitation hair stuff and other mess. Boy, don't play dumb wit' me! You know what I'm talking about."

"What imitation stuff and other mess?" Hiawatha asked, although he knew his mother's concern had nothing at all to do with hair.

"For one thing, havin' all these women 'round here wearin' fake hair." Sista squawked and folded her arms.

Exasperated, Hiawatha said, "I'm not going there with you. Let's go, Charlotte. Mama, you are an original is all I can say. Besides, I'm not even worried. You'll be the first one in a chair on opening day, getting something done to that cast iron scalp of yours."

"Go on away from here," Sista shooed.

Hiawatha eased the screen door behind him and followed Charlotte up the stairs to her room. Charlotte turned on the ceiling fan as soon as she entered the room.

I'm sorry," Hiawatha apologized as he sat in the chair.

With letters in hand, Charlotte sat on the bed. "For what?"

"For giving you the cold shoulder and acting like an ice queen on the way here." Hiawatha appeared to be sincere.

"You're still my buddy, whether you give me the silent treatment or rant and rave like a lunatic," Charlotte said as she opened the next sealed letter. "By the way, are you moving down here to run the beauty and barber shop?"

"Lord, no. I shudder at the thought," Hiawatha said. "No, honey. I would have to paint the town red if I moved here, and I mean that literally. The dude I was talking to is going to be in charge, but I will be making some changes. That dull, drab look has got to go. I'm thinking about re-naming it to Manetain Cutz. The décor colors will probably be a brown and orange. Chocolate and tangerine. I'm not talking about that bright Halloween orange, but I do want it to have fall season feel. A nice rustic look. You thought I was going to say pink, didn't you?"

Charlotte laughed. "No, I did not. I'm impressed. It sounds very classy. I like the name and that whole rustic color theme."

Hiawatha reached in his pocket and pulled out a small velvet box. He leaned over and handed it to Charlotte.

"What's this?" she asked.

"It's the ring I promised to give you."

Charlotte got up and hugged Hiawatha. "Does this mean we're engaged?" she asked jokingly.

"Girl, you look cute in your little cotton dress and all, but you've not mojoed me into falling for your womanly wiles."

Charlotte retrieved another letter from the nightstand. "Okay, I'm going to read this letter out loud." She observed the letter. "That's funny. This letter is addressed to God." She looked puzzled.

"Hmmm." Hiawatha practiced exercising his fingers by opening and clenching his fists. "That is interesting."

Charlotte sat on the bed and began reading.

Dear God,

It's me again. Ramiyah. I don't know why I'm writing these letters to you. I seemed to have ceased from praying and now find myself writing letters to you. Am I crazy? I mean, I feel like a kid writing to Santa Claus. Where would I mail this? Perhaps I'm chronicling something to leave to my children.

As you know, I had been on such a spiritual high after our ministry meetings. But there are times I would be in my cell having equally euphoric pity parties. Why?

He may have been a scoundrel of a father and an absentee dad, but I thank you for sending JT away. Otherwise, I might not have been born, and I say that mainly because of my precious children. They would not have been born if I were not here. Don't get me wrong, I'm still struggling with what my sad existence is worth. Is their life without a mother present worth it? Hesitantly, I say yes because of the ministry. You hold the future.

Why weren't things done differently? Stupid question, huh?

Part of the reason why I'm in here is to help Yvette, right? You know Yvette. The young lady who was a victim of incest, fondled and molested repeatedly as a child by her alcoholic uncle. And what did she do when she became an adult? She's in here because she became a sex offender. It's a vicious cycle that is not her fault.

On a positive note, I am happy to report (as if you don't know) that five new members have joined the ministry. More importantly, they've accepted you in their lives. All honor and praise belong to you, Father!

I do have a question or two. Are you impressing upon me to share my past sexual exploits in our next meeting? Will you give me a sign that it is you leading me in this direction? Otherwise, I will not make a move. Sharing my story will certainly let Yvette know that I have a shameful past also, so in that aspect, she is not alone.

But bestiality? Zoophalia, as she so politically correctly puts it. I've not been there, not to imply that my sin is not as bad as hers. It was all a stench in your nostrils. No wonder you sent us a guest speaker the other day. I was absolutely floored when she told us that the telephone ministry at her church gets inundated with phone calls from people asking for prayer for deliverance from bestiality.

My heart bleeds for your people, God. My heart bleeds for Yvette, who confessed to having dabbled in this despicable practice. Yvette had become so distrusting, so loathsome of mankind that she turned to animals. My mind went numb as she told of an embarrassing phone call made to 911 dispatchers.

Please forgive us. We have totally disrespected and disrupted your plan for procreation. We've literally allowed the enemy to use us to mock you, to slap you in the face.

By the way, Neil . . . Nell, I should say, has been keeping a low profile lately. What's up with that? Are you dealing with her, or is she up to no good? In the meantime, I'll just watch and pray. Thank you for taking care of my boys. Keep them in your loving care. Protect them always.

Love, Ramiyah.

Hiawatha was stunned. Charlotte felt as if her jaws had dropped two inches from the floor.

14

"I used to say my middle name was Mayhem," Hiawatha commented. "That is some true mayhem right there! It makes me question why I would want to associate myself with mayhem."

"Good, because there is power in words; and you are not associated with mayhem. Your middle name is not Mayhem, and I rebuke every negative word spoken by you or *to* you," Charlotte declared.

"Charlotte, Ramiyah has been trying to talk some sense into me. She figured you could drive the nail home. Don't get me wrong. Deep down in my heart, I know what I'm doing is not right, but I don't know another way. I just do not have a desire for females."

Charlotte folded the letter and placed it back in the envelope. "I'm listening."

"I know Ramiyah is praying for me. My mom is praying for me. That's all well and good, but I am what I am."

"What you are *is* a man."

"I've been celibate since my diagnosis," Hiawatha blurted out. "But I do not intend to remain that way for too long."

Charlotte heard Hiawatha. She just was not sure if she was ready to minister to him. *I know we must be ready in season and out of season*, she said to herself. *But Lord, I have no expertise or any remote experience in the gay lifestyle. All I have is your Word.*

Immediately afterward, Charlotte heard the Holy Spirit say, "My Word is all you need."

"Are you judging me?" Hiawatha asked on the defensive.

"What? Do you honestly think that I am? Do I throw stones at you? Do I shun you? Or have I been hanging out with you and confiding in you during our time here?" Charlotte had become tired of people who used the accusation of judging as a means to run from correction.

Hiawatha's body language changed and he seemed less agitated and more relaxed.

"I will say this about judging: Sometimes we think we can be left off the hook by accusing someone of judging as our defense. In reality, while we are not to judge, we are to judge."

Puzzled by the comment, Hiawatha furrowed his eyebrows.

"For instance, you have to judge a character of a person to determine whether or not to make them your friend. We cannot call everyone our friends."

Hiawatha's chest swelled with pride and indignation shone through his eyes. "My question is this: if God was so displeased with my sexual preference, then why do we have . . ." Hiawatha was momentarily at a loss for words. "Okay, what about this? We have churches nowadays presided over by gay leaders. Does that sound like a non-loving, non-accepting God?"

Charlotte picked up her Bible from the nightstand. The holy book was so worn from usage until the pages had turned yellow and their edges curled. At this point, Charlotte did not care if Hiawatha would be agitated or not. She had to do what she had to do. "Remember earlier I suggested that you read Romans 1:26?"

Hiawatha responded with a steady gaze.

Charlotte flipped through a few pages, stopping when she found the Book of Romans. "Hiawatha, this is what the Word of God says, not the word of Charlotte; the Word of God.

> *Because of this, God gave them over the shameful lusts. Even their women exchanged natural relations for unnatural ones. In the same way the men also abandoned natural relations with women and were inflamed with lust for one another. Men committed indecent acts with other men and received in themselves the due penalty for the perversion. Furthermore, since they did not think it worthwhile to retain the knowledge of God, he gave them over to a depraved mind to do what ought not to be done.*

"Now, this applies to a whole lot of people," Charlotte stated. "I'm not singling out homosexuality. That just happens to be the topic you want to address. You see, the problem is an unrepented heart can eventually lead to a reprobate mind. I know a woman who refuses to serve God. In fact, I've even heard her curse God. Every time I turn around, something is happening with her. Her children steal from her. She has had numerous car wrecks and she has all types of health issues."

"Fortunately, I'm not prone to bad luck," Hiawatha replied sarcastically.

Confident that she had done what the Lord wanted her to do, Charlotte decided to trust God by leaving the rest to Him. "Come on, let's go back outside and see what the folks are up to."

Hiawatha followed Charlotte outside. By this time, Esau had returned home and was sitting on the top step eating a cinnamon roll and talking with Sista.

"Hi, Mr. Morley," Hiawatha greeted. Unable to speak due to a mouth full of crumbs, Esau just held up his hand.

Charlotte sat next to her father and traced her index finger along his receding hairline. "Such open space. What's going on here, Daddy?" she asked teasingly.

"What's going on? When you get older you start regressing. That's what's going on. I was bald when I came in the world, so I guess I'll be bald when I leave," Esau retorted, knowing that his daughter was joking.

"All you gotta do is buy some of that imitation hair," Sista added. "All these girls around here swingin' they heads like they slingin' hash."

After spotting something near Hiawatha's neck, Sista leaned over for a closer look. "How did you get those scratches? You been in a fight?"

"Yeah, with myself." Hiawatha took his left hand and crossed it over his shoulder to trace the marks with his fingers. He felt one long and two short scratches, which almost crossed the width of his very broad back.

"Well, duh! Maybe you need to get some of those mittens they put on newborn babies to protect yo'self. What were you and Charlotte in there doin' anyhow?" Sista asked.

"Reading her mail," he answered smugly.

"It takes both of y'all to read *her* mail?"

"You wanted to know, and no, we are not telling you what is in her letters.

Defeated, Sista sucked her teeth. As she leaned forward to pick up her house keys, which had been resting on the floor, a box of Anacin and her change purse came tumbling out of her bra.

Charlotte released a laugh. Hiawatha released a sigh. Esau released some cinnamon roll crumbs along with a spray of spittle.

15

*The beginning of strife is like releasing water; therefore,
stop contention before a quarrel starts*

Proverbs 17:14

Esau stood almost erect over the trashcan, spitting out
watermelon seeds as his mother continued putting the fin-
ishing touches on a heavenly chocolate cake by garnishing
the top layer with rose petals. Mattie Mae's fresh press and
curl had started to lose its vigor.

Sista blew into her bowl of mushroom soup to cool it
down a bit and recalled a burning question she wanted to
ask. "Esau, I've been noticing Betty lately. She looks like
she's bogged down with the weight of the whole world on
her shoulders. Is everything all right?"

Esau tried to make light of the fact that everyone showed
great concern for his wife's welfare. "My wife has been
going through a tough time with her sister being in jail, but
she will be fine. Betty is a trooper."

"God knows that's the truth. Maybe she needs to learn
how to let out some steam," Sista replied while opening a
pack of oyster crackers.

Mattie Mae started humming in an effort to tune out
Esau and Sista's conversation, for she, too, had been con-

cerned about Betty's demeanor. Esau tossed the half-eaten watermelon rind into the garbage and joined Sista at the table.

Sista crushed a few crackers into her soup before dipping her spoon into the bowl. "Sometimes Betty looks like a piece of broken glass. I'm a little worried about her."

"No need to worry, Miss Sista," Esau said, not too convincingly.

"By the way, Sista," Mattie Mae said, "I saw Rachel Robinson the other day and she had one of those handicapped stickers on her car. There's nothin' ailin' her, is there?"

"Sho' there is. She's cracked! That woman is as fool as a tick, and she ought not be drivin' at all." Sista slurped up the last bit of soup with great appreciation. "It sho' would have been nice to have had a grilled cheese sandwich with that soup."

"Now, Sista, you ain't no stranger here. You can still make one," Mattie Mae pointed out.

Esau rubbed his hand across a grainy substance on the table. "What is that?" Mattie Mae asked, coming to the rescue with a damp dishcloth.

"I don't know, Mama; sugar or something. Speaking of Rachel Robinson—" Esau got up from the table to wash his hands at the sink—"did she ever get married?" Esau prepared to pour himself a tall glass of ginger ale with more ice cubes in it than soda.

"Who is Rachel gonna marry?" Sista quickly answered. "A married woman has to consider somebody else's feelings and plans. A single woman don't have to. And Rachel ain't studyin' nobody but herself. Besides, who wants a crazy woman like Rachel for a bride?"

Esau chuckled. "You say she's loopy, Miss Sista?"

"Loopy, loony, cracked, all of the above."

"Stop it, Sista," Mattie Mae scolded while setting the

timer on the stove. A drop of hot grease splattered on her hand. Mattie Mae retrieved some butter from the refrigerator and rubbed a small amount across the back of her hand in order to prevent it from blistering.

"No, you stop it, Mattie Mae. You know that gal ain't got a lick of sense. You remember that year when we had the Christmas parade in town and she walked right through the procession like she didn't see it goin' on. That fool-behind gal crossed the street through a parade to go and talk to her aunt."

Mattie Mae doubled over in laughter. "Yeah, but not before she stopped to talk to her niece, who was ridin' on one of the floats. Rachel can't take care of a husband 'cause she can't even take care of herself."

"You're kidding," Esau said. "Rachel walked right through the parade?"

"That's exactly what she done. If that ain't crack, I don't know what is." Sista was about to go into more detail, but was distracted by a voice most annoying to her.

"How y'all doin' 'round there?" Nellie Moss asked in a slightly hoarse voice as she neared the kitchen entrance. "Edmund told me I could come on back. I hadn't had a chance to see Esau yet and didn't want to miss him befo' he went back to Washington."

"Come on 'round, Nellie," Mattie Mae invited, rattling a set of tea cups as she put away the dishes.

"It's good to see you, Nellie." Esau met Nellie with a friendly hug. Flakes of dandruff encamped around the collar of her shirt.

Sista placed the empty soup bowl in the sink and whispered to Mattie Mae, "Too bad we didn't have a chance to nail everything down. You know how light Nellie's hands are." When it came to dealing with Nellie Moss, Sista was as relentless as a shark that saw blood in the water.

Mattie Mae poked Sista in her ribs. "Can I offer you something to eat, Nellie?" Mattie Mae pointed toward her trusty stove. "I've got a pot of baked deer meat, green beans and potatoes, broccoli, cold water cornbread and a few pieces of fried chicken. Help yo'self to as much as you want. I almost forgot. There is some leftover soup in the microwave dish next to the cornbread."

"That sho' sounds good, but I just ate and can't eat another bite," Nellie said, practically huffing and puffing out her sentence. "I'm tryin' to watch my weight."

Sista lowered her eyes until they landed on Nellie's pudgy mid-section. She grunted. "Yeah, watch it get bigger. And what is she lyin' for? This comin' Sunday is the first Sunday in the month. I wouldn't take communion if I was her. It might burn her lips."

"You forever in the kitchen cookin', Mattie Mae," the rotund Nellie said. Nellie balled her hand into a fist and pounded her chest lightly after firing off a couple rounds of burps.

"Y'all excuse this kitchen." Mattie Mae enjoyed the cold blast from the freezer as she took out some ice. "I know it's hot in here. I've had the oven goin' and all four eyes on the stove burnin' at the same time."

Although everyone in the room heard Mattie Mae, it was clear to all that Nellie was ignoring Sista on purpose. Sista followed Mattie Mae to the back of the kitchen into the corner where the washer and dryer were located. Sista and Nellie had been feuding since the day Sista buried her husband. Sista had embarrassed Nellie for inviting herself into the family procession. This was an outrage considering the fact that they were not kin.

"She has yet to speak to me," Sista noted.

"Hush, she might hear you," Mattie Mae warned.

"She can't hear me back here or see me." This was true

thanks to the double door, sub-zero refrigerator obstructing the view of the corner.

"And I don't care if Nellie did hear me!" Sista continued. "I can't even stand to hear her name or see her name, let alone see *her!* It's so bad until I know the only time I wouldn't mind seeing her name in print is on an obituary."

"Sista!"

"Sista nothing. I'm just saying."

"Well, that's an evil thing to say." Ashamed of her friend's ugly attitude, Mattie Mae refused to look Sista in the face while she loaded the washer with dark-colored clothes after shoving another heap of laundry into the dryer.

"You know I don't wanna hold no hatred in my heart, Mattie Mae. I ain't the only one who feels that way about Nellie and you know it. The Lawd is just gonna have to change my heart."

"Well, why don't you see if the Lawd done already changed it by you goin' out there and being the first one to speak," Mattie Mae suggested. Sista bristled at the notion.

Ignoring Sista, Mattie Mae searched the top shelf for something to hold the torn flap down on the detergent box. All she could find was a dried out rubber band, which she did not want to use for fear of it breaking.

"I wonder why Nellie really came here," Sista said with suspicion. "And by herself at that. I heard that she wasn't lettin' Otis outta her sight much these days. Folks been teasin' that it was so bad 'til they thought she had replaced his shadow."

"Why can't she be here for the reason she said? She came to see Esau. Esau used to be real good friends with one of her brothers when they was chaps in grade school."

"Yeah, and I could never figure that out. Esau was smart as a whip and that boy could not get any darn dumber, but you couldn't pry those two apart with a pair of pliers. The only way you can make an 'A' in class is to either sleep wit' the teacher or sleep wit' yo' books. That boy ain't done either one of those."

Leading the way, Mattie Mae said in a hushed but disciplinary tone, "Come on out here and be friendly." Mattie Mae hoped against hope that her stubborn and strong-willed friend would soften up that mind of stone she had.

Mattie Mae and Sista returned to the front part of the kitchen to find that Nellie had decided to help herself to a hefty plate of food, and Esau was getting in the truck with Edmund. Mattie Mae nudged Sista in an attempt to silence her, but she was too late.

"Told you," Sista said, gloating. After witnessing Nellie pull her meat apart with her hands, Sista decided to dismiss greeting Nellie as Mattie Mae had suggested and uttered a question instead. "Why don't you use a fork?"

Licking her greasy fingers with much satisfaction, Nellie smirked and simply said, "Fingers were made before forks." She then crammed a nice chunk of deer meat into her mouth.

Even though Sista's dislike was more intense when it came to Otis, she often feuded with Nellie. Mattie Mae dreaded having any scenes in her home and attempted to diffuse the situation at hand. "Sometimes a still tongue makes for a wise head. Go on and enjoy yo' meal, Nellie," Mattie Mae said while cutting her eyes at Sista.

Nellie did not keep quiet, but did a wise thing by changing the subject. "Did ya hear about Minnie Wells passin' away?"

"No!" Mattie Mae was shocked.

"She had a heart attack. Happened this morning. And here she was, takin' care of her sick husband."

"A lot of times that's how it is. Sometimes a creaking gate hangs the longest," Sista said.

"That's the truth too," Nellie agreed. "I heard that Min-nie's daughter married a white man up in Chicago."

"Is that right?" Mattie Mae asked.

"Well, some women like a little milk in their coffee," Sista noted.

"And she married a *rich* white man at that," Nellie emphasized.

"A white rich man? If that don't beat all. He must be cockeyed," Sista said before she and Nellie erupted in laughter.

Rarely did Sista and Nellie get along amicably. Rarely did Sista succumb to Mattie Mae's advice or instructions, especially in an obedient, childlike manner. This too would soon pass.

"That gal used to ho 'round so bad when she lived here," Nellie continued. "She'd go wit' any man that would look at her."

"You remember that too?" Sista asked. "Almost every man done near 'bout had her. And it ain't like she's blessed with good looks. But Minnie claimed the man loves that gal so much 'til she thinks if her daughter asks him to grow another toe he would try it."

"Just goes to show ya how a lot of men don't turn down nothin', Sista," Nellie said. Nellie and Sista giggled, hemmed and hawed like schoolgirl chums.

"And then she claims her husband is the father of her baby. I done seen that child and he don't look nothin' like the man, if it's the same man I seen on the pictures. It's a shame she tricked that man into marryin' her by getting pregnant. Oh, well. He's gonna have to keep feedin' the chile 'til he looks like him," Sista added.

"Y'all a mess." Mattie Mae chuckled. "Maybe she's turned her life around."

"You right, Mattie Mae," Sista said. "Thank the Lawd for the blood of Jesus, 'cause any one of us could have been a ho! Thank the Lawd that He saw fit to keep us outta the ho kingdom."

Nellie gripped her sides, doubled over in laughter.

"Nellie, I know you're glad that gal moved away from here and got married. At least you won't have to worry 'bout yo' husband creepin' wit' her no more," Sista slipped.

Nellie nearly choked on her food. If steam could have risen from her head, it would have. Sista could never leave well enough alone.

16

"The *Farmers' Almanac* calls for a full moon all this week.
Fishin' should be good," Edmund pointed out. With a ther-
mos cup of herbal tea in his hand, Edmund led his son to an
embankment where the two men settled down near a large
rock. Esau handed Edmund his favorite rod—a St. Croix
fishing rod.

Edmund lifted the top on the container of mealworms
and carefully baited the hook with half of a worm, while
Esau twisted the cap off of his Diet Dr. Pepper and took a
swig. The soda tasted flat, causing him to grimace.

"Look, Pop." Esau pointed to a school of fish swimming
in the middle of the private pond owned by one of Edmund's friends. Except for a man of swarthy complexion, a
small boy of about ten years old, and their large German
shepherd dog, Edmund and Esau were the only two at the
pond.

The man scolded the boy for throwing stones into the
pond, causing a rippling effect and purling sound, along with
scaring away the fish. The dog frolicked about, barking and

writhing in the wet grass. Soon, the boy wrapped his arms
around the animal and they rolled and roughhoused together in merriment.

The man turned around, revealing his GONE FISHING
T-shirt, and warned the child not to get grass stains on his
brand new pair of Dockers or his shirt, which read, GONE
FISHING WITH MY DAD. He then curled his legs beneath him
on a hard mound of red clay and baited his hook.

This evoked fond memories in Esau of tender moments
shared with his father as a young boy. Edmund had always
been active in the church and in helping his friends, but
when it came to his sons, Esau and Charles, those were
times well spent. Now, the frailty of the once virile Edmund
made Esau a little sad, reminding him of life's inevitable
evolution.

Esau sorely missed the carefree lifestyle that the Caroli-
nas had to offer. He missed the innocence of his boyhood
even more so. Yet, even with all that had happened within
his family of late, he was still able to breathe a sigh of relief.

"Sometimes I think we should have named Charles after
someone in the Bible like we did you," Edmund said out of
the clear blue.

"There is nothing wrong with the name Charles," Esau
said, referring to his bisexual brother.

"No. But still I have to wonder." Edmund stroked his
chin. "I read somewhere that the name Charles means *man*.
Ain't that something to chew on? Man."

Esau took two quick sips from his bottle. "It's only a
name, Pop. My name means *hairy*. I am a hairy man, but
unlike Esau in the Bible, I didn't sell my birthright to my
brother for a bowl of stew. And Charles is still a man. It's his
lifestyle that is contrary."

Always the cautious type, Edmund did not reply. He only
grumbled.

Both men proceeded to cast their lines into the water. Soon, Esau could sense that something was nibbling on his hook. He reeled in a small brim fish, wriggling furiously for his life.

Edmund beamed all the while his line was being tugged, pulled and moved around in a frenzy, swooshing about in the water. Finally, he reeled in a slightly larger brim fish that conceded to his capture much quicker. He tossed his freshwater find inside the cooler. Edmund flung his arm back as if he were about to throw a curveball, casting his line in the water again. Afterward, he quenched his thirst with some herbal tea.

They waited patiently for another yank on the line, enjoying their time together.

"Is everything all right between you and Betty?" Edmund asked his son all of a sudden. His question was almost drowned out by the drones of crickets.

"Yes, sir. Why do you ask?" Esau then yawned and stretched out his arms, arching his back in the process.

"I know that Betty is a caring woman, but sometimes she seems so much sadder than the rest of us. It ain't good to be walking around burdened all the time."

"Well, she's worried about Ramiyah." Esau paused for a moment. "I shouldn't say worried, but you know what I mean."

Esau monitored the slow pace of a turtle trekking across the slightly murky pond. "Now, I know she's worried about her sister; that's understandable. But what can she do?"

"Not a thing but pray."

"That's right. Son, women are carriers by nature. Sometimes they carry more than they should. You gotta let some stuff go. It is a shame about Ramiyah. That's for sho', but how come we humans, who the Lawd considers more than the angels, can't learn to be content like that turtle over there?"

"I don't know, Pop," Esau confessed, wrinkling his nose.

"Look at it. That turtle ain't in no hurry to get nowhere. He ain't on no cell phone talking about stuff that don't matter or stuff that can wait."

Esau chuckled at the disparity and pushed his sunglasses back up to the bridge of his nose. "I know you've got a message coming out of this."

"I do. The people that followed Moses into the desert were never satisfied. We're the same way today and it gets us into trouble sometimes."

Esau gave Edmund ample time to continue making his point, but Edmund remained silent.

"Surely this is not all you have to say about the matter, Pop," Esau challenged.

"No. I know she and her husband lived a fast life, but God has His hands on Ramiyah. We should learn to be content. Don't go stepping out of God's law. Love is a commitment; a decision, not a passin' fancy. If a man or woman don't or can't honor marriage vows, then they should stay single."

"Amen to that. We all assumed Ramiyah lived a charmed life. A good husband. A nice home. Great kids. That just goes to show you never know what goes on behind closed doors. Ramiyah waited until after the trial to tell Betty about the physical and sexual abuse inflicted on her by her husband. For her to end up in prison is devastating."

Edmund sat quietly for a brief moment, rubbing his chin. "It sounds like Ramiyah did not end up *in* prison. She got *out* of one. I know it looks bad now, but I don't think this is how her story is gonna end. This is her beginning. I'll tell you something else too. I believe Ramiyah is gonna be set free from *that* prison too."

"We're hoping so. You really think she has a chance?"

Edmund just smiled and decided it was time to test out Mattie Mae's packed lunch, consisting of burnt bologna sandwiches with a slice of fresh tomato, crisp lettuce, a dash of oregano and a few pats of mayonnaise on toasted honey wheat bread.

As he waited for a nibble on his fishing line, Esau gazed once more at the man and his boy just in time to see the child running away from an ensuing swarm. The man uncurled his legs, got up and rescued his son from a crush of angry bees.

Silently, Esau hoped the boy would grow up to cherish every moment spent with his dad.

17

*As cold water to a weary soul, so is good news from
a far country*

Proverbs 25:25

With Sista and Hiawatha gone, and Edmund and Mattie
Mae retired to their bedroom, Charlotte found some alone
time with her parents in the living room, even though her
dad had nodded off to sleep. Charlotte took the newspaper,
which had slipped from his hands squarely into his lap, and
gently tapped him on the shoulder. "Wake up."

"I'm not sleep," Esau denied, slightly peevish.

"Esau, your neck was jerking back and forth like a peck-
ing chicken. What do you mean you're not sleep," Betty
corrected. "You need to go on up to bed." Betty got up and
lovingly patted her husband on his shoulder.

"I'm watching the news," Esau said without opening his
eyes, then switched his position in the chair.

"No, the news is watching you," Betty insisted.

"Maybe so, but I can still hear it."

Betty shook her head. "Most newsworthy segments are
shoved off and replaced by tabloid journalism anyway."

Charlotte really wanted to talk to her mother alone.
Knowing that it would only be a matter of seconds before

Esau would nod off again, she waited. The next sound the two Morley women heard was that of snoring.

"Ma," Charlotte began.

"Yes?" Betty rubbed her temples with the tips of her fingers in a circular motion to soothe away a minor headache.

"I know I've asked this before, but is there anything bothering you?" Chilly from the cold air blasting from the air conditioner, Charlotte took the lightweight fleece blanket from the armrest, wrapped herself in it and curled up on the sofa.

Betty closed her eyes, leaned her head back and simply said there was nothing bothering her. Charlotte did not believe her. "When do you plan to go see Ramiyah?" Charlotte asked.

Betty held her head down and said, "I don't know when exactly. Soon."

Charlotte noticed that her mother never seemed to want to talk about Ramiyah and felt that it might be due to humiliation. However, Jean gladly stated to anyone who would listen that Ramiyah justifiably sent Cole back to his home . . . hell. Betty, who was quiet and mild-mannered by nature, never commented on how she felt. In fact, Betty refused to say anything regarding Ramiyah the day she came back to D.C. after attending the trial. Jean, on the other hand, was another story. Jean was particularly furious once she found out that Cole's family was planning to file a wrongful death lawsuit.

Having raised Ramiyah as if she were her own, it was understandable for Jean to react like a mother trying to protect her young. But Betty, being the type of person who could easily be embarrassed by the most insignificant matters, was far removed and detached from it all.

"Aren't you curious as to what Ramiyah has to say?" Charlotte quizzed.

Betty lifted her head and made eye contact. "Charlotte, I just talked to Ramiyah before we came down here. All things considered, she said she was doing well. Your aunt is just trying to adjust to her situation. Why do you keep trying to make an issue out of this?"

"I don't mean to make an issue of this, Ma, even though this *is* a big deal," Charlotte rebutted, although she began to feel that maybe she was trying to make a mountain out of a mole hill. "And I did not mean to make you upset. I'm just curious as to why you never want to talk about what happened to Ramiyah."

"I'm sorry. I didn't mean to snap," Betty apologized. "I just don't like talking about it. I hate that she took a person's life. I hate that her life is being spent in prison and away from her children. It's painful. Switching the subject, Charles called today."

"He did? How's Aunt Francine doing? What's going on with Terry?"

"Francine is doing as well as can be expected. Charles said that some intercessors from the church have been coming over to have prayer with Fran. They've hired an attorney for Terry. She's been arrested for vehicular homicide in Dallas, Texas."

Charlotte was speechless and weary of Terry's foolishness. She resigned to the fact that Terry would finally meet justice.

The sound of Esau's nasal snoring caught Betty's attention. "Lord, let me wake this man up. Esau!" Betty got up, took the newspaper and tapped Esau on his head. "Esau, wake up. Let's go to bed, old man. When was the last time you did any farming?"

Esau grunted.

"Poor man worked so hard he nearly took himself out," Betty said as she massaged Esau's shoulders.

A drowsy Esau shrugged his shoulder and reluctantly got up and stretched his legs before going upstairs. Charlotte smiled as she witnessed her parents share a loving kiss. After saying goodnight, she waited until her parents had reached the top of the stairs before pulling out the third letter.

She flipped the toggle switch on the wall to the off position and turned on a lamp for a softer lighting. Just as Charlotte was about to get comfortable, her cell phone vibrated.

It was Hiawatha. "Hey, Charlotte."

"Yes."

"I didn't want to wake up anybody by dialing the phone number to the house."

"What if I was asleep? You don't care about waking me up?" Charlotte kidded. She checked the time. It was half-past eleven.

"Girl, whatever. How much longer are you staying in town?"

"I'm riding back with my parents and I think we're leaving either Tuesday or Wednesday, but I'm not sure. I know I need to leave soon and get back to my job at the church or else I'll be coming home to a dark house and spoiled food."

"I just wanted to talk with you some more before you leave. You picking up what I'm dropping down, Rev?"

"Yeah, I gotcha. We'll talk."

"Well, I just did not want you to leave without saying goodbye. Girl, let me go. The air condition just went out in this house and I'm in here roasting like chestnuts on an open fire. Whew!"

"You are something else." Charlotte laughed.

"I know it. Pray for me. Speaking of fire, I see I'll have to get on my lazy brother before I leave."

"Why?"

"It will be winter before you know it. John Edward is responsible for getting wood for the wood stove, and instead of logs, I see nothing but splinters out there in the barn."

"Well, maybe that's all that's left from last winter," Charlotte reasoned. "Besides, he's got plenty of time. What's the rush?"

"You don't know my brother. He will wait until the last minute to try and stock the barn and have a hard time finding somebody who has wood to sell."

"Still, I wouldn't worry. It's not like they have harsh winters in South Carolina." Charlotte heard her line click. "But you go ahead and handle your business and I'll see you some time tomorrow. I've got another call." Charlotte clicked over. It was Timmi. "Timmi, you are going to live for a long time, as the old folk say."

"Really? How you figure?"

"I made a mental note to myself the other day to call you back, and here you are calling me. The next time you talk to Jeff, tell him that I will mail Tina's obituary to him since he couldn't come for her funeral."

"I will," Timmi replied. "Charlotte, I have so much to tell you, but don't get too excited just yet. When you get back home we need to have a divas' night, complete with champagne—excuse me, I meant to say sparkling apple cider and tiaras for our heads."

"Timmi, I haven't heard you sound this excited in a long time. Again, details, please!"

"I *am* excited. The event was some sort of meet and greet black tie affair fundraiser for battered women."

"Tell me about it. Anything useful I can pass on to Ramiyah?"

"Yep. I'll have it ready for you when you get back. But let me tell you about the reception."

The mere mention of the word *reception* had Charlotte

thinking of food and craving for a stack of blueberry pancakes and country sausages.

"There were buffet tables with generous amounts of food setup everywhere throughout this huge corridor. There was a sea of men in chef hats walking around with trays of food. I've never seen that much food in my life!"

"How was the food? Was it good or just good to look at?"

"The food was fabulous except for this one spicy dish I tasted. They might as well have served a ball of flames. But anyhow, in the ballroom were these trios of black females playing violins, violas and cellos. They were all dressed in black Vera Wang gowns and wore white orchid wrist corsages. The harpist sat on the platform surrounded by orchids and candles. And there was this gigantic ice sculpture of women and children on a table in the middle of the floor of the ballroom."

"That sounds beautiful. Breathtaking."

"It was. But the most breathtaking thing that happened against that backdrop was that Jeff and I really started clicking. We really are becoming fast friends."

"But?" Charlotte stated, excited about Jeff and Timmi's relationship blossoming.

"But this event we attended was packed with all of these celebrities and what-not. I mean, really notable people that would impress anybody, but we only had eyes for each other that night. Before I get into that, guess what?"

"What?" Charlotte hated to be in suspense.

"Do you remember the tobacco stock certificate I bought from the antique store when I was there a couple of weeks ago? It had a picture of slaves on it."

"Yeah, I remember." Charlotte was thankful for Timmi's visit and saw God's hand in it during that time. Timmi was distraught over a break-up and Charlotte's cousin, Jeff, was the guest speaker at the family church. The two met and apparently their relationship was starting to blossom into at least a friendship.

"Well, stuck to the back of it was an actual bill of sale for a negro slave boy."

"You are kidding me!"

"No joke. He was sold to the owner of a railroad depot. This so-called boy was actually a forty-year-old man! This crap still makes me angry. Forty years old and listed as a boy."

"Unfortunately, that's the way it was back then. You know that."

"Yeah, I do. Sad. It's dated 1846 and another thing it states is that this *boy* would be a slave for life to have and to hold. Sounds like some marriages I know."

"Girl, stop. That's a good find. Look. I don't mean to trivialize this, but—"

"I know. I know. Jeff and Timmi sitting in a tree. Yada, yada, yada." Timmi giggled. "Alas, we reluctantly parted ways."

"Timmi, enough with the suspense already," Charlotte sighed.

"Oh, girl, this is my mom on the other line. I've got to take this call. My grandmother fell and broke her hip the other day. Anyway, I'll give you a call back as soon as I can. I promise to give you details when I call back. Smooches."

"Wait!" Charlotte cried out in disappointment after realizing it was too late. Timmi had already hung up the phone.

18

*Enter into His gates with thanksgiving and into His courts
with praise. Be thankful to Him and bless His name*

Psalm 100:4

Sunday was Charlotte's favorite day of the week. She wiped off the soles of her shoes on the doormat before entering Greener Pastures's sanctuary. The small white clapboard country church had recently undergone a much needed transformation. The hard narrow benches had been replaced with padded pews. The baptismal pool was no longer surrounded by tallow candles, but was illuminated by fluorescent overhead lighting and a collection of Boston ferns and mother-in-law tongues. Spider plants took the place of outdated, dusty plastic potted plants.

The church was packed and Charlotte was impressed, remembering that a couple of weeks ago, church attendance was so low that she'd jokingly stated that the rapture had come.

Charlotte felt someone poking her ribs.

"Are you goin' to the chutch picnic after service?" Sista asked.

"I guess so." Charlotte shrugged. "Even though Grandma has a big dinner waiting for us at home."

"You know Mattie Mae. She's gonna cook no matter what. You know, I heard that the person in charge of the food only paid eighty dollars for everything. Tell me how you gonna feed over two hundred people wit' food that only cost eighty dollars? They know this is a big to-do."

"I don't know, Miss Sista." Charlotte tried not to laugh.

"I don't know either, but I *do* know I won't be eatin' it if it looks cheap. No telling where that stuff came from. I-Can-Do-Whatever-I-Want always shows up before Common Sense. Then again, folks lie so much. That might not even be true."

"I'm sure it's not true, Miss Sista," Charlotte said. "It takes more than eighty dollars to feed a church full of people."

Sista turned her head slightly to look for her sons. "I wonder what's taking Hiawatha and John Edward so long."

Charlotte wondered too. She wanted to ask them why they let Sista leave the house looking the way she did. Sista's powder blue suit was fine and even her matching powder blue alligator purse and shoes were stylish. But her hat looked like something emerging from the forest.

Charlotte forced herself to keep a straight face after she caught herself gawking at the strange millinery. Sista's blue hat was adorned with twigs, fake berries and a bright red bird positioned to appear as if he were feeding on the berries. She expected to hear crickets sing at any moment.

Sista eased by Charlotte, tiptoeing across the wooden planks to go join Edmund and Mattie Mae, who were already seated in their usual spot up front. Charlotte sat in the pew behind her parents. The church was packed with members and first time visitors.

Then Charlotte noticed that Sista was not the only woman at church profiling big, kooky hats. In fact, there was a group of women whose hats obstructed the view of those sitting behind them. Charlotte's eyes traced their row, starting with one woman's huge hat filled with rhinestones, yellow plumes and speckled feathers, all the way down to the tiny derby-styled hat perched like a crown on another woman's head. Even 90-year-old Mother Magdalene Archer looked silly in her newsboy cap and large hoop earrings.

Finally, Hiawatha and John Edward arrived and sat next to Charlotte. John Edward was ruggedly handsome in his navy blue pinstripe suit, and Hiawatha was fabulous as ever in his tailor-made Armani. Charlotte tossed them both a look of approval.

Mattie Mae, who was the church announcer every first Sunday, got up to say that the collection plate would be passed around twice. The first go-round would be for tithes and offerings, and the second trip was to raise funds for a member whose house had recently burned down.

Hiawatha whispered to Charlotte how nice Mattie Mae looked in her brown sequined suit. Charlotte smiled and gave a compliment to Sista's suit, shoes and purse. She decided to reserve all comments about Sista's hat to herself. She had to admit that her grandmother did look graceful and elegant in her outfit. Mattie Mae's turquoise earrings and brooch pulled the look together nicely.

The collection plate passed around twice, as promised, while the praise and worship team led the congregation in worship. Charlotte was so proud of the team. She had worked hard in putting it together, and they were certainly proving themselves capable.

The double doors leading to the sanctuary sprang open. Greener Pastures's Mass Choir came marching in. The choir was uniformly dressed in white tops and black skirts or pants. The women wore big purple flowers on the left side of their torsos and the men wore purple neckties.

Apparently, black, white and purple was the Family and

Friends Day color theme, as the altar had been draped with white tulle and purple flowers. The programs had been printed on purple parchment paper, and even the guest speaker wore a purple robe.

Singing "Onward Christian Soldiers," the mass choir marched up to the choir stand in a perfect line reminiscent of a trail of ants.

Hiawatha raised his hand to signal an usher for a program and extra tithing envelope. The round-faced woman promptly responded. As she leaned slightly to give Hiawatha a program, her right breast lightly brushed against John Edward's face, causing a look of embarrassment to come upon her face. John Edward chose to play it off as if no such thing had happened.

Charlotte peeked over to see the impressive design on Hiawatha's program. On the back of the program she recognized a few names listed as new members: Sally Mae Burton, Herbert Make, Gwendolyn Plymouth, Tom and Lessie Anderson, Booker T. Washington, Jerry and Carrie Lee Lang, Mary Alice Witherspoon and Larry Carroll.

Underneath that was the headline SICK AND SHUT-IN, which listed one member who was recovering from a bout of pneumonia. As Hiawatha opened the leaflet, Charlotte briefly read a little of the guest speaker's wife, First Lady Erica's, bio, which stated that she relinquished her pursuit of becoming an opera singer to become the wife of an AME preacher.

Charlotte quickly turned her head and covered her mouth, expecting to sneeze. She didn't. Curiously, the smell of freshly cut lumber from a nearby sawmill wafted through the air, prompting the reaction from her. She looked over her shoulder and discovered a stained glass window had been hoisted and held up by a small stick.

Hiawatha applied a nudge in Charlotte's side. "You didn't

want one?" he asked softly, raising the program slightly in mid air.

"No," she whispered.

"How come?"

"I'm praying that the Holy Ghost takes reign over this service and we won't feel obligated to stick to a program."

Suddenly, there was a thump, thump, thump against the back of Charlotte's pew. Thump, thump, thump again.

Whereas Charlotte succeeded in not showing any irritation to the child kicking rapidly against the pew, Hiawatha failed miserably. Hiawatha hissed. He turned around to give a cold stare at the child and then looked squarely into the eyes of the child's mother.

The child's mother's hair had been pulled back so tightly until Hiawatha was almost convinced it was the cause of her squinting. But then she went into rapid blinking mode and mouthed the words *I am so sorry*, as she steadied the little boy's legs with her hands. The sandy-haired boy feigned innocence and started singing with the choir, "There is powva, powva, wonder workin' powva in the blood of the Lamb. There is powva, powva, wonder workin' powva in the precious blood of the Lamb."

At the conclusion of the hymn and after the introduction of the guest speaker, the entire congregation stood on their feet to welcome Reverend Horace Holmes with a thunderous round of applause.

Reverend Holmes appeared nervous to Charlotte as he gathered his notes and approached the podium. "Amen, church," Reverend Holmes said, flashing a broad smile and white teeth. An assistant raced over to hand him a glass of water.

"First, I just wanted to give honor to God and to the church for inviting me here today." Reverend Holmes looked over to his right. "Before I deliver today's message,

I'd like to ask the church to give a warm welcome to my lovely wife of twenty-one years, First Lady Erica Holmes."

Another warm round of applause along with a few catty looks from the female congregants went forth. No one could deny how smartly dressed the first lady was in her cream-colored suit with black piping along the seams, matching hat and peep-toe pumps.

Charlotte wondered if the Mrs. was as gregarious as her husband seemed to be. First Lady Erica responded to the welcome with a restrained smile. Her lips were overstated with lip liner. Half waving to the crowd, First Lady Erica took only a few steps forward, but moved gracefully, like an African queen. She then took her seat, striking a pensive pose.

"She is the cocoa in my chocolate," Reverend Holmes added before taking his seat.

To Charlotte, First Lady Erica's body language stated that she was a pastor's wife and she had darn well better be treated as such. Charlotte wondered what she was hiding behind those pouty lips and aristocratic posture.

After the choir sang one slow hymn followed by one fast tempo selection, an eager Reverend Holmes went back to the podium, wiping his head and neck with a handkerchief.

"Church," he called out, sweating profusely through his royal blue suit, "I know that you've been without a pastor, but the good news is that a shepherd is on the way. I personally spoke with the Bishop and he informed me that you will have your set man of God in the house next Sunday."

There was a mixture of cheers, moans and suspicious looks throughout the church. However, Reverend Holmes seemed oblivious to them all. Perhaps he was unaware that the last set man of God that the great Bishop had sent to Greener Pastures had robbed the church blind.

"Before I give you the title of today's sermon, I would like to first set you up with the reading of the scriptures." Reverend Holmes held up his burgundy leatherbound Bible. "I will be basing today's text on Matthew 20:20-22 and Psalm 37:1-3."

Charlotte focused her attention on Reverend Holmes, ready to hear a word from the Lord. Reverend Holmes looked down at the underlined text and began to read:

> *Then came to him the mother of Zebedee's children with her sons, worshipping him and desiring a certain thing of him.*
>
> *And he said unto her, What wilt thou? She saith unto him, Grant that these my two sons may sit, one on thy right and the other on the left in thy kingdom.*
>
> *But Jesus answered and said, Ye know not what ye ask. Are ye able to drink of the cup that I shall drink of and to be baptized with the baptism that I am baptized with? They say unto him, We are able.*

Reverend Holmes flipped back a few pages to the Book of Psalms. He adjusted his eyeglasses on the bridge of his nose and began to read again:

> *Fret not thyself because of evildoers, neither be thou envious against the workers of iniquity.*
>
> *For they shall soon be cut down like grass and wither as the green herb.*
>
> *Trust in the Lord and do good so shalt thou dwell in the land and verily thou shalt be fed.*

Reverend Holmes closed his Bible and looked out at the congregation. "Church, I know many of you know what it's like to see people who've done wrong or even done wrong to you and it *looks* like they are prospering while you are suffering. You've been emotionally malnourished due to lone-liness with nothing in your stomachs but bitterness."

The worshippers shouted a hearty collective, "Amen." Everyone seemed pleased, as if a good dose of religion had cured whatever ailed them.

"And I know many of you feel that you deserve vindica-tion. You think you deserve this and you think you deserve that. You serve God and you come to church, but yet *you* are the one getting the short end of the stick and you want to see the tables turn!"

People stood up on their feet and shouted as if they had been waiting on this affirmation all their lives. Even Betty bobbed her head in agreement.

"Oh, but my brothers and sisters, I've come here today with a word from the Lord. How many of you know that God cannot lie?"

Everyone raised their hands and shouted praises.

"That's right. With that said, I've not come here with a weak word, but with a strong message from the throne! The title of today's message is, 'Hold On. Your Suffering Is Not In Vain.'"

As Reverend Holmes preached about patience and main-taining the right attitude while suffering through such things as loss and heartache, over half the congregation wept or shouted as they demonstrated how they could relate to go-ing through trials and tribulations. Emotions were flying high. People even brought down an extra offering as Rev-erend Holmes echoed God's promise to bless those who be-long to Him.

Charlotte watched closely as her father constantly rubbed her mother's back during the sermon. While others seemed to be rejoicing in the spirit, Betty seemed distressed and Charlotte sensed turbulence just over the horizon.

19

*So continuing daily with one accord in the temple and
breaking bread from house to house, they ate their food
with gladness and simplicity of heart, praising God and
having favor with all the people. And the LORD added to
the church daily those who were being saved*

Acts 2:46 & 47

After having proven himself to be a very effectual minister
of the Gospel, there was hardly a dry eye in the house by the
time Reverend Holmes got through with his jaw-dropping,
eye-opening sermon. One female worshiper shouted so
hard until one of her false eyelashes had dangled down from
her eyelid and threatened to fall off completely.

Charlotte, too, had appreciated the fresh manna from
heaven and even considered that she may have misjudged
the august First Lady Erica, who was not ashamed to get her
praise on.

First Lady Erica knew that Greener Pastures was in for a
special treat. After all, she was in position to know that her
husband was truly anointed and carried a "right-now word"
from God in his belly.

After giving the benediction and blessing the meal that
awaited everyone in the fellowship hall, Reverend Holmes
remained behind to greet and shake hands with parish-
ioners. First Lady Erica joined him, standing proudly beside her man.

Edmund, Mattie Mae, Esau, Betty and Sista got in line to pay accolades to the visiting minister while Charlotte, Hiawatha and John Edward, who were motivated by hunger, chose to go to the fellowship hall.

John Edward pointed out two women who were walking ahead of them. He had observed them speaking in tongues during the altar call. "We don't see people speaking in tongues around here. I heard about speaking in tongues, but I've never seen anyone do it."

"And you still haven't. I don't think that was tongues," Hiawatha said. "I didn't need a translator to know that he's-cominginahonda is not speaking in tongues."

"Her friend or whoever the other lady is was worse," Charlotte added. "When the pastor asked everyone to pass the peace, her friend hugged me and whispered something really strange in my ear. She just kept saying, tat-tat-tat-tat-tat-tat."

"Now, see. People ought not play," Hiawatha said.

"No, they sure shouldn't," Charlotte agreed.

"You guys want to sit indoors or out?" Charlotte asked since the weather had presented them with a picture-perfect day.

"Indoors. The picnic area is too close to the cemetery for me," John Edward said, almost shrieking.

"What? Are you afraid the dead will rise and sit next to you, John Edward?" Charlotte kidded.

Even though John Edward found humor in the question, Charlotte could tell that he was *dead* serious about his fear of being around graves. As a show of bravery, John Edward conceded, "We can go outside and eat."

The trio stood patiently in a line that led to a row of oblong tables manned by a crew of women wearing comfortable shoes, white aprons and hair nets. On this day, Greener

Pastures's fellowship hall was definitely the place to be for anyone who was razor thin and in need of a good meal.

Hiawatha pushed the braided purple, white and black streamers and Chinese paper lanterns that hung from the ceiling out of his face as he walked in the room. Each dining table boasted a fresh floral centerpiece that came from the gardens of various members. Later, the floral arrangements would be judged and prizes given to the grand prize winner.

"Sweet," Hiawatha remarked after spying the good eats and treats.

As they got closer to the entrees, Charlotte noticed that the first table offered nothing but a variety of meats, and her mind scrambled to make a decision as her eyes danced to and fro. The smoked ham, herb encrusted pork loin, fried chicken, baked chicken, barbecued chicken, sliced roast turkey breast, fried turkey, barbecued turkey, Swedish meatballs and the grilled hot dogs and hamburgers were, in fact, tempting.

She gave her request for a piece of baked chicken to a food server with gorgeously long, wavy red hair and elf-like ears. Next, Charlotte found her way to the vegetable table where the server's tone was dry, at best. Despite the fact that the veggies were in plain sight and needed no introduction, the attendant said, "We have green beans, collard greens, black-eyed peas, fried okra, stewed tomatoes, carrot soufflé, vegetable lasagna, butternut squash casserole and broccoli casserole. What would you like to have?"

"Are we limited to how many choices we can have?" Charlotte asked.

"Not at all."

After making her vegetable selections, Charlotte moved on to the next table, which catered non-vegetable type side dishes. By now, Charlotte was embarrassed by the mound building up on her plate. Nevertheless, she was not deterred. Years of frowning had clearly taken residence upon this table's food server's face.

Charlotte noted that everything on the next table looked equally mouth-watering with its lineup of macaroni and cheese, yellow rice, Spanish rice, red beans and rice, potato salads, garden salad, mash potatoes and gravy, stuffed bell peppers, crackling cornbread, slices of rye bread and wheat and yeast rolls.

However, the dessert table was a splendor to behold and Hiawatha and John Edward nearly knocked Charlotte down rushing over to it. The two-tier, lazy Susan type table was hosted by two smiling faces that were obviously proud of their post.

"Who wants a piece of cake?" Charlotte heard a young mother ask her daughter.

"Me do! Me do!" the chubby toddler replied, jumping up and down, twisting and turning like an acrobat. The little girl ran over and sat on a small table with a wobbly leg. The table protested against the weight of her body and soon lost the battle. The leg of the table finally gave way, sending the child to the floor and causing her to let out a wail.

Meanwhile, Charlotte, Hiawatha and John Edward gawked and marveled at the various homemade confections. The table boasted sweet potato pudding, coconut pies, pecan pies, eggnog pies, red velvet cake, vanilla pudding cake, chocolate cake, carrot cake, upside down pineapple cake, blueberry cheesecake, apple pie, peach cobbler, a fruit tart, different flavors of Jell-O in lettuce cups and a melon fruit medley.

"Man," John Edward exclaimed. "Look at that chocolate cake!"

"I'm looking at it," Hiawatha said. "I think I would eat my own foot if it was smothered in chocolate like that. But in all honesty, there is so much sugar on that table my teeth are starting to hurt. That table is a diabetic coma waiting to happen."

Charlotte's chuckle at the comment was cut short by the sight of one of the obliging servers at the dessert table. The young woman wore blue contact lenses and a platinum blond weave. "There are obvious identity issues going on here," Charlotte said to herself.

"In fact, they should label all of these tables," Hiawatha continued his summation and pointed his index finger toward the various tables. "Again, that is a Diabetic Coma Waiting to Happen." He then pointed at the meat table. "That is Clogged Arteries and Congestive Heart Failure." He turned to the table behind them. "And that table is Clogged Arteries II, because it's full of fatback, hog jowls and smoked ham hocks."

Charlotte and John Edward both burst out laughing after realizing Hiawatha was referring to the vegetable table, the so-called healthy fare that could not escape his ire.

"I'll just call the other table of side dishes a distraction. But it's all good." Hiawatha patted himself on the back. "A good workout at the gym, plenty of water to flush out the toxins, return back to a diet of wheat germ, tofu and colon cleanser and I'll be as good as new."

Now that the main course and dessert selections had been made, and due to the amount of salt, sugar and starches on her plate, Charlotte decided on having a bottle of spring water to go along with her meal.

John Edward spotted a lone knotty pine picnic table and rushed over to claim it.

"Are you coming?" Hiawatha asked after realizing Charlotte had fallen behind several paces.

"You go ahead. I'll catch up with you guys in a minute. I

see our family members standing in line. I'll let them know we're going to be sitting outside," Charlotte said, changing her direction.

"Tell my mama to grab an extra crispy fried chicken breast for me. I didn't have enough room on my plate. And tell her no cussing either. Remind her that she is still in the house of the Lord." Hiawatha winked. "And hurry back. We've joined hands, sang old Negro spirituals and now it's time to break bread together."

Charlotte headed toward her family. Just as she got within inches of her parents, she and First Lady Erica almost collided as they crossed paths. First Lady Erica apologized in a voice sweet as dripping honey, and went on about her business, gliding across the room as if she were floating through a current. In the meantime, Charlotte caught Sista raising her eyebrow as First Lady Erica whisked by carrying an aluminum tray filled with cucumber sandwiches cut into perfect little squares.

Charlotte bit into the drumstick she held securely between her index finger and thumb. She grimaced. The chicken may have looked tender and juicy in the serving tray, but it tasted dry and bland in her mouth. After swallowing the piece of meat, she told her mother that Hiawatha and John Edward had reserved seats outside for everyone.

Just as Charlotte turned around to go outdoors, she nearly bumped into Reverend Holmes. They both exchanged apologies. She noticed that he had removed his hot and heavy robe, which had been damp from sweat. Reverend Holmes maintained a gallant, priestly stride that said *I am somebody* as he walked across the room.

Charlotte chuckled to herself as she watched Sista check out Reverend Holmes. She knew what Sista was looking at specifically and why she had a baffled look on her face. Reverend Holmes had a handsome head of curly black hair. His sideburns were graying and neatly trimmed. It was a stylish look nonetheless. However, the wide part in his scalp made him look like a nineteenth century barber.

Once outside, it didn't take Sista long to start with the wisecracks.

"You look prosperous," Sista said, touching an obese woman's stomach and wincing at the woman's behind. "*And* highly favored."

"I thought you were saved," the woman pointed out, sounding insulted. "How would you like it if I said you looked like you could use a sandwich? You ole bag of bones!"

"I *am* saved!" Sista joked back. "And call me a bag of bones one more time. I'll have you singin' 'Nearer My God To Thee.'"

Heads turned immediately toward what seemed to be an ensuing altercation, unaware that Sista and the woman were actually first cousins who were just playing around.

"I know we're not about to get alley on church grounds by having a slugfest, right, Miss Sista?" Charlotte, who was also unaware that the two women were only jesting, asked.

"No, we're not." Sista grinned mischievously. "I don't have time for sugar-honey-iced tea on chutch grounds, or anywhere else, for that matter. Charlotte, this here is one of my favorite cousins, Ruby Jones. We always cut the fool like that."

"One of yo' few living cousins," Ruby added, rubbing her elf-like ears. "I can't stay too long. This ole arthritis got my toes all bent up."

"You want me to step on 'em?"

"What?"

"Do you want me to step on yo' toes? Straighten 'em out." Sista snickered.

"Sista, you better not step on my toes. I ain't got time to fool wit' yo' crazy self." Ruby's stomach began to growl like waves crashing against the rocks. She pulled her matted wig down for a snugger fit, said goodbye and boldly wobbled toward a table with her plate of food.

A biscuit from Sista's plate fell onto a piece of concrete slab, making a thumping noise in the process. "I won't be eating that," Sista declared. "That thing sounded like a jackhammer falling on the floor."

One of the deacons made an announcement that the judges were about to select the winners of the floral arrangement contest. A group of volunteers presented the flowers before a panel of judges. The four female judges confessed that it had been tough, but after some debate they had finally made their decision. In fact, one of the judges claimed that it would have been easier to sweep the ocean with a broom than to unanimously pick a winner.

Mattie Mae Morley's "Pretty in Pink" took first place to the grand prize winner, Pearl Cleveland's "Dark Beauties" after final voting. Although the judges liked Mattie Mae's arrangement of African daisies, tiger lilies, peonies and pink velvety roses, they simply fancied Sister Cleveland's romantic collection of baby blue-eyes and pansies, which were wrapped in a brownish-gold organza ribbon, fashioned with a nice tidy bow and placed in a lead crystal vase.

Susie Mae Johnson's "Tall Treat" of Calla lilies and amaryllis won the honor of second place. The winner's grand prize was a twenty-five dollar gift certificate at Miss Millie's Millinery Shop and dinner for two at the Turtle Island Boathouse Restaurant.

Pearl Cleveland, who was also last year's winner, strutted and grinned her way toward her blue ribbon and gift certificates. And like last year, Sista made a churlish remark under her breath.

Most people knew, whether they would admit it or not, that Pearl had a talent for arranging flowers and deserved to win. It was her high and mighty attitude that sucked and made folks roll their eyes. Pearl deliberately veered down the row of tables, passing by Mattie Mae and displaying such haughtiness.

Then something caught everyone's eyes as Pearl sauntered to the front in such pageantry. There appeared to have been something traveling at great speed up the back of her dress.

"Miss Pearl!" a short, middle-aged man screamed as he hit and jerked on her dress. Frightened, confused and angry, Pearl lashed back at the man, not realizing that the back of her dress had been ambushed by an army of red ants.

Some of the crowd jeered and snickered at the sight of the spectacle. The man struggled to brush the ants off of Pearl, but she struggled to maintain her dignity. Pearl's dress flew up and her hat flew off. In his continued attempt to knock off the insects, the man delivered Pearl a final blow of humiliation by giving her one good whack on her bottom, sending Pearl head first into her prize-winning "Dark Beauties."

20

And it happened, when Elizabeth heard the greeting of
Mary, that the babe leaped in her womb and Elizabeth was
filled with the Holy Spirit. Then she spoke out with a loud
voice and said, "Blessed are you among women and blessed
is the fruit of your womb."

Luke 1:41 & 42

Charlotte slowly pushed opened the door to the spacious
ladies' lounge. The first thing to greet her was the purple
and pink floral wallpaper and a strong lavender scent. She
then pushed back the door that led to the stalls and porce-
lain sinks. At first glance, she assumed the bathroom was
unoccupied until she noticed First Lady Erica standing before the mirror, combing her hair.

"Hi, First Lady," Charlotte said. "I wanted to introduce
myself to you earlier. I'm Minister Charlotte Morley. I truly
appreciated the word your husband gave earlier."

"Thank you," First Lady Erica said as she approached
Charlotte with her arms extended. Charlotte was somewhat startled by the embrace. Although First Lady Erica
did strike her as polite enough, she did not seem overtly
friendly.

"You're welcome," Charlotte responded as she turned
slightly to turn on the faucet and squirt a small amount of
soap into her hands. Charlotte vigorously washed her hands,

looked in the mirror and noticed that First Lady Erica had not budged. "Is there something wrong?"

"Well," First Lady Erica hesitated. "First, I wanted to say I'm sorry about the suffering your family has been going through. It's a small town, honey. I also heard about all you've done to help during your stay here."

Charlotte dried her hands. She wanted to say something back but couldn't. She could not speak. The Holy Spirit told her to just listen.

First Lady Erica slipped her wide-tooth comb back inside her purse. "If you have a moment, I would like for you to indulge me for just a bit." She snapped the clutch back in place.

"Sure. What's on your mind?" Charlotte asked.

"Right after you and I nearly bumped into each other in the Fellowship Hall, God told me to get transparent before you and solicit your prayers."

Charlotte turned to face the first lady, giving the woman her undivided attention. It was at that moment when Charlotte sensed that the first lady was grappling with heartbreak and hardness of heart despite her soft demeanor.

First Lady Erica sighed. "Are you married, Minister Morley?"

"Divorced. And please call me Charlotte."

"I see. Charlotte, a year ago around this time, I was on the threshold of filing for divorce from Pastor Holmes," she said as she unfastened the laminated name badge from her lapel and tossed it in the trash.

Charlotte was stunned by the revelation.

"Believe me. I don't enjoy airing dirty laundry, especially mine, but I truly believe that the Lord wants me to tell you this, not only for my sake, but for your sake as well."

"For my sake?" Charlotte was puzzled.

First Lady Erica nodded her head. "Now, I don't know

what it is, but I definitely got a clear unction about this. All I ask is that you pray for me and my husband because I'm sure you know there are good ole boy systems in the church too."

"Boy, don't I know," Charlotte answered wearily.

"I promise I will be brief," First Lady Erica said.

"Take your time. I am a listening vessel."

"I certainly appreciate that." First Lady Erica smiled.

"Do you mind my asking you how you and Reverend Holmes met?" Charlotte inquired.

"I don't mind at all. First, let me say that he and I are as different as oil and vinegar." First Lady Erica covered her mouth with a monogrammed handkerchief as she sneezed. "Excuse me. I tend to have allergies to one thing or another lately."

"God bless you. How are the two of you different?"

"I grew up in New Jersey surrounded by asphalt, row houses and industrial smog. My husband, on the other hand, spent the majority of his life around clucking hens, John Deere tractors and pot belly pigs."

Charlotte chuckled. "Those are different backgrounds all right."

"Indeed they are. I also grew up in the Pentecostal church and my husband was born and raised AME. We met in college, we later got married and he was called to preach at churches where the people were annoyingly rigid. I was not used to that. We really had a hard time at first. Those folks weren't coming to church on Sundays to praise God and receive a word. They were coming to their weekly routine meeting. The deacons blatantly smoked cigarettes right outside the church doors and the kitchen committees were nothing more than gossiping cliques. It was awful."

Charlotte felt that she could probably finish the rest of First Lady Erica's story, but didn't. That would be presumptuous. "Why don't we have a seat out here in the ladies' lounge," she suggested instead.

First Lady Erica grabbed her designer purse and followed Charlotte through the swinging double doors, her stiletto heels tapping against the marble floor as she walked. Before the first lady even took a seat in one of the burgundy leather armchairs, she began to pour her heart out again.

"Pastor and I have been married for fifteen years."

"That's quite remarkable for this day and age," Charlotte stated.

"Yes. For this day and age, I suppose it is. The first year of our marriage was a year-long honeymoon. By year two, the honeymoon was abruptly over. I found out that he was drinking, running around with other women, you name it. Fellow clergy, and by that I mean good ole boy acquaintances who pastored churches, offered nothing in the way of counseling." The first lady spoke frankly and in measured tones.

Charlotte was not at all shocked. In fact, she understood all too well and knew that sometimes you simply had to have the fortitude to dig yourself an out. Reverend Holmes sounded much like her ex-husband, except that her ex-husband had never been a man of the cloth.

"My husband started talking down to me, and I'm the type of sister who does not stand for that. Either you will leave my presence with it, or stay to be on the receiving end of *my* tongue-lashing."

"Let me guess," Charlotte interjected. "He would leave."

"Yeah, girl. Every single time. Although I think many times that was a ploy to leave. You know, create an argument so you can leave the house to cool off."

Charlotte nodded. That tactic was familiar to her as well. "I know what you mean. There were times when I wanted to straight head butt my ex-husband right out that door. Save him the trouble of playing games."

The first lady chuckled. "Where can a pastor's wife go for help without being scrutinized? I wanted to start a support group for women at the last small church where we served. Actually, I wanted to hide behind a support group. Help others without letting them know I needed help myself."

"I know what you mean," Charlotte concurred. "It doesn't stop at being a pastor's wife. It can be trying for female ministers as well. I got more support from my bras than from the staff at my former church."

"There is something very malignant about holding this position and refraining from being transparent. The wife of a pastor has a better chance of escaping from her own shadow than escaping from the microscopic eyes of onlookers," First Lady Erica confessed while sounding eerily detached.

"I don't mean to interrupt," Charlotte stated, "but I minister to hurting women back home in D.C. I'll be happy to give you my phone numbers and resources."

"That's so kind of you. No wonder the Lord led me to you. My husband and I are doing fine now after having gone through some extensive counseling. I even prayed that his influence be broken from that good ole boys club, as I like to call them, and since then, the Holy Ghost has been dealing with him about pastoring the church His way instead of man's way."

"Praise God." Charlotte gently squeezed First Lady Erica's arm, feeling that she had met a kindred spirit. Charlotte appreciated her candor.

First Lady Erica crossed her legs and rested her arms on the arms of the chair. She was relaxed, composed and comfortable with confiding in Charlotte. "You know, I did manage to get a monthly women's prayer breakfast started, much to my husband's chagrin."

"Why was he upset?" Charlotte asked.

"Because he only wanted me to sit on the front pew and look pretty. But I have a heart to serve the Lord too, so that was a constant battle between us. A battle me and the Lord won," she said candidly.

"All right then."

"The prayer breakfast was an immediate success. The ladies and I would meet every first Saturday of the month in the new members' classroom. We'd pray, worship, enjoy a hearty breakfast; you know, the usual. But then I came up with the idea of us sponsoring a person each month. And by that I mean if any female needed financial assistance or resources to better herself, we would pool our monies and resources together to assist that person."

"That's ministry." Charlotte was impressed.

First Lady Erica smiled and then burst into an infectious laughter. Charlotte chuckled along with her, waiting for the punch line.

"I'm sorry," First Lady Erica apologized. "I'm just recalling a particular incident where someone took advantage of our little program. It's kind of funny, and then again, it's not."

"What happened?"

"One of the deacons' wives brought her niece to our prayer breakfast one Saturday, which is fine. We encourage members to bring a guest or two along. However, this particular guest really tried to test us."

"What do you mean?" Charlotte asked.

"Well, the young lady requested that someone pay to get her hair done for an upcoming job interview. Now, keep in mind we have a limit on monetary contributions because this is coming out of our personal pockets until we figure out how to get a cash flow."

"Sure."

"So one of the members, Sister Michelle, agreed to pay for this. No problem. We believe in mentoring our young women, teaching them basic life skills, how to present themselves for job interviews, so forth and so on."

"Right." Charlotte nodded.

"How about the girl calls Michelle from the most expensive hair salon in Columbia, which is owned by a personal friend of Michelle's, who was willing to put the fee on Michelle's tab? The girl has the nerve to say she needs more money to get her hair colored."

"Hair color?" Charlotte could not believe her ears. "Wasn't she satisfied with getting her hair washed and styled?"

"Washed and styled? Apparently not. Michelle finds out that the girl went there for a hair weave at first, but then decided she wanted her natural hair colored instead."

"Okay, now I know you're kidding."

"I kid you not. Michelle was kind enough to give her enough money for a hair relaxer, and you know how expensive that can be. She wasn't trying to pay for the works."

"I know she wasn't."

"Listen. Not only that. Michelle told her that neither a weave nor hair dying was in her budget. So then the girl broke down with this sob story about her boyfriend being in jail and she was short on cash to bail him out. The boyfriend had a job waiting for him, and she promised that the boyfriend would pay Michelle back with his first paycheck."

"Oh, my God. She probably didn't have a job interview but wanted her hair done to look nice for this man when he got out. You've got your work cut out for you. She needs some serious mentoring."

"True, but I don't think she seriously wants it. Michelle

informed me that that girl paused over the telephone as if to say, 'Go and get the money.' "

"How much did she want?" Charlotte asked.

"Honey, I didn't even ask."

Charlotte was all too familiar with such episodes of brazenness. "Some people are past being bold. Believe it or not, one of my toughest counseling sessions was with a fifty-year-old female who was battling the aging process tooth and nail. She wanted to remain a part of the mini-skirt girls' club. She was very well preserved, but she acted if she saw a relic when she looked in the mirror."

"Well, I'm not too thrilled about wrinkles and sags myself." The first lady laughed. "But you know what? I don't know why I segue like that. I didn't stop you to talk about some girl out to hustle the church. Even though I am a stranger to you, Charlotte, I feel strongly that the Lord has led me to you. Yet, what I am getting ready to say, I say with fear and trembling, so to speak."

"Trust me. I know what it is like to try to be obedient in what you believe God is saying, but still fear man," Charlotte reassured her. "So, please, tell me what you believe you heard."

"I wrote this down and memorized it. God said that it was no accident that you were given a heart for ministering to hurting and abused women. Up until now, it has all been training for you. It's one thing to help a stranger or even an acquaintance, but it is another thing when it is a blood relative. Your loved one will be used mightily by God, and I hear the words *sentence overturned*."

Charlotte did not view the first lady as some sort of parking lot prophetess and felt comfortable with her. Tears welled up in Charlotte's eyes as she talked about the rocky road that led Ramiyah to prison, and eventually, her prison ministry. She also spoke about Terry. Although she could definitely see how God was using Ramiyah, Charlotte admittedly held on to a slim chance of hope for Terry.

"Well, there you go," First Lady Erica responded. "Changing the subject, I couldn't help but notice a young man admiring you on our way here to the ladies' lounge."

"I saw him too," Charlotte gushed. "No offense, but aside from a man who loves God more than David, I like them preferably Hershey-chocolate dark and tall as skyscrapers, or at least taller than me in heels."

"So you're not willing to take someone with chapped, cracked lips and crust around the eyes and clean him up?" First Lady Erica asked jokingly.

"I don't think so," Charlotte said, smiling and nodding with certainty that she did not have a curious taste in men and standards.

The two women giggled together like old school chums.

Charlotte was surprised that she and First Lady Erica had not been interrupted during their little visit in the ladies' lounge. Then again, she knew that was just like God to set up an uninterrupted divine appointment for such a time as this.

She and First Lady Erica ventured back outside and noticed the crowd had thinned out considerably. There were a few hangers-on who walked around somberly visiting the gravesites of their loved ones or huddled in circles saying their goodbyes. Charlotte never stood before a tombstone to reflect. She knew the final end for the dearly departed was not placement in the ground surrounded by earthworms.

After exchanging telephone numbers and saying goodbye to First Lady Erica, Charlotte moved on to find her family, carrying with her the words First Lady Erica had spoken into her life.

21

*Do not forsake your own friend or your father's friend, nor
go to your brother's house in the day of your calamity;
better is a neighbor nearby than a brother far away*

Proverbs 27:10

The sun hung from the sky like a bright, humungous pumpkin. The early Monday morning fog indicated that a scorcher of a day was imminent. Nevertheless, Charlotte preferred Carolina mornings over its starry but humid summer nights. A pesky mosquito, thirsty for blood, buzzed around her ear before landing on her wrist. After failing to kill it with the slap of her free hand, she finally taught it a lesson with a squash by the *Reader's Digest* from her nightstand.

Charlotte woke up to a new day, determined more than ever to have a talk with her mother, even though she wanted to crawl back underneath the covers and lie in a fetal position. But going back to sleep was an impossible dream.

She picked up the letter and clutched it tightly in her hand. Charlotte re-read the letter that had cost her a good night's sleep.

Dear God,
I am in a lonely place, a hard place, and I need to vent! I want to go off on a tangent so deep and with such velocity until all heaven and earth shakes.

I'm in prison (my fault) trying to serve you, trying to get others to serve you, trying to behave as if I'm all right. I have questions and I want answers. How could you let me be a product of incest? He was her father! She is my sister! Why didn't you protect her? I grew up thinking for the longest time that Betty was my sister. Not my birth mother!!

And to have my husband be the one to cruelly inform me of this fact only added fuel to our already engulfing fire. Not many people know that's the real reason I killed him. That's when I snapped. That's when I went over the edge and emptied the bullets into his body. The last cruel joke. No child asks to come here and they certainly don't ask to be conceived through incest.

No wonder, as memory serves, Ma (or should I refer to her as Grandma or even Gladys) was so mean to Betty. And she didn't treat me all that great either. It was not Betty's fault. I know I'm saved now, but my flesh sincerely wishes that someone had taken a skillet to JT's head a long time ago. Oh, God! Forgive me. Am I still saved, sanctified and filled with the Holy Ghost? Has my flesh developed a taste for blood now that it has crossed the line?

Here I sit, a murderer who has a sister who is really my biological mother. I've been sired by a man who held the title of father AND grandfather. There should be a movie based on this. I suppose I've grieved the Holy Spirit with my frustration, but I feel as if I'm about to explode. Clearly, I am not having a good day.

What do I tell my children? I don't know how to explain my own mess to me let alone to them. There seems to be no end to these thresholds of madness. The skeletons in my family closet are too many to number. And then there is Charlotte, who does not know about this. Betty is going to have to tell her. Soon!

As a child, I used to think that Betty was schizophrenic. It was confusing to me to be treated with scorn one day and lovingly the next. I guess she was confused too. Who could blame her? Honestly, I was all too glad to see her marry Esau and leave the house.

You certainly did have a hedge of protection around her mind. I guess because it's a miracle Betty was not the one who hung herself. I suppose Ma lived with unbearable guilt for as long as she could and then hung herself. Guilt to having a blind eye to havoc going on in her own house. I was so young when Ma died, but I gathered that she was a piece of work herself. Oh, but I do remember the awful day she died.

My brother, Wendell, had gotten into trouble at school. He always had a skill for getting into trouble. Wendell knew that his teacher had called the house and Ma would be waiting to greet him with wrath and an extension cord when he got home. I vaguely remember her having a low tolerance for bad grades and rude behavior.

It was during the last days of school. Jean was at work at a local department store and Betty was working a temp job downtown. She and Esau had not too long ago gotten married and I was in my class, learning how to make paper flutes. Art has always been my favorite subject. I noticed the principal peering through the glass as he knocked on the classroom door. When my teacher opened the door, our neighbor, Mrs. Carmichael, followed him inside. The principal whispered something in my teacher's ear and soon afterward, we all heard my teacher gasp.

I didn't have to be an adult to know that something was terribly wrong. While the teacher and the principal looked horrified, I could not help but notice that Mrs. Carmichael looked kind of smug. In my mind's eye, I can still see that teacher's fat lips quivering. That day would also mark the beginning of Wendell's corkscrew spiral into alcoholism.

Although Jean would end up raising me, she would not

have to put up with Wendell's antics for too long. One year to the day after "my mother's" funeral, he enlisted in the Army. Of course, you know all of this, Lord. It's just that writing is therapeutic for me and besides, I'm thinking about leaving my letters, or at least copies of my letters, to my sons. Some legacy, huh? Maybe it will help them to understand.

Mrs. Carmichael drove me home that day, looking straight ahead with that mean face of hers and listening to some preacher scream and yell on the radio. She would not tell me what happened. Her only response was, "God hates sin." I just wanted to go home and get as far away from Mrs. Carmichael and the smell of her cheap toilet water. Did she douse the whole bottle of that stuff over her body?

As soon as we turned the corner of North Capitol and Florida Avenue, we were met by glaring red lights and a growing crowd. My little adolescent mind could not understand why two patrol cars, a rescue squad truck and a black car with white lettering, which I later learned belonged to the coroner, were parked in front of my house. Next came the stares from neighbors and other curiosity seekers. They made me feel as if I had done something wrong and was about to be ripped from my family forever.

Then I saw Wendell, sitting on a stoop with a fuzzy powder blue blanket wrapped around him. I remember wondering why he had that thing around him as hot as it was. He looked helpless, hopeless and not saying a word. When I got out of the car and started running toward the house, it seemed as if everyone else was moving in slow motion.

A procession was led by two muscular paramedics, pushing a gurney, carrying Ma's lifeless body strapped to it. It was veering toward me as if I were some sort of bullseye. Jean, who was being helped down the steps by two other neighbors, appeared dazed. I don't think she saw me at first.

I remember seeing Betty and one of her coworkers running down the street and then I screamed. The rest of that day is still a blur.

My memory of that era is sketchy to say the least. Of course, I have no memory of JT. At first, I was told that he had been banished from the house before I was born and had died a few years later. I grew up wondering if he ever missed us. I was never told why Ma hung herself until that night I killed Cole. I grew up with so many questions, like where was she when JT was busy violating Betty?

It's a small world indeed, isn't it? Who would have thought that years later, the woman Cole would threaten to leave me for would be Mrs. Carmichael's daughter, Anjenette? She and I used to play together as kids. The wretched night Cole was killed was the night I got answers to so many questions.

Disturbed by the contents of the letter, a choked up Charlotte rushed toward her parents' bedroom. After knocking on the door and calling out to them twice, she pushed the door open only to find the room empty.

She then looked out the open window but saw no one in sight. Plumes of smoke began to rise as a neighbor burned trash in his yard. She looked for a vehicle but saw tire impressions instead.

"I don't even remember coming upstairs to get in the bed last night. No wonder I slept in my clothes," she said to herself while observing her wrinkled attire.

Charlotte turned around to go down the stairs, calling out again to anyone who might hear her. "Ma. Daddy. Grandma. Granddaddy." She nearly clashed into Hiawatha as he strolled through the front door.

"Chile, calm down. Your family is not here. Ms. Mattie Mae and your mom went to the flea market and took that stubborn mother of mine with them. Of course, my mother *knew* I wanted to have a consultation with her doctor. That woman! I think the men folk went there too." Hiawatha paused after seeing Charlotte's disheveled appearance. "Whew, chile! You look a hot mess. Aren't those the same clothes you had on yesterday?"

"Not now, Hia." Charlotte shook her head and burst into tears.

Gently pulling Charlotte away from the bottom step, Hiawatha led her to the sofa. She tried to speak, only to have muffled noises come out.

"Calm down. Let me get you a glass of water," Hiawatha offered as he made his way to the kitchen. When he came back, Charlotte was blowing her nose.

He handed her the glass. She took one sip of water before thanking him.

"What has gotten you so upset?" he asked. Hiawatha sat slanted, facing Charlotte with one arm resting on the back of the sofa. "So, what's going on here?"

Charlotte drew a deep breath and said, "I'm usually the one telling people to pray, to have faith, be steadfast and unmovable. But what do I do when the wind gets knocked out of me? I fall to pieces." Charlotte blew her nose again.

"It can't be all that bad," Hiawatha suggested with uncertainty.

"It's bad enough," Charlotte refuted through her sniffles. By now, her nose was Rudolph red. "I should wait until my mother gets back, but I—"

Hiawatha grabbed Charlotte's hand. "If you need to get something off your chest, go ahead and do it now. Now, if it's that private, I'll understand if you just go on and have yourself a good cry instead, but you need to do something."

Suddenly, Charlotte jerked her hand away and slammed the letters down on the coffee table. "Read those while I take a shower. I won't be but a minute. I'm going to be praying while I shower, and when I come back, hopefully I will be in a better frame of mind."

Hiawatha leaned back against the sofa and read one of the letters. He was so taken aback that he had to read it twice—slowly dissecting every word, each sentence and all paragraphs. He already knew that Cole had literally sent Ramiyah over the edge on the night of his murder, and figured Cole's threat of divorce was the straw that broke the camel's back. He was wrong. Dead wrong.

A warm summer breeze started wafting through the opened window behind Hiawatha as he reviewed in his mind all the drama he and his close circle of friends had experienced over the years. He could draw no comparison to the shock Charlotte must feel or the shame Betty had endured. And then there was Ramiyah.

As the warm breeze continued to blow, he caught a slight whiff of jasmine that had circulated throughout the room. It emanated from Charlotte, who was descending the stairs. Hiawatha thought she looked totally refreshed in a crisp white sleeveless blouse and a pair of wide-leg linen pants that buttoned down the side from the waist all the way down to the ankle.

Charlotte sat adjacent to him. "Did you finish reading them?" she asked.

"Them? I couldn't get past the one I read. Man, I don't know what to say." Hiawatha leaned forward and dropped his head down.

"Which one did you read?" Charlotte asked, crossing her legs. She seemed cool as a cucumber. In fact, Hiawatha thought her to be a little too cool and collected.

"The one about Ramiyah being your sister. Tell me why you're so upset." As soon as Hiawatha asked the question, he felt he came off sounding stupid and insensitive.

"Wouldn't you be?" Charlotte stared blankly at him, realizing she was not an only child after all. "I don't know. I'm not sure, really. I know it's not because Ramiyah is my sister. Naturally, I'm shocked; but we don't choose how we come here. I've always wanted a sister. It's just disturbing to find out you have a sister via incest! I mean, come on."

"Yeah, this is pretty deep," Hiawatha admitted. "How do you pray in a situation like this?"

"I asked the Lord for healing and forgiveness to take place in the hearts of my mom and Ramiyah. I can only imagine how deep their scars are. I asked the Lord to give us *all* strength and wisdom, for I have a nagging feeling that something else is brewing."

"Believe me, Charlotte. I had no idea about this. Ramiyah and I talked, but she did not share this with me. I wish I knew what I could do to help you guys through this."

"Just be my friend. For now, I want you to read this letter." Charlotte removed another piece of stationery from the stack. "This one was written to Ramiyah by my mother. Apparently, Ramiyah wanted to share with me something that my mother could not."

22

"I still have many things to say to you, but you cannot bear them now."

John 16:12

Dear Ramiyah,

I know you're grappling with your true family history. I know I have been for years. Please forgive me. Forgive me for not being able to be the kind of mother you deserve to have. I don't know exactly how much Cole and/or Anjenette has told you, but let me help clear the air.

It's unfortunate that you could not divulge the whole truth to me until after your trial. You were so upset. I still don't blame you for not wanting to talk to me then. But why didn't you tell your attorney the real reason why you killed Cole? Why didn't you tell the attorney about any of this? There might have been some leniency.

It could have been ruled as temporary insanity. I'm sure the jury would have been more understanding about the circumstances surrounding your birth more so than the run-of-the-mill infidelity excuse. Anyone would snap under those circumstances. I nearly did. Were you worried about added embarrassment? Did you fear I would be too meek to testify on your behalf?

I was so young when I had you. Too young. When I was gearing up for my high school graduation, you had already started kindergarten. A year later, I met Esau and the year after that, I had Charlotte. I named Charlotte after Ma, whose name was Gladys Charlotte Hines Patterson. I named you after a friend of Jean's.

It was Mrs. Carmichael who pointed out to Ma that I might be pregnant. She was the neighborhood watchdog. Of course, Ma being Ma, she claimed I was just gaining weight, getting plump. She knew. She had to. Ma never liked facing the truth. I suppose I take after her with that one.

You want to know something strange? Since the identity of your real parents had always been kept a secret, we all got used to life being as it was. However, I always dreaded the day you would need your birth certificate. I was so dumb and naïve. I did not know that Ma and her mid-wife pal, who delivered you, had doctored it. More illegal stuff to deal with.

One day, Ma finally admitted that the "pudginess" centered only in my mid-section had to be due to a little more than daily consumptions of chocolate donuts and cheeseburgers—my cravings. By the time I got to the doctor, I was diagnosed as being five months pregnant. Ma was livid. What would her church members think? What would the neighbors think? Who was the no-good boy who did this to me? She had not seen me acting all goofy over any boy. All of us neighborhood kids were just friends. Most of us were too young and too uninterested in being anything else.

I couldn't tell Ma that her husband, my own father, did this to me. So, I lied. I told her that a gang of boys had jumped me one day after school and I didn't know who it was. I was floored by the words and names that spewed from her holiness's mouth that day.

The next thing I know, we were on a train to her sister's

house in Tennessee. We returned to D.C. shortly after you were born. Ma was crazy enough to think that Mrs. Carmichael and the rest of the neighbors would believe you were her baby.

Ma and JT's fights were legendary and everyone knew that JT strayed more than he stayed, so their separation came as no real surprise. However, I'm sure her "allegedly" having another child by the man set tongues wagging.

Thus, the lie went forth. Ma had announced to certain neighbors that SHE was pregnant and packing up the family to stay with her sister so that she could deliver her baby in a peaceful atmosphere. Luckily for us kids, you were born in the summer, so it was not like Ma had to take us out of school.

The first and only time JT raped me was after one of their notorious fights. I had just started having my period four months prior to that. Ma went off with her church group to play bingo at the hall and Jean was down the street babysitting, so Wendell and I were left alone with JT and his bottle of Jim Beam. No wonder Wendell eventually turned to the bottle himself. He was forced to live with this secret along with the rest of us, and that was how he dealt with it.

I won't go into detail simply because I want to spare you the sordidness, and I don't care to relive the pain. I'll tell you this much. As you can imagine, it was horrible. Wendell had fallen asleep in front of the television. I was in my bedroom, studying for a test. JT came in drunk and covered my mouth with his filthy hand. After he was finished taking away my innocence, he threatened me not to ever say a word. When he left my room to go sleep in his own, I threw the bloody sheet in the garbage outside.

I remember crying myself to sleep and JT leaving the house for good, two nights later. He and Ma were fighting about the electric bill money being missing and JT carousing with some woman who lived around the corner. In my heart, I believe that was a ruse, although he did leave to live with this woman for about a year. After that, either she threw him out or he left on his own. Either way, he was gone. A couple of years later, we heard that he died in Florida from tuberculosis. None of us attended his funeral.

Be patient with me, Ramiyah. This is a slow process for both of us, but I am glad that we are starting to open up to one another. I am going to try and get the boys sometime soon. Hang in there. I am praying for you, for us all.

Love,
Betty

Hiawatha's hands felt clammy as he placed the letter on the coffee table. He shot Charlotte a questioning glance, thinking she did not look as pale and tragic as when he first arrived at the Morley home.

Raising his perfectly arched, crescent-shaped eyebrows, he asked, "How do you feel about this? I mean, you were so upset when I came through that door, but now you seem so composed."

"How do I feel?" Charlotte sounded as if she thought the question to be ludicrous. She leaned back in her seat and sighed, staring blankly at him again.

"Now, I don't *think* that was a loaded question, so you don't have to go off and have deep legal thoughts on me." Hiawatha smiled, trying to make light of the situation.

"No. It was not a loaded question," Charlotte replied. "But I'm sure you can understand why I have mixed emotions. On one hand, I find out that someone I've known all my life to be my aunt is actually my sister, and on the other hand, I find out my mom has been living a lie. But I can't be angry at her, can I? She went through a terrible ordeal brought on by a very sick man."

"True that. I may have my issues, but I don't understand what makes a person attracted to children; especially their own."

"Oh, there is a source. You know, I'm already struggling with this revelation, and now there is this internal battle of resistance." Charlotte's voice died away.

"What resistance?"

"The resistance to not hate a dead man whom I've never met—my grandfather."

"Yeah, life can make you want to drink a Molotov cocktail."

"Do you want to hear something interesting?" Charlotte asked, spinning the ring, given to her by Hiawatha, around her finger.

"What's that?"

"Right before I took my shower, the Holy Spirit instructed me to read something. Now, the other night, I thought He told me to read II Samuel 4:10 or something-14. It turned out that was not what I heard."

"It wasn't?"

"No. I was sleepy at the time, trying to write a letter, and I wasn't clear about the chapter or verse. Anyway, upstairs He said it again, and I heard it more clearly this time. It was II Samuel 13:14."

"Did you read it?"

"Yeah, and it was the last part of verse 14 that hit me like a ton of bricks. It says, *'but being stronger than she, forced her and lay with her.'* "

"Whoa!" Hiawatha's eyes widened.

"If I had been obedient and opened to hear, I would have known about this a little earlier," she spoke plainly.

"I don't know if you would have put two and two together so easily. Think about it. Would you have allowed your mind to believe something like that had happened to your mother?"

"No," Charlotte replied, almost coldly.

"I may not be a Bible scholar, but I know enough to blame life's heartache on Adam and Eve eating that apple."

"It wasn't any apple. It was the pair."

"Okay, I'll leave it at that. Look. Believe it or not, John Edward parted with his car and is letting me drive it. He had to work today, so I dropped him off and came over to see what you wanted to do. It's not like we have many choices on this godforsaken island."

"I'll be right back." Charlotte got up to go upstairs to change. She needed to get out of the house, but was in no mood to spend the day tugging and pulling on a tight undergarment that was trying to make its way into her flesh.

After spraying a little oil sheen on her hair, she returned downstairs with her purse and a carry-all bag hanging from her shoulder. "Come on. Let's just go."

Hiawatha knew all too well how to make a scene. Now he was concerned that Charlotte was on a secret mission to create a scene of her own by seeking to confront her mother.

23

Rescue those being led away to death; hold back those staggering toward slaughter

Proverbs 24:11

Meanwhile, against the backdrop of fruit and vegetable stands, pickup trucks and peddlers' booths, Mattie Mae, Sista and Betty trekked slowly down aisle two of the county's largest indoor/outdoor flea and farmers market.

As Mattie Mae and Betty continued to move forward to check out a vendors' collection of crocheted blankets, pillow shams and shawls, Sista sequestered herself over at The Cozy Corner.

The Cozy Corner was an alcove located inside the southwest corner of the flea market, and a favorite spot for hodgepodge lovers. It was also anything but cozy, as customers awkwardly maneuvered their bodies around the tight space.

The owner was a middle-aged woman of auburn hair, Irish green eyes and dried, cakey makeup that nearly disfigured her face. She sat quietly behind the counter, gently scouring and scrubbing a brass tea pot with a toothbrush soaked with white vinegar, water and salt.

Out of the corner of her eye, Sista caught a glimpse of her least favorite person in the world, Nellie Moss. Bargain hunters who were trying to reach the half-price rack had a difficult time squeezing by the full-figured Nellie. Nellie, who was busy flipping through a handful of old nostalgic black and white postcards, was unaware of Sista's presence.

"Nellie," Sista said forcefully, with her arms folded.

Nellie quickly turned around with a frown on her face. "Sista, you know me and you don't get along worth two cents, so I hope you did not come in here to start nothin'."

"I'm just sayin' hey to you, Nellie," Sista rectified. "My God! A person can't say hey these days? I see you found some postcards. For some reason, my daughter-in-law likes to collect that kind of stuff. Did you see any more around here?"

"No, I did not. And don't go getting no ideas about these postcards. It will be a cold day in hell befo' I believe you wanna make nice wit' me," Nellie, who had more size on her than Sista, huffed brusquely.

Now agitated, Sista raised her voice, causing the ears of those around her to perk up. "What's wrong wit' you? Here I am, tryin' to make nice, but let me tell you something. A cold day in hell already came, and today hell freezed over! I know good and darn well you had no intentions of buyin' all those postcards. You're just bein' spiteful 'cause you figure I want to get 'em for my daughter-in-law."

Spectators, whether they walked away or came closer, were thoroughly convinced that the two women were about to go for each other's jugulars. An unsuspecting elderly gentleman, fumbling with his cane, tried to walk in between the two in an effort to reach the sales rack.

Sista and Nellie stood as still as two ships anchored at sea when suddenly, Sista felt a hand gripping her elbow. Mattie Mae pulled Sista's waifish body away, allowing the old man to pass through. Nellie politely nodded at Mattie Mae and headed straight toward the cash register with her postcards, where the owner waited as her husband stood over her, sipping from a brandy glass and watching the entire thing.

Even Mattie Mae was baffled by Nellie's extra sour attitude and decided it was best to leave rather than stick around and watch the area be cordoned off as a crime scene.

The woman's husband reached for Nellie's money with one hand, while cradling the glass between the middle and ring finger of the other hand—sipping. He then slipped the money in his pocket and walked away. His wife gave him a look that was generally produced by drinking pickle juice. After pinning down a rebellious curl that kept dangling in her face, she returned to the chore of scouring a tea pot.

"I can't take you nowhere," Mattie Mae whispered in Sista's ear as she led her away from The Cozy Corner. "They're fixin' to have a gospel concert outside. You need to focus on the Lawd and not Nellie."

"I do focus on the Lawd. I ain't studyin' Nellie," Sista protested, even though she was actually madder than a woman scorned. She glanced back at Nellie, who had a smug look on her face. "Look at her. She's just bein' spiteful, but that's all right. God don't like ugly. Why are they havin' a concert outside anyway? It's too hot out them doors for a concert."

But what sounded like angels caroling had soon placed a smile on Sista's once sour face. She recognized the voices as belonging to her favorite singing group, The Gospel Harmonettes.

Mattie Mae led a very excited Sista out the side exit to where Betty was enjoying the music. A crowd formed around the large stage where The Gospel Harmonettes were performing.

The lead singer of the group signaled a nearby stagehand to do a sound check before belting out the next tune. Decked out in rhinestone earrings and matching pink and peach chiffon dresses, The Gospel Harmonettes were a smash as they delighted the audience with a medley of songs. Sista was pleased as punch.

"One time, The Gospel Harmonettes was singin' at The Coliseum over in Columbia, and they was chargin' sixty dollars a ticket," Sista commented, while keeping her eyes on the group. "I refuse to pay that much money to see any woman *or* man, 'cept maybe Jesus."

Meanwhile, Betty turned her head slightly to the left and thought she had seen a familiar face as Mattie Mae urged her companions to move closer to the front. Feeling disturbed, Betty continued looking for the face that was now lost in the crowd.

Mattie Mae squealed as she watched *her* favorite quartet take center stage. Betty jumped as a pair of muscular arms wrapped around her waist.

Esau kissed her on the cheek. "Are you having a good time?" he asked.

"Esau!" Betty was pleasantly surprised. "That *was* you. What are you doing here?"

"I thought I'd spend a little bit of time with my wife," he answered lovingly.

Hiawatha and Charlotte casually strolled along the park, which was across the street from the flea market. Delighted by what she saw, Charlotte stooped down to pick a few buttercup blossoms and threaded them throughout her hair.

A woman with a round, freshly scrubbed face, carrying a round white object, was quickly approaching them. As the woman drew near, Charlotte recognized the object as being a coconut cake topped with thinly sliced lemon wedges. The woman smiled proudly at Charlotte as she rushed by.

"That looks like one of Ms. Mattie Mae's cakes," Hiawatha said. "No one's cakes can wake up all my senses like Ms. Mattie Mae's cakes. Not even Mama's. Listen. I take it we're over here until you build up the nerve to go across the street and confront your mom—in a public place?" Hiawatha asked. "You'd be wrong for that, preacher woman."

Just when Charlotte was about to defend herself, she felt a firm tap on her shoulder.

"Excuse me, Miss; but do you know if they sell socks over at that flea market?" the scruffy-looking man with sallow skin and thick muttonchops asked. He bent over to pick up the coins that had showered down to the ground from his shirt pocket.

"I have not been over there in years, but I'm sure they do," Charlotte replied.

The man tipped his baseball cap and proceeded toward the flea market, walking a path littered with chewing gum wrappers and stubbed-out cigarettes butts. After the odd-looking fellow crossed the street, he looked back at Charlotte, tipped his cap again, and disappeared into the crowd.

As Hiawatha and Charlotte continued to walk, it became clear to them that the garbled sounds they had heard earlier were actually voices singing.

A voice, one decimal below a scream, came over the loudspeaker and said, "Is everybody having a good time? Next up, we have a special treat for you. All the way from Jackson, Mississippi . . . give it up for the Baxter Brothers!" In a mad dash to make it to the concert, people trampled across the lawn, forcing the blades of grass to yield beneath the weight of their feet.

The roaring cheers nearly drowned out all other sounds.

"Getting back to what you were saying," Charlotte said, "don't worry. I'm not going to make a scene. I don't even plan to go over there to look for my mom. For me, there is something about being near water or being in a tranquil setting like a park that gives me peace. Usually, those are times when I hear from God," Charlotte explained. "That's why I wanted to come here. I can't help it if the park just happens to be in close proximity to the flea market."

"Uh-huh. How much you wanna bet our kinfolks are over at the singin'?" Hiawatha said. Then he noticed Charlotte's half smile. "Do you feel like talking, or would you rather continue licking your wounds undercover?"

"I want to talk. Not about my mom and Ramiyah, but about *you* and Ramiyah. Why is Ramiyah guiding me sideways into your issues?"

Hiawatha shrugged his shoulders, but Charlotte did not buy into his clueless act. She located an unoccupied area shaded by a huge cypress tree and led Hiawatha, who dutifully followed, to the secluded spot. Next, Charlotte covered the ground with a tri-colored plaid blanket, which had been stashed at the bottom of her carry-all bag.

Charlotte sat on the blanket with her legs crisscrossed and arms folded. Hiawatha stretched out his long legs and pressed his back against the tree.

"Okay, here's the real," Hiawatha started confessing. "When Ramiyah and I first started this pen pal thing, we were both angry people. She was angry about how her life had turned out, and me, I was just plain angry."

"Angry about what? We all know Ramiyah's anger. Help me understand yours."

"Well, it all started when Ramiyah got religious."

"You mean when she received Jesus," Charlotte corrected.

Hiawatha rolled his eyes. "At first, I became resentful toward her because she sounded all sanctimonious; but actually, she was challenging me."

"Challenging you how?"

"You know, making me face things, making me think. I didn't like that, 'cause I was comfortable in my thoughts and beliefs."

"None of us like being shaken from our comfort zones," Charlotte acknowledged.

"No, but let me ask you some things."

"Go ahead. Shoot." Charlotte relished the position of Christian vessel. She hoped this opportunity to minister to Hiawatha would fully take her mind off of her own issues.

"I know you're a member of a large church, a mega-church. Did you join it because of some smooth, slick-oil message, like a promise to get houses and cars if you sow an extra seed? You know, the whole wealth and prosperity message."

"Is that what you think?" Charlotte looked hurt, not only because Hiawatha did not give her credit for being led to a house of worship, but because there was some truth to his statement as well.

Hiawatha's body seemed to relax as he leaned forward and then rested his back against the tree.

"I can't speak for all churches or their pastors, but my pastor does not entice people with promises from man. As for wealth and prosperity, Deuteronomy 8:18 states that it is *God* who gives man the power to produce wealth. God gives us creative minds, and we must listen to Him for direction. Prosperity and wealth is not limited to money and things. Besides, there is much more to God than 'bless me, give me mine.' We live in a dying world. It does sadden me to see the games out there, but God's got it."

"Oh, so you admit all is not well in the church?"

"Of course," Charlotte replied swiftly. "The message and the methods are often twisted."

"Okay, but these mega-churches seem so impersonal. Do you get to see your pastor?"

"Of course I do. I'm on staff. But even if I wasn't a staff member, I wouldn't need to shake his hand after service or need his hand laid on me. I'm anointed to rub oil and lay hands on myself."

"Didn't you find a large congregation to be intimidating?"

"I must admit I was awestruck at first, but I was really going through it at the time. That congregation started looking more like a couple instead of a crowd. Trust me. A large crowd will be insignificant to anyone who wants to feel free to worship or is desperate to hear a word that speaks to their spirit. Funny. People complain about mega-churches, but if truth be told, everyone would like to see their church grow. Heaven and hell will be crowded. Hey, I think Moses was the first pastor of a large congregation."

A somber Hiawatha spoke just barely above a whisper. "Maybe so, but it seems like the church is big business."

"It is! At least, it should be. The church is supposed to be about our *Father's business*. Look. Each passing day symbolizes time winding down. No church started out big. As more and more people join a church, guess what? I'm not saying that everyone who attends a so-called mega-church or even a storefront church is there for the right reason."

"True that. A friend of mine goes to a mega-church just so he can try and hook up with the pianist. I told him to keep hope alive, honey. Seriously, how can a pastor of such a large church get to know his entire congregation?"

"He can't," Charlotte answered in a matter-of-fact tone.

"Right, and he can't possibly eulogize every funeral or counsel everybody or—"

"Right again. Okay, think about this, the story of Moses. Moses was actually the first person to shepherd a large group of people. One day, his father-in-law recognized that Moses could not possibly do it all. So he suggested to Moses that he delegate some of his duties to others. Our example today is that we have assistant and associate pastors, deacons, elders, so forth and so on. Does that make sense?"

"Okay, I've got one more thing to say," Hiawatha added.
"What's that?"

"I have a problem with hypocritical Christians."

"Hia, I have a problem with hypocritical Christians too.
But please understand that many people are calling themselves Christians these days when they don't even know
what being a Christian means. For example, the minute something unscrupulous happens, those very same people will attack true Christians for standing up to the issue, forgetting
that at times, they call themselves Christians. The first thing
out of their mouths is, 'Those Christians.' "

"You know, you're right. I guess folks tack on the title of
Christian when it's convenient for them, or just because they
go to church every once in a while."

"Exactly. Most of the time, I just say that I'm a believer.
Since the world wants to define what Christianity means,
what Christians can or cannot do, so forth and so on, saying
that I'm a believer usually dumbfounds people."

"I bet it does; but then it'll get to where they want to
know what you believe in so they can find a way to attack
that."

"I don't doubt it. But let me say this also: while we are not
to judge folks, we are to judge each other's fruit, and we
need the gift of discernment to know one's character. By the
way, mega-churches are nothing new. It's the phrase that is
new."

"Huh?"

"Greener Pastures, with its three hundred plus members,
has always been the largest black church in this community.
That's *mega* for a town of this size."

Hiawatha nodded. He and Charlotte sat silently, watching children nearby scream and play outdoor games and young
adults play fetch with their dogs. Couples in love walked

about holding hands, purring and cooing at one another. The air smelled of hickory and mesquite-scented chips burning over charcoals in a nearby pit.

As Charlotte watched a vendor lose a bundle of floating balloons to the sky, she grew anxious to speak with her mother. She looked over at Hiawatha. "Thank you for being my friend."

"No problem. And let's not lose touch after we leave this town. Let's remain friends through the good, the bad and the butt ugly."

Charlotte dug around in her bag for her brush. The afternoon heat forced her to pull her hair back into one long braid. She smiled as a gospel soloist sang in the background. No longer tightly wound, she felt herself loosening up. "Looks like rain."

Hiawatha looked up and drew a deep breath. "At least a light drizzle for shizzle."

24

And Jesus answered and said to her, "Martha, Martha, you are worried and troubled about many things. But one thing is needed . . .

Luke 10:41 & 42

During the drive home, Charlotte noticed Mattie Mae walking toward Sista's house. She also witnessed Edmund and Esau pass by in the truck. Assuming that Betty was home alone, she rehearsed in her mind several times what she would say to her mother.

"Looks like your mom might be home alone," Hiawatha astutely noted.

"Yep, it certainly looks that way. At least, I'm counting on it." Charlotte drew a deep breath.

"Are you going to be all right?" Hiawatha reached across Charlotte to open the car door for her.

Charlotte got out and said, "Yes," as she waved goodbye to Hiawatha. Usually not one to suffer from jittery nerves, Charlotte could feel her stomach churning. She asked the Lord for strength as she walked up the steps. "Ma," she called out. "Ma!"

"What is it?" Betty asked as she hurried out the front screen door. "What's happened?" Her eyes were bright with worry.

"Nothing. I just wanted to—"

Betty placed her hand across her chest. "You sounded as if somebody was chasing you. You scared me."

"I'm sorry. I didn't realize I was coming off like that." Charlotte stood on the top step, standing face to face with Betty. "Ma, I want to talk to you before everybody comes home."

"Okay. Let's talk," Betty conceded with a pinch of courage in her voice.

"Why didn't you tell me that Ramiyah was your daughter?" Charlotte blurted out.

Betty remained calm. "Because considering how Ramiyah was conceived, I never grasped the reality of it myself."

"Does Daddy know?" Charlotte leaned against the post.

Betty sat close by and showed no sign of apprehension. "Yes, your father knows everything."

Charlotte was stunned. Betty reached out and lovingly held Charlotte's hand as only a mother could. "He is the only person in the Morley family that does know."

At that moment, Esau drove up. He was alone. Cool, calm and collected would best describe Esau Morley. Like his father, he was a man of wisdom who spoke few words. Hardly one to move at a brisk pace, Esau took his time approaching two of his favorite women.

Charlotte found herself facing reality, forced to downscale her picture-perfect family to a mere illustration.

"Charlotte, are you pouting?" Esau asked, passing by Charlotte to sit next to his wife.

"Sorry. For someone my age, I guess a pout is not an attractive look," Charlotte replied.

Esau and Betty made eye contact. Somehow, through their unspoken language, Esau knew exactly what was going on. "Come sit down, Charlotte," he commanded.

"Daddy, I know all about Ramiyah and I have some mixed emotions going on right now."

"None of which includes anger toward your mother, I hope," Esau stated. "Here's an idea. Why don't we deal with one emotion at a time—as a family."

As a family, Charlotte thought. She then irrationally toyed with the idea that perhaps there was a secret held about her, such as being a black market baby. Disappointed that she did not have the chance to steal away some alone time with her mother, Charlotte chose to accept her father's presence and suggestion as divine intervention.

"I don't know where to begin. I suppose I feel betrayed." Charlotte sounded unsure.

"By who?" Esau asked.

Charlotte looked at him as if he had lost his mind. "Well, at first by Ma, but then I just found out that you knew about Ramiyah also. So my answer is I feel betrayed by both of you. When did you guys think I would be adult enough to know that Ramiyah was my sister?"

For the first time since their confrontation, Betty held her head down in shame and embarrassment. Again, Esau came to the rescue. "Betrayed, huh? We understand. Now, do you understand that your mother also felt betrayed when her own father came in her bedroom and—"

Not wanting Betty to become unglued, Charlotte interrupted. "Ma, I'm so sorry that this has happened to you. A part of me wishes I could hurt the man who hurt you." Charlotte practically sprang from her seat and was now kneeling before her mother. As Betty fought back tears, Charlotte lost control of hers, and the two women held each other.

"Guys, I am not a child. Why has this been a secret for so long? Forget about me. I can only imagine how this has affected Ramiyah. Forgive me for how I've acted. But, Ma, just as Daddy has supported you, don't you know that I am your support too?"

Betty kissed Charlotte on her forehead. "There is nothing to forgive you for, baby. Forgive me, because I've totally dismissed the fact that not only are you now a woman, but you are a woman of God. For years, I have been hiding in my pain. It's amazing how a person can smile on the outside and cry a river on the inside."

The married couple smiled as Betty continued to relay the story. "But Esau was very patient and loving. It took me a while to realize that God sent him to me."

"Boy, the irony," Charlotte said.

"What do you mean?" Esau asked.

"The timing. The snowball effect this has caused. This one secret came out because some woman had an adulterous affair with Cole and she wanted him. Ramiyah murders him, and I'm sure Ma has been forced to relive painful memories. What's next?"

Esau and Betty gazed into each other's eyes again, but this time, Charlotte read their language. There was something else.

Betty pulled an envelope from underneath a clay flowerpot on the ledge behind her and handed it to Charlotte. "What is this?" Charlotte asked.

"This came in the mail about two days ago," Betty answered. The envelope was addressed to Mrs. Betty Morley and it came from Ramiyah.

Suddenly, the sun started hiding behind the clouds. The clouds burst and the gray sky gave way to a heavy downpour with blowing winds. A group of crows that had gathered at the front of the cornfield immediately fled the field. The flowers took a beating and bowed their heads to the whipping rain, losing a few tender petals in the process. Even tree limbs bent in submission to the blowing winds.

With one more revealing letter to read, all Charlotte could think about was the fact that the rain would undoubtedly cause some ponding on the roads, an anticipated event for the parched earth.

She wondered if it was raining back home in D.C. She envisioned downtown D.C. experiencing the same gray, melancholy day, marching under a sea of umbrellas that bobbed up and down as people sought shelter. Thoroughfares like the 14th Street Bridge and Pennsylvania Avenue were virtual parking lots on days like this, with people trapped in their cars, drudging through traffic congestion. The nation's capital, like so many other metropolitan cities, had been drowning in crushing gridlock for decades.

"Let's go inside to get a snack," Esau said, looking back at the pounding rain and glaring headlights from passing cars. "The ground could use a good soaking, and I could use a cup of coffee anyway."

With her heart racing faster than a speeding bullet, Charlotte followed her parents inside the house and soon began reading:

Dear Betty,

I don't know how I honestly feel about your being my birth mother. How can any human being process something like this so quickly? But I am praying. Thank you for committing to raising my children—your grandchildren.

Undoubtedly, it will be difficult for them to understand how your role has changed from auntie to grandma, but at least they won't continue to grow up living a lie.

We are like wheat, you and I, wheat that has been threshed and tossed about in high winds. We ARE valuable grain. I am valuable. At least I know that now. Life's beating has been brutal, but it was to separate and is separating us from worthless chaff. I made a bad decision—murder. However, the Lord still found a way to use me through prison ministry. Betty, remember what you told me? What will you do with your gift?

Up until recently, I have kept my promise to you. I've been silent and you have been silent, but time is running out. I agree that it was best that you and I try and work this out amongst ourselves, and I wanted to allow you the time to tell Charlotte.

I don't know any other way to do this but to say it. Betty, someone came to the prison to see me. It was JT. Betty, JT is not dead!

I've only seen one picture of JT, which had been taken years before I was even born, but I easily recognized him. He has hypnotic eyes like Uncle Chester, only his are dark and soulless. Looking through them was like traveling through a tunnel with no light in sight.

JT is a tall, slender man, lanky to the point of being almost hunched over. Although I believe he was sober on the day of his visit, years of drinking alcohol caused the scent to seep through his pores.

For the longest time, he just sat there watching me without saying a word. It made me feel uncomfortable, and when he finally did introduce himself simply as JT Patterson, the moment officially became awkward.

He waited for me to respond, obviously unsure as to whether or not I knew who he was. I could not resist. Out came my reply that was completely unrehearsed. "It has recently come to my attention that you are actually my father and not my grandfather. So, you're alive after all?"

Just like that, all curt and precise. There was a sinister-looking smile on his lips, but the crow's feet around his eyes could not hide the guilt. It then turned into a contest . . . a challenge to see who was going to speak next.

I held my ground and my breath, for I am already struggling with painful revelations. He spoke next. Except for a short stint in jail for assault and battery, JT had been living in New Jersey with his second wife.

He earnestly informed me that I had his mother's glorious red hair. Honestly, I was not interested in learning any more about my family tree. I knew enough. It was infected and diseased. But that was his opening statement. I was not prepared for his next.

In essence, JT has squirreled away over $400,000 and wants to pay the legal fees for my appeal. My attorney thinks I should have a really good case regarding battered women's syndrome. Imagine me being exonerated. Again, thank you for agreeing to allow yourself to be transparent in court when that time arrives.

I was speechless. Where did he get that kind of money? I mean, the man looks like a pauper. Apparently, JT has had a very hard life: barroom brawls, poor health, alcoholism, etc., and then his wife took ill about ten years ago. She went in for surgery and there was a mishap with the anesthesiologist and she died.

JT had stockpiled his windfall from the malpractice suit along with most of his earnings and retirement. As he puts it, "I have no need for money, and I have a family that I need to make amends to."

He has been keeping tabs on us through someone from the old neighborhood. He would not say who it was. Finally, he said the words, "I'm sorry," in a gravelly voice, his chest echoing signs of bronchitis.

"Sorry for what?" I had asked with cynicism in my tone.

He just held his head down low. My flesh wanted to scream, fight and tear up the place, but fortunately, my spirit spoke up instead. I heard myself saying, "I forgive you." Betty, I swear to you, JT lifted his head back up and his whole countenance had changed.

We (mostly he) talked some more, but I will let him tell you the rest. If you have not already seen him, expect a visit from JT.

Love, 'Miyah

Betty was just about to enter the living room to check on Charlotte.

Charlotte's ears perked up to the sound of a gentle tapping on the frame of the screen door. It was the man from the park.

25

*If your enemy is hungry, give him bread to eat and if he is
thirsty, give him water to drink*

Proverbs 25:21

Betty was well aware of the identity of the peculiar-looking
man with the thick muttonchops and soaking wet clothes.
Her knees buckled and she fainted on the living room floor,
knocking over a stack of books in the process. Not knowing
what else to do, Charlotte immediately ran to prepare a cold
compress while Esau, after hearing the commotion, thought-
lessly invited the stranger inside.

A very nervous JT apprehensively entered the home. He
stayed close to the door. While Esau tended to his now alert
spouse, Charlotte focused her attention on the dowdy-looking
man standing before them. She could see a family resemblance and guessed the identity of the man to be that of JT
Patterson.

As Esau helped a visibly shaken Betty up on her feet,
Charlotte saw a look on her mother's face that she had never
seen before. It was a mixture of fright, disbelief and anger.

Betty cleaved to her husband like a newborn suckling, her
breathing labored, as if JT's presence were suffocating. "I'm
sorry, sir," Esau started out saying.

"No, please. Pardon me for the intrusion. My name is JT Patterson." The man watched Betty cautiously.

"Your name is JT who?" Esau questioned in a raised voice. Esau's posture stiffened and his nostrils flared as he released Betty from his arms. Like everyone else, Esau assumed that JT was dead. This indeed was jarring news.

The room grew still as it yielded to two minutes of disturbing silence.

JT looked as if he didn't know whether to inch closer toward Betty or run straight out the door. Charlotte could not believe her ears or her eyes. She instantly remembered seeing the man in the park only hours earlier. He was the same man who asked about socks. Now, she wondered if that meeting was happenstance or deliberate. "He really is alive," she said to herself.

JT's presence was not commanding. Not in the least. Then again, he couldn't behave as if he were an invited guest or some sort of special delivery. Even though Charlotte knew JT probably came seeking redemption, perhaps measuring his last days here on earth, she was still baffled by JT's courage to show up at the house. It was as if he were a long lost relative returning to the family fold after completing some sort of odyssey. Clearly, Betty was struggling with forgiveness and other emotions. JT's resurfacing certainly raised a few eyebrows and stirred up unwanted ghosts.

After witnessing Betty and JT share the same tension-filled air space, Charlotte tried to guess what could possibly be going through her mother's mind. This was not a Kodak moment. Dumbfounded, Charlotte took this opportunity to study her infamous grandfather more acutely.

JT had gray eyes and skin the color of pumpernickel bread. His salt-and-pepper sideburns could have used a good trimming or been done away with all together. His pants were worn from years of washing and ironing. She also noticed the pair of dollar-store slippers on his long, narrow toes.

According to one of Ramiyah's letters, JT had money. Loads of it. And if that were the case, he certainly had enough to upgrade his wardrobe from pauper to decent. For a man with so much bank, he looked as if he had pawed and clawed his way to their house.

Betty moaned. Although her face showed heartbreak, she fought to keep her emotions from bubbling to the surface. It was the kind of pain that lingered long, like a toothache. Charlotte wanted desperately to comfort her mother, but her father stood by Betty like a fortress, making it obvious that he was the family's protector.

While Charlotte appreciated his guarded stance, she was concerned about the fire in his eyes. Esau was angry, and he looked like he was ready to explode. He clenched his right fist tightly.

All of a sudden, Charlotte started praying. Loudly. "Father God, we need you this very moment. This very hour. Father, cover this family with your peace, which surpasses understanding. Please impart in us your wisdom. In this hour of need, help us to not frustrate your grace or your mercy, and I command peace be still, in the name of Jesus."

Charlotte started to breathe heavily and evenly. She closed her eyes and flailed her hands about in the air. "Oh, Lord, bring about forgiveness. I thank you for hearing my plea, for your Word states that you know what we ask of before we even ask it. That is awesome. You are awesome. Thank you for being a loving God. All things are in your control, in your capable hands. Thy will be done, in Jesus' name. Amen."

When Charlotte opened her eyes, she discovered Betty sobbing and sitting on the edge of the coffee table. Kneeling beside Betty was the devoted Esau, with his arm wrapped around his wife's shoulders. JT stayed put near the door. Standing quietly behind him were Mattie Mae and Sista.

"What in God's name is going on here?" Mattie Mae demanded to know.

Sista looked to and fro, waiting for an answer also as she double-knotted the thin cotton belt attached to her shift dress.

Betty shot JT a cold, icy glare.

Suddenly, a loud clap of thunder jarred everyone's senses. After Mattie Mae finished looking from one person to the next, she extended her hand to introduce herself to JT.

"Mama, that man is not welcomed in this house!" Esau announced firmly. His voice burned with anger. His veins throbbed. Pulsated.

"Daddy!" Charlotte exclaimed. But Esau merely held up his hand as a strong gesture to hush up. Esau's stance was sturdy. His gaze steady. His blood pressure rising.

Mattie Mae was bewildered and could not care less if she had a dog in this fight or not. Something was up, and she intended to get to the bottom of it. She was the very vein, the major artery of this family, and she was not having any mess. Meanwhile, Sista was equally shocked by Esau's abrasive behavior, yet practically salivated in anticipation.

Mattie Mae took a tissue from her apron pocket and wiped away the droplets of sweat from her forehead. "Now, normally I trust what my chi'ren say and let it go at that. But the last time I checked, this was still *my* house. Me and Edmund's. Now, when I came through that door, I asked a question. Is anybody gonna answer it?"

"It's okay," JT said ruefully. Dried saliva had tracked down from the corners of his mouth. "Maybe I shouldn't have come."

"You should not have come?" an undoubtedly cross Esau shouted, believing JT's remark to be terribly accurate.

Betty rocked back and forth with Charlotte, now included in the huddle with her parents, rocking along with her.

"Esau, please," Mattie Mae said sternly. "Mister, I don't know who you are or what has got my family so upset, but I intend to find out one way or the other."

By this time, Sista had slithered past Mattie Mae and JT, and was now sitting comfortably in one of the arm chairs. Legs crossed. Arms folded.

"This man is my father, JT Patterson," Betty muttered in a frosty, flat tone.

"He's your father?" Mattie Mae was confused, but she resisted the temptation to badger for an explanation.

"I thought your father was dead," Sista screeched, leaning forward in her seat.

JT, whose facial color had changed due to embarrassment, started to turn around, but Mattie Mae placed a firm hand against his back to keep him from bolting out the door.

Esau and Charlotte gently assisted Betty up from the edge of the coffee table. "I'm taking Betty for a drive," Esau said, still fresh with outrage. "I mean no disrespect to you, Mama, but he had better be gone by the time we get back." Esau looked to his daughter. "Do you want to join us, Charlotte?"

"No. I'll stay here," Charlotte replied without reservation.

Sensing that her son was about to object to Charlotte's decision, Mattie Mae looked directly at her son. "From the looks of things, it might not be a bad idea for you to go on and take that drive, Esau."

Mattie Mae was so baffled by what she had walked into that she had not even considered asking Sista to leave. Then again, whatever was going on, Sista would eventually find out anyway. There was very little that Mattie Mae kept from her best friend.

Meanwhile, Charlotte fought feelings of anger. Nonetheless, she found herself in a very unique position. Charlotte may have been saved and understood God's command for all to love and forgive one another; however, she felt no urge to run into her *grandfather's* arms.

Esau and Betty had slipped out the back door and had already gotten into their vehicle. Everyone's eyebrows rose to the sound of the engine starting up.

JT looked apologetically at Mattie Mae. "Please, I did not come here to cause any trouble. I'll leave. What I had to say, I really came to say to my daughter."

Charlotte thought his addressing Betty as his daughter sounded ludicrous.

In spite of the heinous act he had committed, JT looked downright pitiful, and Mattie Mae encouraged him to get whatever he had to say off of his chest.

Sista eyed him suspiciously. Something about the man did not sit well with her, and she was all too ready to spearhead a thorough interrogation. Although Sista kept her mouth shut tight as a clam for the moment, she was anxious to see what explanation would ooze from his lips.

"I did a shameful thing," JT volunteered, none too eager to recount that chapter in his life.

"What did you do?" Sista baited.

Mattie Mae rolled her eyes. "You look like you could use a bite to eat," she suggested in an effort to clear the air. Mattie Mae took JT by the arm and led him into the kitchen. Charlotte and Sista automatically walked behind them.

JT settled down at the table in the chair nearest the door, all the while fixating his eyes on Charlotte as she sat across from him.

"You look just like my mother," he blurted.

Mattie Mae and Sista darted glances back and forth at each other.

"I do?" Charlotte responded, feeling slightly unnerved by his stare; an unwelcome stare by the man who had hurt her mother so badly. Ugly thoughts slipped into her holy head. The thought of punching JT in the face came first; then one of lunging for his throat and wrapping her hands around his narrow neck, giving it a hard squeeze.

Of the three women present in the room, only she knew of the hole in Betty's heart that JT had caused. Only JT and Betty knew how deep and how dark that hole really was.

"Yeah," JT answered. "She was an evil woman, but I don't sense that about you."

"You're right. I am not an evil person," Charlotte said, startled by his comment and battling with emotions. "Why do you say your mother was evil?" Charlotte was surprised at how she was able to hold a civilized conversation with a man who initially had her flesh screaming to curse. But, she was familiar with and understood God's enabling grace.

"Because she just was. Some women should not be allowed to have children." JT looked off in the distance as if he were recollecting some horrible memories of his mother and believing his statement to be clear as water.

"She was?" echoed Mattie Mae. "I'm sho' she wasn't that bad." With a plate in one hand and a large dipping spoon in the other, Mattie Mae piled hefty portions of beef barbecued ribs, cabbage and carrots and brown rice onto the plate.

"And the Bible says to honor thy father and thy mother," Sista chimed in. "*Evil* is a harsh word to say."

"That may be true, but it is what it is," JT stated.

"What would you like to drink?" Mattie Mae asked as she

laid the plate before JT. "We have orange juice, cranberry juice, white grape juice, iced-tea and water."

JT bowed his head and stared straight down. "I'll have a glass of white grape juice if you don't mind."

"I don't mind at all," Mattie Mae answered as she went to pour JT a glass of juice.

"You're awfully kind to me, but if you knew what I had to say, you'd have second thoughts about offering me this fine meal and a cool drink."

"I already know what you have to say, or at least I know what it is about," Charlotte spoke up. "So why don't you eat first and then we can talk."

JT was stunned by Charlotte's statement, especially after revealing that she knew what was on his heart. Mattie Mae and Sista, however, were clearly confused.

"Thank you," JT said after accepting his drink and before approaching his meal with enthusiasm.

Charlotte pondered whether to ask Mattie Mae and Sista to allow her some time, alone with JT. She wanted the alone time but could also use their wisdom, even though Sista's frankness was something of a concern. Alone time these days had been an illusion.

Charlotte felt anxious. Whenever she felt anxious, she would either pray, or yield to taking a trip to her favorite bakery, I Kneed Bread. Charlotte prayed silently. She worried that Betty might be upset once she found out that the four of them had been discussing her past behind her back. She wondered if her mother would return to the house seeking a pound of JT's flesh. Charlotte decided to risk a little "deep interrogation" of her own. After all, Betty did leave JT alone with them.

Charlotte imagined JT slept with one eye opened these days, with a guilty conscience whipping him every time he tried to lay his head down at night. A life filled with grief and empty of joy.

She noticed that JT had slight difficulty in grasping his fork.

"Arthritis," he explained after spotting her gaze.

"Oh, I'm sorry. I didn't mean to stare," Charlotte apologized, not realizing that JT had finally lifted his head.

By this time, all three women had joined JT at the table.

"So what brings you here after all this time? Were you sick? Are you sick?" Sista asked. But JT avoided the question like falling debris.

"You know what?" Charlotte banged lightly on the table after realizing she, Mattie Mae and Sista must look like a convoy of Indians on horseback, circling the wagon. "Maybe we should leave JT alone to eat instead of us gawking at him like he's some circus animal."

Besides that, Charlotte quickly grew tired of observing JT's lack of table manners. It was painful to watch him scoop up his food with his fork *and* fingers, then to eat with his mouth open. JT plowed through his food like a horse at the racetrack.

"No, please. I want you all to stay," JT said sadly, after licking the grease from his fingers. "Besides, Betty may never ever speak to me again, and I need to talk to someone. Been carrying this weight for far too long." JT wiped his hands on his napkin and laid it on the plate.

"You don't want to finish your food first?" Mattie Mae asked.

"Oh, no. This was one of the best meals I've had in a long time. Reminds me of my late wife's cooking." JT looked straight ahead toward Charlotte. "Ramiyah told me a lot about you."

Charlotte felt a cold chill go down her spine.

"When did you see Ramiyah?" Sista interrupted. No one seemed to mind Sista's presence or interrogation. One thing was definite: Sista would challenge JT and dare to go where Mattie Mae and Charlotte may not. Mattie Mae would provide fairness and wisdom. Charlotte was the peacekeeper and could provide spiritual guidance. They were indeed a motley crew.

26

"Therefore be merciful just as your Father also is merciful

Luke 6:36

Remarkably, JT had transformed from the nervous outcast who first arrived to a slightly more relaxed man. Perhaps the notion of releasing a heavy burden made him feel lighter, or perhaps he no longer felt threatened since the atmosphere was no longer hostile.

The fact was that JT did, indeed, feel a relief. He had thought long and hard about what he would say before his arrival—only he expected to be saying it to Betty instead.

He had planned his words carefully, so as not to garner any sympathy. He did not deserve it. But his children did deserve to know their family history, and since Ramiyah had informed him that his granddaughter, Charlotte, was a praying woman, he thought that maybe it was a sign from God to have her in the room with him.

"Charlotte, you said you knew why I was here?" JT rubbed his temples as if he had a headache.

Charlotte nodded. "I know what happened," she said stiffly as she thought about the proper way to address this man. JT? Grandfather? Granddaddy JT? He didn't feel like a grandfather to her. But he was the man who fathered her mother, which made him her grandfather, and she was given the grace to be kind to him. "God, that can only be you," she said softly.

Silence and frowns emanated from Mattie Mae and Sista, confirming to JT that they did not have a clue.

"Like I said, I did a shameful thing and I am not proud of it," he continued. JT's lips quivered.

"We can't afford to judge you, JT," Mattie Mae stated. "We can confess our sins one to another and pray for one another. God is in control of everything."

"God," JT whispered. "I didn't grow up in a religious family. When I was a boy, an old woman who lived down the road from us said God told her I was to preach. I come from a long line of number runners, alcoholics, thieves, hustlers and whores, but no preachers."

JT paused.

No one gasped as he had expected, and Charlotte wondered if JT was stalling or laying some sort of foundation. And then the Holy Spirit brought something back to her memory. It was the dream from the other night. The dream of the shadowy figure and the words *generations of stains*.

"Shucks, is that all," Sista said. "One of my uncles used to be a traveling salesman and would put washin' powder in cigarette wrapping paper, roll 'em up and sell 'em. Uncle Gene was a scoundrel. So, ain't no telling what will fall out if you shake anybody's family tree."

"That's right, and it don't matter where you come from. It matters where you're going," Mattie Mae said reassuringly.

"I appreciate what you're saying, but if someone came along and shook either one of your family trees, would a child molester fall out of it?"

Apparently, what JT said took a second to register, for the gasps and bug eyes took a minute to manifest. But even Charlotte did not know fully what JT meant. She asked herself if she was really ready to listen to JT's account of his incestuous deed.

"What do you mean? What are you saying?" Mattie Mae rambled.

Charlotte held her breath. Sista's mouth fell open.

"Ramiyah is not Betty's little sister. She is her daughter," JT said ruefully.

Mattie Mae clutched her chest. "Ramiyah is Betty's daughter and her sister? What do you mean? Who is Ramiyah's father?"

Charlotte figured Mattie Mae had to know what JT was saying and was in denial.

"I'm Betty and Ramiyah's father," JT confessed sullenly.

"YOU ARE!" Mattie Mae and Sista both shouted, with Sista bellowing the loudest.

Mattie Mae looked questionably at Charlotte. "And you knew about *this*?"

"Yes, ma'am. But only recently, after reading Ramiyah's last letter," Charlotte admitted. A feeling of shame washed over her.

The words *generations of stain* haunted her again. Now she understood how JT's disclosure related to it. *Generations of stain* was actually generational sin governed by lust and lunacy. Sin passed down from God knows how many generations. Charlotte thanked God that it seemed to have stopped with JT. She knew that she had to commit to serious warfare in seeing to it that this craziness never reared its ugly head again.

"No wonder Esau was so upset," Mattie Mae said, still clutching her chest as if this gesture would stop an impending heart attack.

For once in her life, Sista seemed to be at a loss for words.

"Forgiveness," Charlotte started out saying.

"Forgiveness?" Sista shouted.

Charlotte reached across the table and placed her hand over Sista's hand in an attempt to quell another outburst.

"Forgiveness is something I don't deserve, but I came seeking it anyway. And to talk a little about my family," JT admitted.

"What about your family?" Charlotte asked. Sista slid her hand from underneath Charlotte's hand. Mattie Mae kept shaking her head in disbelief.

"Earlier, I said that my mother was evil. I know all about the Bible commanding us to honor our mothers and our fathers, but my mother was meaner than a chained dog. My brothers and sisters and I didn't know who our fathers were because my mother slept around with so many men. When she couldn't find a man to sleep with, she would sleep with her own sons."

"Wait a minute." Charlotte felt a little uneasy. "Are you saying your mother molested you? You and your brothers?"

"Unfortunately, that is exactly what I'm saying. Now, it's no excuse for what I did, but I know now that I acted out on what I knew. I forced my rage on my child. It wasn't right. It wasn't right for Betty, and it wasn't right for me and my brothers."

As JT continued to pour out his heart and history, the tears started flowing. Charlotte left the table to get the travel-size packet of Kleenex from the utility drawer.

"Whatever happened to your mother?" Charlotte asked. Charlotte pictured JT's mother as a plump, severe-looking woman with a backhand slap heavy enough to knock the wind out of a tornado, marching through a cornfield, knocking down rows of corn as she searched for enemies.

"She died when I was a teenager. The wife of the married man she was messing around with caught the two of them together and introduced my mother to the business end of her twelve-gauge shotgun. Shot right through the heart."

"Whoa! What about your brothers and sisters? Who took care of you guys after that?" Charlotte wanted to know everything there was to know about the Pattersons. She wanted to know what needed covering in prayer.

"Well, there were three of us boys and two sisters. The oldest was a girl. She had ran off and got married while Mama was still alive, and we never heard from her again. To this day, I don't know if she ever found out what happened to Mama or not. I don't even know if she is still alive.

"My youngest brother used to stay in trouble all the time. He ended up in county jail, where someone stabbed him to death. He was about twenty-five at the time."

"My other sister was an alcoholic. She died from cirrhosis of the liver at an early age. My brother, Chester, was the only one who turned out all right."

"My memory can be sketchy sometimes, but I vaguely remember hearing Betty mention Chester," Mattie Mae said. Her face looked chalky.

JT acted as if he hadn't heard Mattie Mae speak.

"Does my mom know about all of this?" Charlotte asked.

"No. An old woman who lived down the street from us had prophesied over my family once. She said I was to preach and if I was disobedient, the Lord would raise up someone else in my bloodline to do His will." He looked directly at Charlotte. "I guess I wanted to meet the granddaughter who was willing to do what I wasn't."

"Well, what I want to know is what were you thinking?" Sista asked. "I mean, I'm sorry about what you and your brothers and sisters went through, but to turn around and do the same thing to a chile! Your own chile! You can offer any no-count woman a shot of whiskey and she'll turn up her skirt. Why chi'ren?" Sista argued.

"Sista!" Mattie Mae shouted, although she felt the same way. Mattie Mae reached inside the fridge to throw out the tired-looking celery sticks and dying tomatoes while it was on her mind.

"It's all right. She is right. The best way I can describe it is as some kind of disease or out of body experience. Believe me; I felt bad afterward. Real bad. I felt bad for years." JT's voice was strained.

"It was a disease. A demonic seed that passed down, but that madness has ended in the name of Jesus," Charlotte nearly screamed. She realized that she must have come off sounding certifiable. She did not care, because finally, she understood what the Holy Spirit meant by the word *unveiling*.

27

*Do no fret because of evildoers nor be envious of the workers
of inequity. For they shall soon be cut down like the grass
and wither as the green herb*

Psalm 37:1 & 2

No one even noticed that the heavy downpour had finally
scaled down to a light drizzle. Nor did they hear Betty come
in. Not even Sista, who had need of the bathroom but was
willing to risk making a puddle on the floor in order to hear
JT's entire story.

"Why can't I use the downstairs bathroom?" Sista had
asked with a bit of irritation on her tongue.

"Because the downstairs toilet won't flush and Edmund
hadn't looked at it yet," Mattie Mae explained, relieved that
Sista would be out of the room for at least a minute. Sista
was prone to ask improper questions, but somehow, Mattie
Mae felt this was not a time to banish her away. Sista had
been pretty tame so far. Surely she would not stir up even
the mildest of trouble.

Betty had returned to the house unnoticed and without
Esau. She had assured him of her intentions and encouraged him to go join Edmund and Busta. She and she alone
would hammer the nail in *this* coffin. There would be secrets

to unearth as far as she was concerned. She *had* been a victim, but now she was a victor.

The initial shock of the resurgence of her violator, thought long gone, had now worn off. Betty arrived with a new determination, realizing that she had been busy surviving, raising one daughter while denying another and pretending to feel normal.

She could hear voices coming from the kitchen and quietly followed the sound of low chatter. Betty made deliberate steps, no longer shivering in fear at the awareness of JT's presence as she did as a child. All fear had been removed and replaced with the Spirit of the Lord.

Betty was comforted by a peace that surpassed all understanding. She was also comforted by an unction; an unction that said both of her daughters, Ramiyah and Charlotte, had been praying for her. She could feel the love and support of her children and kept a stiff upper lip, knowing the serious task at hand.

JT was the first to see her from the corner of his eye. Now, it was he who felt intimidated by Betty's presence.

"I don't mean to sound rude, but can I have some privacy with JT and Charlotte?" Betty turned to Mattie Mae.

"Of course," Mattie Mae said as she directed a reluctant Sista out of the kitchen.

Betty remained august, standing in the doorway with her hands behind her back. Charlotte braced herself.

"Charlotte, I strongly believe the Lord wants to speak through you about the threshing floor," Betty sternly announced.

Confused, Charlotte raised her eyebrows. "The threshing floor?"

JT squirmed about in his seat, displaying discomfort and nervousness.

Just as Charlotte was about to refute Betty's notion, a

scripture came to mind. "Ma, I had no idea what you were talking about, but I just thought of something in the Book of Joel."

Betty half smiled as she revealed what had been hidden behind her back. Betty handed over to Charlotte a small white Bible, to which JT showed obvious relief, seeing a Bible as opposed to a handgun or carving knife.

Charlotte started to feel queasy. It was the kind of queasiness that only a large cup of hot tea and a few soda crackers could cure. She flipped through the pages until she found the Book of Joel. After scanning the first two pages, she began reading aloud.

"Chapter 2 of the Book of Joel, beginning in verse 24 and ending at verse 27, says:

The threshing floors will be filled with grain; the vats will overflow with new wine and oil. I will repay you for the years the locusts have eaten, the great locust and the young locust, the other locusts and the locust swarm—my great army that I sent among you. You will have plenty to eat, until you are full and you will praise the name of the Lord your God, who has worked wonders for you; never again will my people be shamed. Then you will know that I am in Israel, that I am the Lord your God, and that there is no other; never again will my people be shamed."

"What do you think God is saying to us through the scriptures, Charlotte?" Betty asked, refusing to look at JT.

Once again, Charlotte found the Holy Spirit to be faithful as a message began to rise in her being. "First off, threshing is a process used for separating wheat grains from their outer shell. Farmers would toss the beaten wheat into the air and the wind would blow away the shells, which are light in weight."

Betty had a faraway look in her eyes. "I remember as a

child, wanting to feel the very breath of God, a wind of His Spirit or even the hair to stand on the back of my neck, anything, as long as I had some tangible assurance that God had not forsaken me."

JT opened his mouth slightly, but Betty's swift and fleeting glare warned him not to speak. A bluish-green vein in his forehead began to throb.

"My spirit was wounded and my faith crushed," Betty continued, the coldness still in her voice as memories of empty liquor bottles covering the floor like toss rugs flooded her mind. She walked over to the kitchen island, rested one arm on the granite countertop and placed one hand on her hip. "It's a miracle I'm able to string two sentences together coherently."

Finally, Betty stared squarely into JT's eyes. He felt a lump in his throat the size of a golf ball as he swallowed. Hard. He dared not return the stare. In fact, JT wanted to pull out a cigarette, light it, take a drag and blow a puff of smoke into the air big enough to cloud his escape from the room.

"Threshing wheat," Betty stated almost mindlessly. "Beaten. Separated. I used to think all men were the same underneath those washed faces and aftershave lotions."

The more Betty rambled, the more Charlotte became concerned. Charlotte wondered. She wondered if her mother was standing there somehow nourishing her anger. Was she about to snap? Would she haul off and knock JT into the fiery bowels of hell?

JT constantly and annoyingly cleared his throat. JT coughed a cough so rattling it should have cleared his lungs. He pushed his plate aside. His eyes pleaded for mercy at Charlotte. Charlotte took deep breaths.

A fly landed on Betty's hand but quickly scurried away as if it could smell trouble looming.

"Years later, after my mother's suicide," Betty continued, looking at Charlotte again as if JT were not present in the room, "Mrs. Carmichael told me that my mother had actually confessed to her about knowing of JT's fondness for children. She couldn't be sure, but she believes my mother *knew* I hadn't been telling the truth. I did not get pregnant by some boy in school."

JT's eyes were downcast.

Betty's posture was rigid as she turned to face JT. "What was it, JT? We had family honor to maintain?" she asked curtly. "No one should know about the evil that was in that house?"

JT remained silent. The rain spots on his clothing had finally dried.

"Ma," Charlotte interjected. "I was under the impression that Mrs. Carmichael was a busybody, a gossip. It sounds to me like she came to you years later to pour salt in the wound, and I think that's awful."

"Maybe so, but no child should grow up feeling guilty for something they have no control over. That is just as awful," Betty said. "Mrs. Carmichael was remorseful about keeping a secret instead of coming forward."

"Louise Carmichael was a busybody. She always minded everybody else's business," JT spoke boldly.

"You have the nerve to downplay your role in this by trying to avert the attention off of you and onto Mrs. Carmichael's love for gossip?" Betty shouted, her eyes turning red. She drew deep breaths to calm herself down, knowing her blood pressure could be rising.

Charlotte could hear fumbling in the next room, guessing Mattie Mae and Sista were listening close by. She felt as if she were watching a tennis match between JT and her mother, except the tennis ball would be words. A war of words. Hurtful words. Revealing words. Healing words. Charlotte was caught in the middle and felt powerless. But she knew where the help would come from.

"That's not my intention at all, Betty," she heard JT defended himself, his voice elevated slightly.

"What *is* your intention then?" Betty roared before remembering her promise to God that she was willing to forgive JT if He would help her. Betty understood that saying she could forgive someone was one thing, but truly feeling it in her heart was another. She did not feel it.

28

There is one Lawgiver Who is able to save and to destroy.
Who are we to judge?

James 4:12

After all these years, Betty thought she had forgiven her father. Seeing him made her realize that she hadn't. And since true forgiveness sometimes takes time, she was determined to take this time to vent, release, purge or whatever it took to put her on the road to healing.

"Ma, why don't you have a seat?" Charlotte suggested. "JT came all this way after all these years. JT, why don't you tell my mom what you just told us." So far, JT appeared sincere to Charlotte, which was good. Insincerity with Betty was not going to fly.

Betty moved with obvious trepidation to a chair on the opposite side of JT. A part of her viewed JT as a monster from her past. She did not want to hear what he had to say. She wanted to continue lashing out. Yet, another part of her, a little girl, longed for the daddy she never knew, and she wondered why she had been singled out that horrible night.

Unbeknownst to Betty, JT also wished things had been

different. He wanted to give Betty a fatherly hug without it
being misconstrued. He dared not take the chance.

Charlotte waited for some sort of sinister display to appear on JT's face. It never came. In fact, at times he seemed deeply remorseful. At others, strangely apathetic. She could feel the peace of God filter throughout the room. Tension was starting to break.

Betty's once trembling hands now lay still on the table. Even JT's posture shifted from a cowardly slump to upright and confident.

Betty's eyes swelled with tears as JT repeated his hard-scrabble background to her. She felt she never had a fair chance, especially after learning a little bit more about her mother's own imperfections.

According to JT, Gladys was a Bible-thumping, scripture-quoting religious fanatic who was also a closet drunk, a mean drunk who provoked most of their fights and came from a family of moonshiners. While JT's drink of choice was usually a fifth of Jim Beam or Puerto Rican rum, Gladys favored vodka mixed with fresh squeezed orange juice.

JT went on to explain that after major blow-ups with Gladys, he would go on a serious drinking binge. "I wasn't faithful. I'll admit that. But I never walked through that door and instigated a fight with your mother."

"More diversions." Hostility and impatience resonated in Betty's voice. She fought desperately to shed her show of bitterness or relief that night.

Charlotte stayed silent during this whole time, obedient to the command of God to do so, even though she worried about her mother's feverish attitude.

Betty, however, found herself mellowing, easing. She did not want to, even though she had asked the Lord for help with forgiveness.

JT looked harmless, a thin shell of the monster who attacked her so many years ago. She felt sorry for him. Sorry for herself for having come from such sorry stock. Then she looked over at Charlotte, her God-fearing daughter, her pride and joy called by God. She then thought about Ramiyah, the daughter that reminded her of her shame, the daughter who God had also called.

JT mustered up the courage to continue. "Gladys also knew about my family. Our dark secrets weren't so dark to her."

Betty gritted her teeth, unable to part her lips, but her eyes asked the question.

"The married man who my mother was killed over was Gladys's uncle," JT volunteered. "That's how we met. I mean, you can only imagine the family feud behind that. The stories that came out. True and false. We were bound to meet."

"You must have been some prize," Betty blurted in a low voice.

"Not to make light of the situation, but Gladys was no angel either."

Just as Betty was prepared to argue there was no comparison to apples and oranges, devils and saints, nor JT and Gladys, decades of old memories came flooding back. Memories of a mean-spirited Gladys, braiding switches together or grabbing the iron cord to beat Wendell for looking like his father.

That had to be the real reason for the beat down. Although Gladys would call Wendell in the house for roughing up a neighborhood kid or getting into trouble at school, she berated him every time with every blow and every strike for having JT's prominent features.

Another memory popped up. It was of pillow cases saturated with tears, followed by sounds of shouts and glass shattering and the sight of bruises and black eyes on both parents.

Betty tried to shut off the memory flow. She needed to do it before things got ugly. Lamenting was a burdensome and draining task. "I used to scream at night," Betty announced in an effort to quiet her soul. "Not the kind any human can hear. I screamed quiet screams. The kind that only the keen ear of a dog could hear."

Charlotte felt a churning in her stomach again and wondered if her mother was about to go off the deep end.

Betty turned to Charlotte. "Every Sunday, my mother would dress us girls in our little organza dresses, frilly socks, patent leather shoes, white bonnets and gloves. Wendell wore either a black or blue suit, which he would outgrow by Easter. We would then catch the bus to the church on Seventh Street, where we smiled and sang as if all was well."

JT opened his mouth to say something, but Betty insisted on pouring out her heart. "I want you to know, JT, that I really don't remember seeing your face that night. I might as well have had my face on backward. I blocked so much out. When Ramiyah was born, I wanted Mama to dote on her like most grandmothers do. And she did. In public. But in private, she pretty much shunned Ramiyah and me."

Charlotte and JT stole glances at one another as Betty kept talking.

"Now that I look back, I can compare dinnertime to still photos. We sat at the table, rigid. You weren't there most of the time," Betty said, looking at JT.

Meanwhile, having spent most of her times with the Morley side, Charlotte was utterly shocked at how dysfunctional her mother's side of the family was. The Pattersons sounded like headline news. Not to mention Gladys's family. And she was curious about what they were like after discovering that they, too, apparently favored the sauce.

Gladys Patterson. Gladys, Charlotte immediately opined, was no Mattie Mae. Mattie Mae exemplified genteel Southern charm. Gladys sounded confused. Ruling with an iron hand, professing a God who she did not lean on for guidance in raising her children or helping her in not giving up on life.

Charlotte imagined chain-smoking relatives, sitting around a table stocked full with beer, gin, whiskey, vodka, scotch, bourbon and corn liquor, getting lit up like Christmas trees. A bunch of alcoholics drinking their way through life. A label and a hobby her Uncle Wendell took on as well.

Charlotte sat there pondering on how she never would have guessed her mother came from such bleak beginnings. Betty had always seemed so perfect to her, or at least as close to perfection as one could get.

Although Betty did not welcome the family home wearing high heels and a gingham apron, she was the consummate housewife and nurturer, devoted PTA mom, guidance counselor, good neighbor, prayer warrior, supporter, etc. Charlotte knew, without a shadow of a doubt, that for Betty to be a woman of such grace, it had to be the grace of God. To narrowly escape by the skin of your teeth from a lineage of drunkards, adulterers, molesters and murderers had to be by the grace of the Almighty.

Charlotte sat there thinking about how many women she had counseled who'd traveled along paths similar or worse than her mother's. Charlotte could still see their faces, not knowing that her own mother's face belonged in that room at church also.

"I want to know why," Betty nearly shrieked. "Why me?"

To Charlotte, it was as if time stood still, preparing to rewind to a track not even she wanted to view. However, life taught her that confrontation was sometimes the first step toward resolution.

JT lowered his eyes and buried his face in his hands. "I can't explain—"

"It's not that you should have abused Jean or Wendell," she interrupted. "But why did you single me out? Not that I wish any harm to Jean or to Wendell, but why me?"

JT rubbed his hands up and down his thighs. Perhaps he did not know what else to do with his hands. He lifted his eyes as he began to pour out his heart. "There is no excuse for what I did to you, Betty. I shouldn't say this, but I will say it anyhow, because it's the truth. You were my favorite child. I saw more potential in you."

Betty was stone-faced.

"My state of mind at the time," JT continued, stopping for a moment, and then regaining his thoughts. "Let me say this: it takes a monster to touch a child in that way, especially his own child. A sick monster. Jean looked like my mother, who I resent to this day, even though she's dead and gone. Wendell looked too much like me. So, unlike my brother, I was never into boys or men. But you. You reminded me of my sister, Stella."

"Stella?" Betty whispered, tired of his stalling.

"Stella is the one who got married, left home and we never saw or heard from her again. She took care of us kids as best she could when she was at home. That included running interference with our mother whenever she was on one of her evil prowls. I missed Stella when she left, and then I found myself resenting her for leaving us."

"So, let me get this straight. Your attacking me was your way of bringing Stella back or getting back at her?" Betty asked in a tone icy enough to chill boiling water.

"No. Like I said before, there is no excuse for what I've done. Only facts. The facts are I was a raging drunk. Angry at Gladys. Angry at myself. Angry at the world and feeling sorry for myself. I snapped."

"I'll say you snapped," Charlotte said to herself as she carefully studied their facial expressions. By now, JT appeared spent. Betty was nonchalant at this point. Maybe even slightly annoyed.

"There is something else Mrs. Carmichael told me," Betty spewed. "On the day Mama committed suicide, Mrs. Carmichael thought she saw you leave the house. Is that true? Were you there that day?"

JT lowered his eyes again. "Yes. It's true," he muttered.

Suddenly, Betty jumped up from the table with such force, startling both JT and Charlotte. She stood with her back straight. The palms of her hands lay flat on the table and her eyes welled up with tears. "Why did she hang herself, JT?"

It was now clear to Charlotte that her mother wanted to hear JT take responsibility for his actions.

"When I left you guys, I left feeling so guilty for what I'd done," he admitted. "I came back to see Ramiyah and to make Gladys stand up to her part in this, this . . . to make her share in this guilt."

Betty peered over to a very perplexed Charlotte, knowing what JT was about to confess. She believed every word Mrs. Carmichael told her some time ago. Since God allowed her mother to go on to the great beyond before she could confess and saw fit to bring JT back to her, she wanted to hear the truth from JT's mouth.

"There is something about being sober for a year. It does something to a person. The cobwebs in your head start to clear out," JT continued.

Betty started tapping her feet, an indication that her patience was growing paper thin. She felt like she was seconds away from pulling an apology straight from JT's mouth.

29

But may the God of all grace Who called us to His eternal glory by Christ Jesus, after you have suffered a while, perfect, establish, strengthen and settle you

I Peter 5:10

A typical warm summer breeze flowed through the kitchen, a soft wind coming from out of nowhere. It increased the humming noise from the ceiling fan that circulated on low speed. Dusk was approaching, sneaking up on them.

Betty waited. So did Charlotte, who wondered how this Mrs. Carmichael came to know so much.

"I honestly don't know how or who started the rumor about me being dead, but I'm willing to bet it was Gladys," JT said.

Betty sat back down, but this time she faced the sink and not JT. She crossed her legs.

A faraway look entered JT's eyes as he recalled his dark past. "Gladys told me that Ramiyah was in school. But long story short, I told Gladys that I didn't know if incest was a crime or not, but I couldn't keep living like that. I was willing to turn myself in to the police."

"Five years after the fact?" Betty pointed out.

"It took five years of having my conscience constantly

whipped. Five years of living in squalor while watching Gladys walk around like she had a ticket to heaven."

Charlotte was stunned to know that he had been spying on Gladys. Betty, even more so.

"Did Louise Carmichael tell you that I kept in contact with her every now and then?" he asked.

"She did," Betty answered, sounding upset. "And I was not too happy about it either."

Charlotte was anxious to learn what part Gladys had played in all of this, and she found it hard not to ask any questions. Hard to the point of biting her lip.

"I suppose Louise also told you that not only was I willing to report myself but—"

"Then why didn't you?" Betty interrupted.

"Ma," Charlotte said simply and sternly, breaking her vow of silence. But she recognized Betty's interruption as a nuisance that broke JT's train of thought.

JT looked appreciatively at Charlotte and ignored the question. "It's one thing for me to go running off to the authorities, but to implicate Gladys? That woman had to uphold her reputation. Her image."

As morbid as the entire ordeal sounded, Charlotte could not deny its intrigue.

JT stared at the wall and said, "You see, if I had gone to the police, I would have also told them about the fight that led up to, you know. As usual, Gladys picked a fight when I got home. Said she saw how I had been looking at Betty. She dared me."

Feeling uneasy, Betty shifted her body in the chair.

JT finally faced Betty. "Gladys even made a cruel bet that I wouldn't touch you. Said I wasn't a man."

Betty felt sick to her stomach. Tears rolled down her eyes. Charlotte's too. The thought of Gladys egging on such an event and JT following through with it made Charlotte sick to her stomach.

JT's voice cracked as he continued. "Gladys left the house to go play bingo or something and I allowed her and alcohol to turn me into my mother. I did it. I snapped, and I am so sorry. I am so sorry, Betty." His face was ashen.

Betty wanted to get up and run out of the house. Run until her legs gave way. But she didn't.

"When I returned to that house years later, I also promised to expose her, too, but the thought of being investigated for being an unfit mother or the thought of neighbors seeing her children being taken away was too embarrassing. What would the neighbors say? What would her family say? What would the church say? Everybody thinking so high and mighty of the upstanding Gladys Patterson. Poor Gladys," JT went into rambling. "Poor Gladys; married to that no-good drunk, JT. Huh? Little did they know."

Charlotte was appalled. Everything was so hard for her to believe. To digest, even.

JT cleared his throat. "Louise got word to me about Gladys's death. After that, I don't know. I got to thinking I'd be making a mistake showing my face again. Let sleeping dogs lie. You all would be better off like you were, without her and without me. I never would have thought Gladys would take her own life, but she did. I know she lived with guilt also. She had to."

"Tell me something, JT." Betty sounded less combative. "Was there ever a time that you know of when she really believed some boy at school impregnated me?"

"No. She knew the whole time. Why do you think I left?"

Betty shook her head. Charlotte sniffled and wiped her nose, wanting the whole discussion to end.

Betty stood up again. Her posture was commanding, like

that of a CEO about to adjourn a staff meeting. "Is there anything else you have to say?"

"Just that I came to beg your pardon."

Betty looked down at the table to avoid the risk of shooting a harsh glance in JT's direction. "I chose to forgive you some time ago. You and Mama. But now, I must ask you to leave. Not only this house, but leave my family alone as well. Now, I do understand that you want to lend Ramiyah some financial support. I won't stand in the way of that. However, until I am totally healed of this, I can't pretend and I cannot force a relationship with you. Forgiveness does not mean that I have to do that, especially when there is an issue of trust."

"I understand," JT said as he got up slowly from the table. He placed his cap on his head. "It was nice to meet you, Charlotte. I don't deserve you for a grandchild."

Charlotte could not exactly say the feeling was mutual, only that she wished him well.

"I'll see my way out," he said. But Charlotte got up to escort him to the front door. She looked back at her mother. Betty stood trembling slightly. Her lips were pouty and stiff.

"Are you going to be all right?" a concerned Charlotte asked softly.

"I will be fine."

30

*But they do not know the thoughts of the LORD; they do
not understand His plan, He who gathers them like sheaves
to the threshing floor*

Micah 4:12

Drained from passing out a surprising amount of common
courtesy to JT, Betty spent the rest of the evening with Esau
in the bedroom. Charlotte had joined Mattie Mae and Sista
in the front room to watch the local news.

The headlights on Edmund's pickup truck glowed through
the curtains as he drove up the lane. Shortly thereafter, he
came stomping up the steps like a Clydesdale to loosen the
muddy red clay from his boots. Edmund dragged himself
inside the house and joined the clan.

"Evening," he said as he plopped down in his recliner,
raising the back of the chair to an upright position.

Everyone spoke except for Charlotte, who was preoccu-
pied with listening for sounds from upstairs. There were
none. Not even a creaking floorboard from her parents'
room. She assumed that her mother was curled up in her father's arms, sobbing and talking quietly. Decompressing.

The once humid and intense climate that hovered in the
house had started to cool down to comfortable as Mattie
Mae and Sista restrained themselves from prodding and
pumping Charlotte for information.

The sportscaster, dressed in a plaid polyester blend sports jacket, starched white shirt and a wide silk tie with large horizontal stripes, was an obvious throwback to the seventies in Charlotte's opinion. A seriously devoted fan of the era. All he needed was an afro complete with an afro pick (handle carved in the form of a fist, of course) and a pair of tube socks.

Charlotte sensed the questioning eyes of Mattie Mae and Sista bearing down on her as she listened to the final scores of various baseball teams. Edmund also noticed the attention given to this granddaughter, but said nothing.

"Well," Sista said, "do we have to beat it out of you?"

This time, the equally curious Mattie Mae made no attempt to quiet her habitually intrusive friend.

Meanwhile, Edmund continued to pretend to be oblivious and totally enthralled in the game highlights.

Charlotte heard the question. Loud and clear. After feeling confident that Betty and JT's conversation was safe to discuss and she hadn't been sworn to secrecy, she opened her mouth. "You guys didn't hear anything? Because I thought for sure I heard a noise in the dining room."

Sista looked as guilty as a puppy caught lounging on a sofa. "I was in the dining room for only a minute just to get a piece of hard candy out of the dish. I didn't hear a thing."

Charlotte figured she may be telling the truth. There had been brief moments of silence in the kitchen during JT's visit, and Sista's tongue did have a bright red stain on it, perhaps from savoring a piece of cherry-flavored candy.

Unable to fake it any longer, Edmund asked, "Hear what? What are y'all talkin' about?"

"Betty's father dropped by here today," Mattie Mae answered.

"Who? Betty's father?" Edmund appeared dumbfounded.

"Yes, Betty's father," she repeated.

"I thought he was dead."

"So did everybody else," Charlotte added. "Granddaddy, there is something else you don't know."

Edmund pulled the lever on the side of the chair to raise the foot rest.

"He raped my mom years ago."

"He did what?" Edmund shifted in his chair and leaned forward slightly.

At this point, Charlotte was convinced that neither Edmund nor Mattie Mae were hard of hearing. They just had a hard time grasping such deplorable news.

"When my mother was very, very young, her father, JT, molested . . . raped her. Ramiyah is actually their daughter." Charlotte could not believe she had conveyed the story of such a despicable act against her mother in a matter-of-fact tone. Her awareness was not only heightened by the existence of incest, but that it existed within her own family.

A full twenty seconds had elapsed before anyone said anything else. All the while, Edmund kept his pupils aimed at Charlotte. Sista worried that she would not get the full story before John Edward or Hiawatha came to take her home. And although curious and concerned, Mattie Mae was at peace, somewhat, since she had gone in her "prayer closet" while Sista was roaming around in the dining room in search of candy and a chance to eavesdrop, no doubt.

Sista might have been nosey, but Charlotte was prepared to gladly welcome any unsolicited comment she had to offer. Sista's tongue was sharp and cutting, but at least she told the truth.

Charlotte wiped her forehead with the back of her hand as if it were washed down in sweat. It wasn't. She decided to start talking—fast—before Sista started gunning for her again. "As everyone knows, I've been receiving letters from Ramiyah lately. In the latest letters, she mentioned finding out that she was really my mom's daughter."

As Charlotte continued telling the story up until the part where JT left, the room was saturated with outbursts of sighs, groans and gasps. Surprisingly, Edmund listened intently, not saying a word, but only staring into the fireplace the entire time.

"Oh, he's goin' to hell," Sista declared. "And he might as well dig his way there wit' his bare hands. Po' Betty. That's too much heartache to go 'round totin' for years."

"It sho' is," Mattie Mae agreed. "But who are we to say who's goin' to hell or not?"

Sista sucked her teeth.

"That's true, Grandma. He's already approached Rami-yah. He came here to ask for forgiveness from my mom. We don't know what he has said to God or what God has said to him," Charlotte replied rather dryly.

Sista grunted. "All that is fine and dandy, but how would y'all feel if that happened to you? You telling me you wouldn't be mad?"

"It did happen to me." Charlotte caught herself speaking in a raised tone. She glanced up toward the ceiling half expecting to hear movement because of their near-loud discussion.

"I don't mean me directly," she said after composing herself, careful not to let her volume spike again. "But this happened to my mother. My mother. And yes, I'm angry. Yes, I'm hurt. So is she. But she knows the right thing to do is to walk in forgiveness, and that's hard. It takes the Lord's help for sure."

"Some things are real hard to forgive," Sista insisted.

"Some things are," Charlotte agreed. "But I know you know that we will all go through times where we're going to have to forgive somebody for something. Unfortunately, we don't get to choose what that thing or those things are."

"Amen," Mattie Mae said. "Ain't that the truth. Charlotte, don't let Sista fool you. She knows all of this."

"Yeah, I do," Sista conceded. "But I don't understand

why we can keep some laws from the Old Testament, like bring a tenth of what you make to the temple for tithes and offerin', but God did away wit' an eye for an eye. I wouldn't take a log out of his eye. I would shove one in it."

Charlotte wondered how she could explain to Sista that being human, having a sour attitude would be perfectly understandable. However, sizing down such an event to nihility would certainly be unrealistic. One has to lean on God for supernatural help.

Incest was indeed a taboo subject, but it was nothing new. Charlotte recollected the biblical story of Lot and his daughters. Lot's daughters initiated the act of incest out of fear of not finding mates to father their children. Now, incest was prevalent and threatening to become commonplace.

It also made her want to join forces with Ramiyah somehow in establishing a ministry specifically geared toward sexual abuse against women and children.

"Don't forget, there is one bright side to all of this," Edmund interjected. "Actually, there is more than one."

The room grew still, as if preparing for some great announcement to bounce off the walls.

"Well, you're lookin' at one." He pointed at Charlotte, who smiled modestly.

"And Ramiyah is another. Now, we may not agree wit' God's way of bringin' Ramiyah into the world or what it took to get her attention, but we can't deny He is usin' her. Esau told me about the letters Ramiyah wrote to Betty and about her prison ministry. Both of Betty's girls are being used mightily by God."

Mattie Mae nodded her head in agreement.

"And another thing," Edmund continued, proving that he not only paid attention, but also gave it considerable thought. "This goes to show how mindful we should be."

"How so, Edmund?" Mattie Mae asked.

"Well, this made me think how easily folk say such and

such ain't of God. Keep in mind, I'm not sayin' He winks at incest. I'm just sayin' He'll use any circumstance to get His glory. People so quick to think that God don't allow struggle or sufferin', or He can't speak in different ways. Now, the Holy Ghost speaks in a still, small voice like He did wit' Elijah. I understand that He wasn't in the earthquake. He wasn't in the wind. He wasn't in the fire. At *that* time, He wasn't in those things. We must learn how to listen to God."

"You better preach, Granddaddy!" Charlotte nearly screamed.

"But we can honestly say that God sometimes uses the weather or anything else He wants to use to get our attention." Edmund's voice rose with excitement. "God used the flood wit' the people in the days of Noah. He used a donkey wit' the prophet, and He used a burnin' bush wit' Moses. God can do anything."

By this time, Charlotte was ready to give an altar call.

Ten o'clock had rolled around to the honking of John Edward's car horn, alerting a very exhausted Sista that it was time to go home. After Edmund and Mattie Mae said goodnight and excused themselves to go upstairs, Charlotte thought twice about telephoning her good friend, Timmi.

Since it was so late, Charlotte decided to wait until the morning, while she was traveling in the car, to call Timmi. Hopefully, she would catch Timmi during her morning coffee hour, which was actually quiet time Timmi allotted herself before going to court, if she was even scheduled to appear in court. Timmi's weekly calendar was pretty generic and simple.

Scrolling through the channels on the remote, Charlotte settled on watching an old black and white film on the Turner Classic Movie channel. Although slightly disturbed by her family history, she felt at peace and looked forward to going home in a couple of days.

31

*This is the day the LORD has made; let us rejoice
and be glad in it*

Psalm 118:24

It was a brand new day, a day that had never been seen or touched before. After saying her prayers and meditating on Psalm 41, Charlotte discovered a color chart pressed in between pages in the back of her Bible.

"What color am I today?" she asked herself while imagining a color defining a mood or position. "Gray from age," she said out loud as she rummaged through the closet. "Green with envy. Seeing red. Sad and blue. None of these will do. Today, I choose to be tickled pink."

At that declaration, she retrieved a pale pink, form-fitting dress with an empire waist and V-neckline from a hanger. After pressing out a few wrinkles, she checked the time on her cell phone, thinking she could probably catch Timmi before her lawyer friend got too busy at work.

Charlotte got back in the bed and dialed Timmi's direct number at the office, bypassing the main line, which was answered by the secretary. The telephone rang three times, with Timmi picking up after the third ring.

"Crawford, Bing and Crawford. This is Attorney Timmi Rogers speaking. How may I help you?"

"Hey, girl. It's me, Charlotte. Did I catch you at bad time?"

Instrumental jazz played in the background. Timmi, a self-described jazz connoisseur, had a diehard passion for jazz music. Fusion, progressive and a particular love for violinist Ken Ford, and old tunes of saxophonist David Sanborn. Timmi listened to jazz a lot on days when she was in a particularly good mood. On bad days, she couldn't stand to hear a pin drop.

"Well, hey to you too, Charlotte. I'm not busy. Just going through my email, phone messages and woofing down a hard boiled egg. I was about to make an appointment for a pedicure. If I don't get these toe nails clipped soon . . . well, let's just say they are about to run away. How are you?"

Charlotte hesitated. "Good."

"You sure?"

"Yeah.

"Then why the hesitation?"

"It's nothing that can't wait until I see you. Just some family issues."

"Terry?"

"Not this time." Charlotte pushed the bed sheet back. "She's in jail and will probably be there for a while. We've had another major issue come to the light."

"More drama?"

"I'm afraid so," Charlotte said firmly.

Timmi constantly gasped over the phone as Charlotte filled her in with the latest family drama. After Timmi expressed her heartfelt sorrow, Charlotte immediately chose to change the topic in an effort to not dwell on the matter.

"What's up with you and my cousin?" Charlotte asked almost breathlessly.

"What do you mean?" Timmi gushed.

"You know exactly what I mean, so quit stalling. I refuse

to be disconnected because you got called to some emergency meeting or summoned to put out some brush fire. Start talking."

Timmi laughed. "Testy little thing, aren't you? Oops. Hold on for a sec."

Charlotte hissed.

"Just a second. I promise."

"All right."

Charlotte heard rustling of papers and the muffled voice of another person in the room.

"Okay. I'm sorry about that," Timmi said. "I was just given a fax I had been waiting for. Okay. Jeff. What can I say? The man is sweeping me off of my feet in slow motion. He'll be here in about two weeks for a business conference at the Hilton."

"What happened? I mean, you guys gave me no indication; well, he gave no indication that he was interested."

"I know, but you know how men are. They can be checking you out from head to toe and you'd never know it." Timmi started shuffling papers.

"That's true." Charlotte lay flat on her back and dangled her legs over the edge of the bed. "So did he tell you he was interested?"

"Yes. After we talked the nights away. But he said he knew that long distance relationships can be hard, and that I was in the process of healing from past broken relationships, so we had to take it slow."

"So he's not asking that it be exclusive."

"Might as well be. As far as my part is concerned, I'm not seeing anyone."

"Girl, you've practically been a part of this family since we were in Pull-Ups. You might as well make it legal."

Timmi laughed. "They didn't have Pull-Ups when we were tots. When are you coming home?"

"I think we're leaving tomorrow morning. I'm not sure, but I hope so."

"Ooh, ooh, ooh. Before I forget, I ran into your ex-husband, Anthony, the other day."

"Really?" Charlotte said in a deadpan manner.

"He was sporting a goatee beneath those bloated cheeks and a nice round beer gut to match. Can we say treadmill?" Timmi chuckled. "I kept calling him Bowflex just to make him mad. Ever seen a black man turn red? It's like a burgundy hue."

No, Charlotte thought as she held back her giggle. She was surprised to learn of his new physical description. Anthony prided himself in having a muscular and toned physique, a physique he used to strut around women like a rooster in a hen house.

"Although, I must say, the goatee looked nice on him. He had sort of a sexy salt-and-pepper whiskers thing going. He asked about you too."

"What did you tell him?"

"The truth. That you were doing great and hadn't gained a pound. I had never seen a person's face sink so low."

"Timmi, you're a mess."

Once the two friends concluded their conversation, Charlotte went to the bathroom. She took a bar of oat soap, lathered her washcloth and scrubbed her face in a circular motion. After brushing her teeth and gargling with mouthwash, she then proceeded to take a hot shower. As the water pounded against her skin, she couldn't help wondering about her mother.

Charlotte found Betty in the kitchen, where she appeared to be remarkably relaxed. Less disturbed. Less guarded. Mattie Mae made a remark about her fresh clean scent, to which Betty credited Crabtree & Evelyn goat milk products. She wore a very flattering white rib-yoked peasant blouse over a pair of denim capris complemented by a pair of Chinese Laundry shoes. Her arms were covered in suds from washing the dishes.

Mattie Mae walked out, saying that she was going over to Sista's house.

Charlotte, who was overcome with an intense feeling of gratefulness, thanked God quietly for her mother's rejuvenation as Betty dried off her arms and poured herself a full cup of percolated coffee. It was no Starbucks nor Brew-Ha-Ha (her favorite neighborhood coffee house) but it would have to do, especially since she was more in the mood for a strawberry-banana-honey-milk-yogurt protein shake with a healthy sprinkle of wheat germ. She even lusted for some of Brew-Ha-Ha's freshly baked black walnut and butter cookies, known for their rich, chewy-gooey goodness.

"Are we still leaving tomorrow?" Charlotte asked her mother as she nibbled on a piece of turkey bacon.

"If life lasts." A cheeriness had returned to Betty's voice. "Esau wants to pull out around five A.M."

"I am so ready to go back home," Charlotte stated as she grabbed another piece of bacon.

"I know you've been concerned, but I promise you, I'm fine."

"Sorry, Ma, but can't a child behave like a concerned parent sometimes?"

"I hope so. When I reach my golden years, I want you to change my diapers just like I had to change yours."

Charlotte burst out laughing. Betty then followed suit. It was a welcoming sight to see Betty laugh again.

"I love you, Charlotte," Betty said with her back turned, loading up the dishwasher with pots and pans.

"I love you too, Ma." Charlotte went over and kissed her on the cheek, feeling confident that her mother was experiencing God's grace and not internalizing pain. She washed and rinsed out her cup. "Hey, listen; I think I'll go over to Miss Sista's house. You'll be all right?"

"I'm not old and decrepit yet. Or upset," Betty said as an afterthought. "You go ahead. I need to do some laundry. God knows your dad's things look like he's been playing underneath the dirt. Speaking of which, I suppose I'll have to throw out the overalls he's wearing today."

"Why is that?"

"Because he and your granddad are over at Busta's house building a new pig pen."

Charlotte scrunched up her nose at the thought.

"I plan to get my grandsons as soon as we get back home," Betty mentioned in a mater-of-fact tone.

Charlotte had momentarily forgotten about Ramiyah's boys. "That's great, Ma. I'm looking forward to being an aunt."

Betty nodded. "Do you want me to wash your clothes?"

"Would you mind?"

Betty flung a handful of soapy suds toward her daughter. For the first time in her life, Betty truly felt as if a weight had been lifted off of her shoulders.

32

Light is sweet, and it pleases the eyes to see the sun.
However many years a man may live, let him enjoy
them all. But let him remember the days of darkness
for they will be many. Everything to come is meaningless

Ecclesiastes 11:7 & 8

Charlotte slipped out the back door and trekked along the path forged by the Morleys and the Joneses over a span of sixty-plus years.

A family of baby chicks had gotten loose from Sista's hen house and was scurrying about frantically in front of her feet, leaving a path of droppings behind. Sista's house was only a short distance away; however, by the time Charlotte reached the front door, she had to remove the sand from the bottom of her shoes that hitchhiked along the way.

"Come on in," Sista yelled from a chair situated near the entrance. "How you doin' this mornin'?"

"I'm doing well, and yourself?"

"Can't complain. You lookin' for Mattie Mae? She's in the back room goin' through some material to make a patchwork quilt out of."

"No. I'm here to see Hiawatha."

"Oh, he'll be down in a minute. I think he's in there takin' a bath or shower. Either way, that boy stays in the bathroom more than any female I know and smells better too. Have a seat. You ain't no stranger here."

As Sista continued to make small talk, Charlotte realized that it had been years since she had stepped foot inside Sista's home. At first glance, the room was virtually a religious shrine.

A collection of Bibles in various translations were stacked up over in a corner. A curio cabinet was adorned with Christian-themed picture frames, crystal figurines, crosses, candleholders and other ornaments. The bookcase contained an equally impressive collage of Christian materials—books, brochures, pamphlets, CDs, DVDs, tapes, ink pens with inscriptions and a calendar.

Ceramic candy dishes, displaying the words *Jesus Is The Sweetest Name I Know* were placed throughout the room on end tables and the mantlepiece. The Roman numeral wall clock featured the imprint *As For Me and My House, We Will Serve The LORD*. A beautiful embroidered quilt with scriptures stitched around the edges rested on the back of the brown leather sofa.

Regardless of—or perhaps, even because of—religious excess, the room was inviting and tastefully done. Churchgoer or not, Sista could carry the fury of a stick of lit dynamite, so Charlotte surmised that she needed reminding of Who was actually in control.

Shortly after Mattie Mae had entered the room with an arm full of plaid, floral and solid-colored cloth swatches, Hiawatha emerged. He was looking good, smelling good and still gay as ever. "Greetings, my lovelies," he said, snapping those soft, manicured fingers of his.

"Good morning," Charlotte and Mattie Mae greeted back.

"Hey, Ma. I couldn't find the scissors to cut open something. Do you know where it is?" Hiawatha asked.

"No. Just use a knife," Sista told him.

"A knife?" he responded gruffly, preferring to use scissors for cutting strips of cheesecloth. "What kind of a knife?"

"A sharp one," Sista answered sarcastically.

Mattie Mae grunted. "Sista, what are we gonna do wit' you?"

"Lord, have mercy. Ms. Mattie Mae, you can't do anything with my mama. She's done." Hiawatha snapped his fingers again before leading Charlotte outdoors and narrowly escaping Sista's complaint about him wasting her cheesecloth, which she used for dusting.

"Where are we going?" Charlotte asked.

"I want to pick some plums and pears. We might as well check out the watermelon patch while we're out here as well."

Perfect, Charlotte thought, given this opportunity to talk with him before she left. However, what she wanted to say and what God would have her to say were probably two different things. Her personal thoughts would be held hostage. She planned to play it by ear, leaning on the Holy Spirit.

A wheelbarrow layered with strips of cheesecloth waited for them by the side of the house. Charlotte followed Hiawatha and the wheelbarrow over to a fruit tree heavily burdened with plump yellow plums.

Two minutes of quietness passed by as the two of them picked plums and dumped them in the wheelbarrow. Charlotte decided to open up dialogue between them since the unusually hushed Hiawatha showed no sign of breaking the silence.

"I'm leaving in the morning." There was slight sadness in her voice.

"You are?" Hiawatha started plucking from the lower limbs of the tree. He then bundled up the plums in the top layer of cheesecloth, securing it by tying a knot. "Wait here a minute."

Hiawatha walked briskly across the street, where there was a cotton field. He stood near the edge of the road and pulled up a tall cotton stalk. By the time he returned, Charlotte had rinsed off a plum under an outside water pump and was thoroughly enjoying it. Juices spattered with each bite.

"I want to take this back to the receptionist. She's never seen a cotton stalk before," he explained. "People can't believe I'm from a small town in the South. Shoot. *I* can't believe I came from the South, especially from a place that might as well have been named No Niggras Are Created Equal, South Carolina."

"Yeah, you've come a long way from that little boy who ran around barefoot in his big brother's hand-me-downs."

Hiawatha looked odd to Charlotte, out of place and out of character in his Rocawear, pushing a wheelbarrow around to gather up a harvest. Next, he led her to a track of land in the back, where a watermelon patch was located.

Charlotte laughed.

"What's so funny, Miss Thang?"

"I'm sorry, but you are." Charlotte spat the pit from the plum onto the ground.

Hiawatha was puzzled.

"Come on. Farmer Brown you are not, with those three cotton balls. Back in the day, you wouldn't have received a wage equal to a penny candy. I can see why people find it hard to believe you're from the South. Look at you. Working it out... in the fields... in Rocawear." Charlotte pulled out her cell phone.

"Don't you dare!"

But it was too late. A few quick movements of her thumb

ended with pressing the capture function on her camera feature.

Hiawatha took three long strides toward her. "You wrong for that. You know that, don't you?" he said, looking at a picture of himself standing in front of a wheelbarrow with a cotton stalk sticking out. "This looks like I came straight from the cotton field. Picking cotton!"

"You did come straight from the cotton field." Charlotte chuckled.

"Careful what you laugh at," Hiawatha said as he stepped over a busted watermelon in search of a nice big ripe one.

Halfway down the row, a small garden snake slithered by. Charlotte screamed. A quick-thinking Hiawatha grabbed a hoe, which had been left behind in the next row. He found the snake coiled neatly near some leaves and chopped its head off.

"I'm going to miss you, Charlotte."

"I'm going to miss you too," Charlotte said, still a little shaken. "And thank you for holding my hand through all of this."

"Chile, please. Thank you for the insight you gave about the church. About God, I mean."

Something inside of Charlotte wanted to jump for joy. Had she reached him?

"Ma told me about Ms. Betty's father coming over there. I already told you. My brother. An ambulance. We can make some folks go missing."

"It's cool, Hia," Charlotte replied truthfully.

"Yeah?"

"Yeah."

"All jokes aside, how is Ms. Betty doing? How are you doing, and what was the tension like in *that* house yesterday?"

"All things considered, my mother seems to be fine. I'm

good. Slept like a newborn baby that was bathed, fed and powered down. As for the tension in the house, I have to tell you; there were moments when I wasn't sure if she was going to keep it together. Heck, I wasn't sure if *I* was going to stay holy."

Hiawatha grunted. "I can guarantee you I wouldn't have been holy or kept it together. He would have walked out that door having had a homemade sex change!"

"One thing is for sure."

"What's that?" he asked.

"This will be a summer to remember in more ways than one."

A neighbor's pigs squealed loudly as they wallowed in the mud. They squealed and pushed and raised their snouts as their owner approached the trough with a bucket of slop.

"Soo-ee. Soo-ee," the neighbor twanged as he poured out the noisome rations.

Hiawatha lifted a medium-sized watermelon, placed it in the wheelbarrow and covered it with the second layer of cheesecloth. "You know, Charlotte, if I were a straight man, you'd be the type of woman I'd pursue."

"I'm flattered." Charlotte smiled. "Have you ever been with a woman? I don't mean sexually, necessarily. But like out on a date."

"Are you flirting with me?" He grinned.

Charlotte regretted not having the plum pit to throw at him. It was too dirty, too gritty to pick up.

"Nope. I've never been interested. But I do want to thank you for being a good friend, being bold enough to speak what you know as the truth and not beat me up about it." Hiawatha walked behind the smokehouse, where a lush green garden of collard greens, bell peppers, pickling cucumbers and onions lay in wait. "Girl, you'd better come over here and get some of these groceries."

"After seeing a snake? No, thank you." Suddenly she was developing an obsession for plums, and nervously walked back to the tree to retrieve another one.

"Why don't you get more than that to take back with you?" Hiawatha suggested after witnessing her take only one.

But Charlotte, who was too busy noting her surroundings, especially for anything in the reptile family, did not hear him. A group of chickens in the henhouse moved about somberly like a pack of pallbearers, reminding Charlotte of the runaway chicks out in the field.

"Hia, I forgot to mention that some of your mom's baby chicks are loose over by the path."

"Now, I have my limits. I will stoop out here and pick bell peppers and onions. I'll even kill a garden snake. Nothing bigger than a garden snake, mind you. But running after something that travels all willy-nilly at the speed of forty miles per hour in every which direction, I will not do."

"They're only baby chicks. Now, you know you can smoke a yard bird. They can't outrun a grown man."

"I'm not hearing you," he said in a high-pitched tone. "If I fell down in my two-hundred-dollar outfit because of some biddy, I will chase it down and make chicken noodle soup out of it!"

Charlotte heard the motor of a car rolling up not far behind her. It was Jack, the traveling salesman. "How you doin'?" he asked. The question hung in the air momentarily.

"Doing well," Charlotte answered. "How about you?"

"Doin' fair. Doin' fair. Is Miss Sista at home?"

"Yes. She's inside." Charlotte watched as the middle-aged man waved and moved like a man on a mission of utmost importance. He walked up the steps and rang the doorbell.

She shook her head in amazement, remembering Jack when she was a child, coming to her grandparents' house to sell Watkins flavor extract, Fuller brush and combs sets, cheap perfumes and colognes, bedspreads and fake Oriental rugs, and on occasion, bags of boiled or roasted peanuts. Jack was one of the friendliest white men she had ever seen. He used to drive around in a station wagon full of wares. These days, he drove a Ford Expedition for more cargo room.

"I didn't know Jack still came around selling stuff," Charlotte said.

"Neither did I."

"I wonder why he doesn't just go and work in a store as a salesman."

"Maybe this is more profitable for him. He could be doing this and getting a monthly retirement check in the mail for all we know."

"This is true," Charlotte agreed.

Hiawatha looked up at the rolling clouds, which made the sky look angry. "Are you joining us for dinner later?"

Charlotte drew a deep breath and smiled. "And miss your mom's words of wisdom? I'll be there for food and food for thought."

"Oh, God." Hiawatha grimaced. Secretly, he had enjoyed Charlotte's company and hoped to stay in touch with her. Unbeknownst to him, Charlotte shared the same feelings, and knew in her heart that one day, she would get the chance to truly witness to Hiawatha.

33

*Better is a dinner of herbs where love is than a
fatted calf with hatred*

Proverbs 15:17

Charlotte and her family found themselves at Sista's house swapping stories one last time. After consuming a delicious meal prepared by Sista and Mattie Mae, everyone gathered in Sista's spacious family room, where the men sat on one side in front of the television, enjoying back to back episodes of *COPS*, the reality show known for nabbing fugitives, lawbreakers and occasionally, a lost snake or two. The women sat on the opposite side, half chatting, half watching. And everyone had a comment or two.

"Now, why you reckon that person thinks he can outrun the police?" Sista commented.

"He probably thinks he's got a chance of getting away," John Edward stated, stretched out on the floor with his legs crossed.

"No. Idiots like going to the lock-up," Hiawatha, who sat parallel to his brother, said.

Mattie Mae and Betty cringed and gasped as they watched the juvenile criminal lead the cops on a high speed chase through a busy interstate during rush hour. Meanwhile, Edmund grunted and Esau chuckled at the outrageous behavior.

Charlotte, on the other hand, allowed her mind to stray as everyone else continued talking. Something on the wall got her attention. There were two portraits hanging side by side. One was of Sista seated and surrounded by all of her children. The other was of Sista standing over her grandchildren, who were all seated. It symbolized a mother being looked after by her loving children and a grandmother who was watching over her grandbabies. Charlotte thought it was touching.

Conversations shifted between generations. The older generation spoke of taking baths once a week in tin tubs with water heated on pot belly stoves, washing with soap made out of lye and lard, and feet-washing every evening before they went to sleep on homemade feather mattresses. The soft beds were comfortable if they could avoid getting poked by feathers sticking through.

Betty shared a tender memory of meeting her sister, Jean, for lunch when she was a teen and Jean worked as an elevator operator in a downtown department store. "Yes," she told the shocked audience, John Edward and Hiawatha. "There was a time when the public did not press a button on their own to go to the floor of their choice. We used to have elevator operators."

The brothers thought that was one of the craziest things they ever heard. Charlotte, too, was fascinated by the tales of the days of mule and buggy and true neighborly love. Mattie Mae brought up fond memories of making quilts for hours on end, a hobby she still enjoyed from time to time.

Aside from missing family and friends who had gone on to be with the Lord (or elsewhere), Edmund stated that he missed the old-time religion church the most. The times when they did the right-hand-of-fellowship, gave testimonies, held tent revivals and baptized folk near the edge of the ocean. Esau and Hiawatha exchanged golf-lovers' tales like war stories.

A knock came at the door, causing everyone to hush up like folks ready to surprise the guest of honor at a birthday party. Sista smacked her lips and got up to answer the door. Her skirt was twisted around her waist. John Edward, who had gone into the kitchen, heard the knock as well. He stood in the doorway with an empty milk carton in his hand and a milk mustache on his face. Sista sneaked him a scolding glance.

"What wind blew you over this way?" Sista was overheard asking.

"Can't I come to visit you?" the voice jokingly snarled.

It was Sista's cousin, Ruby, who entered the family room clutching the hideous necklace that hung from her neck. "Oh. I didn't know you had company, Sista. How is everybody doin'?"

"Fine. Well. How are you? Doin' good," were the various responses.

"You know good and well we ain't no company, Ruby," Mattie Mae clarified. "We all were raised up together like family."

"Ain't that the truth? But you know how I like to cut the fool, Mattie Mae."

"Ruby, where did you get that pretty necklace from?" Sista asked, snickering behind Ruby's back at the jewelry's grossness.

Ruby pulled on it and beamed as if it were the most opulent thing anyone had ever seen. "My husband gave me this for our anniversary," she replied happily before carrying on about their anniversary celebration. Sister, however, knew that Ruby's husband was a ne'er-do-well who was cheaper than the cost of kerosene back in 1945.

"Oh, that's . . . that's something else," Betty said, refusing to lie by paying a compliment. Charlotte stretched her eyes in disbelief at its gaudiness. It certainly was not a high ticket item.

Sista was eager for Ruby to start the gabfest, since she had a way with stimulating gossip and felt certain that Ruby came with news to share.

"We just finished eatin'. Go in there and fix you a place," Sista offered.

"Watcha fixed?" Ruby rubbed her belly.

"Me and Mattie Mae fixed a big pot of rice, some great northern beans with ham hocks in it, sweet peas, fried chicken, some beef short ribs, homemade bread, and I just took an apple butter pie out the oven to cool off." Sista turned her attention toward her son. "John Edward, go and get one of those foldin' table trays so Ruby can sit in here and eat."

A drowsy John Edward rubbed his eyes with the balls of his fists and did as he was told, while Ruby went in the kitchen and fixed a plate of food. John Edward walked over to the corner where a set of four folding table trays were located, and placed one of them next to Charlotte.

Charlotte inched over on the loveseat, giving Ruby, who soon came back with a plate of short ribs and pie, room to join her. Moments later, Charlotte, John Edward and Hiawatha were laughing and howling as Edmund, Mattie Mae, Ruby and Sista recalled stories involving people with nicknames such as Peg Leg Willie Williams, who lost his leg in a railroad accident and loved to fight; Sad Sam, whose short-lived smiles always evaporated into a poker face whenever anyone brought up the fact that none of his children looked like him; Rabbit, a woman who gave birth practically every other year, resulting in eighteen children that included two sets of identical twins; and Mud and Monkey, who, ironically, were two exotically beautiful sisters with long, silky hair, hourglass figures and Hollywood glamour faces with green eyes.

John Edward and Hiawatha concluded that their beauty was due largely to their African and Blackfoot Indian (ancestors who migrated to the South from Montana) and Caucasian heritage. They joked that the Turtle Island beauties were given the monikers out of hateration.

Before long, Betty was back to her old self, laughing, talking and commenting on how the plastic toys of today get recalled and her generation survived on toys made of tin and lived. Everyone agreed it was a shame that kids today didn't play outdoor games such as lemonade, red light-green light, hopscotch, mother may I and hide-and-seek.

"Sista, what do you put in yo' apple butter pie and how do you make yo' pie crust? Mine always come out bone dry." Flakes of pie crust landed on Ruby's chin as she spoke. She nudged Charlotte on her arm. "I always like to test the dessert first."

"Well, I use brown sugar, butter, vanilla flavor, allspice, self-rising flour, lemon juice, nutmeg, syrup, milk and apples. Now, I can't tell you how to make a flaky pie crust except make sho' you use Crisco, cold water and knead yo' bread wit' a rollin' pin, or you can even use a glass," Sista advised.

Charlotte felt more like a spectator than a guest or participant of the group assembled in the family room. For a finicky eater, Ruby practically licked her plate clean before picking out the piece of meat stuck in between her teeth.

It was good to see John Edward and Hiawatha recapture the playfulness of their youth, and even funnier to Charlotte as she watched Sista scolding them for rough-housing it and daring them to break her oblique-shaped clear glass vase. John Edward scrambled to his feet before Hiawatha could catch him by his britches.

"Mind, I ain't that old and feeble, and y'all ain't that big that I can't wear yo' behind out wit' a strap," Sista yelled.

"Can you believe it's September already?" Edmund asked no one in particular.

"Time sho' is flyin'. Christmas will be here in a couple of days," Sista commented.

Everyone looked at Sista as if she had grown two heads.

"Don't believe it, wait and see. Christmas will be here before you know it."

They all knew she was right, of course.

From time to time, Sista and Hiawatha would zero in on each other and exchange barbs. Every now and then, someone would make a comment about the abusive spouse or prostitute or car thief or drug dealer arrested on *COPS*.

"That ain't nothin' but God right there," Sista said, referring to an overweight police officer's ability to chase down and catch a young man who had robbed the owner of a pawn shop.

Hiawatha mentioned to Esau his disgust over drug store over-the-counter medicine being diluted and worthless thanks to meth fiends and crack heads. Being a pharmacist, Esau understood the customers' frustrations, especially when it came to costs, especially for the elderly.

It was now 9:30 P.M. It was getting late. Without notice, the burnt orange sky had swiftly changed to a bluish gray as night began to fall, and it didn't matter that a good night's rest was needed in order to get up at the crack of dawn. No one was willing to yield to giving up a good time, nor could they deny that, just for a moment, they were able to put life's concerns in the deep crevices of their minds.

All may not have been right in the world, but Charlotte

felt that her world was all right. There was no mention of JT, or fretting over Ramiyah's or Terry's troubles. At least the family finally knew where Terry was, and perhaps, she would allow God to work on her heart while incarcerated, the same way Ramiyah had allowed Him to work on hers.

There was only love and laughter in the room, oscillating like a gentle breeze.

Eventually, Charlotte did become a game-playing participant, sliding off the love seat onto the floor to join in on a fun-filled game of Monopoly. "God is good," she said softly. "And all things are in His hands."

Charlotte understood that God had ordered her steps and maneuvered paths to cross, as was the case with Jeff and Timmi. She also knew that it was now finally time to go home. Maybe next summer, she'd plan to return to Turtle Island and perhaps, have a drama-free visit. But as she'd learned over the years, her plans weren't always God's plans.

Readers Group Guide

1. The church was without a pastor because of the unsavory actions of the former pastor. Do you think it's time for leaders to stop "winking" at sin and moving pastors from church to church without repentance? **Luke 17:3**

2. Mattie Mae and Sista were lifelong friends. Do you know your Jonathan(s) from your Judas? **Proverbs 27:10**

3. Charlotte had a relationship with God. She was an intercessor and the Holy Spirit spoke to her. Do you believe God still speaks to us today? **John 16:12-14**

4. Although Ramiyah was in prison, she was no longer imprisoned. Prison is not limited to a cell block, and God saw fit to use her while there. Can you name other forms of prison? **Isaiah 42:7**

5. Hiawatha had some major issues and concerns, one of which was regarding the large church. Do you think Charlotte addressed his concerns properly? **II Timothy 4:2**

6. Charlotte's cousin, Terry, committed atrocious acts. Do you think justice was served? **Psalm 37:1-2**

7. Edmund was a man of few, but wise words. Looking at today's generations, would you say **Proverbs Chapter 2** is good scripture to study, pray over and practice? Or do you think most people are filled with wisdom?

8. Ramiyah and Betty suffered extreme emotional pain. Have you ever felt sorry for yourself only to discover there is always someone else worse off than you, or have you seen God turn your situation around? **Habakkuk 1:5**

9. When forgiveness was asked of Betty, do you think she acted accordingly? **Matthew 18:34-35**

10. Esau stood by his wife knowing her family secrets. Do you agree that a husband should love his wife as Christ loves the church, or are there exceptions? **Ephesians 5:25-28**

Author's Bio

A native of Baltimore, Maryland and a former Systems Administrator for the Social Security Administration, Sharon Oliver resides in the Atlanta, Georgia area.

Urban Christian His Glory Book Club!

Established January 2007, *UC His Glory Book Club* is another way by which to introduce to the literary world Urban Books' much-anticipated new imprint, **Urban Christian** and its authors. We are an online book club supporting Urban Christian authors by purchasing, reading and providing written reviews of the authors' books that are read. *UC His Glory* welcomes both men and women of the literary world who have a passion for reading Christian-based fiction.

UC His Glory is the brainchild of Joylynn Jossel, Author and Executive Editor of Urban Christian and Kendra Norman-Bellamy, Author and Copy Editor for Urban Christian. The book club will provide support, positive feedback, encouragement and a forum whereby members can openly discuss and review the literary works of Urban Christian authors. In the future, we anticipate broadening our spectrum of services to include online author chats, author spotlights, interviews with your favorite Urban Christian author(s), special online groups for *UC His Glory Book Club* members, ability to post reviews on the website and amazon.com, membership ID cards, *UC His Glory* Yahoo Group and much more.

Even though there will be no membership fees attached to becoming a member of *UC His Glory Book Club*, we do expect our members to be active, committed and to follow the guidelines of the book club.

***UC His Glory* members pledge to:**

- Follow the guidelines of *UC His Glory Book Club*.
- Provide input, opinions, and reviews that build up, rather than tear down.
- Commit to purchasing, reading and discussing featured book(s) of the month.
- Agree not to miss more than three consecutive online monthly meetings.
- Respect the Christian beliefs of *UC His Glory Book Club*.
- Believe that Jesus is the Christ, Son of the Living God

We look forward to the online fellowship.

Many Blessings to You!

Shelia E. Lipsey
President
UC His Glory Book Club

**Visit the official Urban Christian His Glory Book Club website at *www.uchisglorybookclub.net*